SmokeFire!

Copyright © T. Judson Kennedy, 2000

All rights reserved. Copyright under Berne, Universal and Pan-American Copyright Conventions. No part of this book may be reproduced or transmitted in any form or by any means, electronic, mechanical or by any other information storage and retrieval system, without permission in writing from the publisher.

Published by
Bedside Books™
http://www.american-book.com
Salt Lake City, Utah,

Printed in the United States of America
12   10   9   8   7   6   5   4   3   2   1

Cover Design, Jeff Jones, jgj@mont.mindspring.com

Library of Congress Cataloging-in-Publication Data is available upon request.

ISBN 1-930586-04-3

Publisher's Note: This is a work of fiction. Names, places characters, and incidents either are the product of the author's imagination or, are used fictitiously, and any resemblance to actual persons, living or dead, events, or locales is entirely coincidental.

SmokeFire!

By T. Judson Kennedy

For my mother, Barbara
Who imparted to me a love of writing,

and

In loving memory of my father, Thomas
Who conveyed a love of reading

And for Judy, who gave me faith

Thank you!

Prologue

**Sunday night, February 24, 1951
Korean War Theater of Operations
Ninety-two miles south-southeast of Seoul, South Korea
en route to Poun, South Korea**

The small convoy of three army trucks and two jeeps, an obscure detachment from General Ridgway's 8th Army, inched its way along the dirt "highway" at thirty miles an hour. Corporal Alan Cummings was driving the third cargo truck, commonly referred to as a "six-by." After leaving Seoul eight hours ago and contending with driving snow, potholed roads and a twenty-five mile per hour wind, Cummings was exhausted. It was now eight-thirty p.m., and the convoy of two jeeps and three six-by's was overdue for a rest stop.

The two-way field radio crackled to life with the voice of the convoy commander, Colonel William "Wild Bill" Anderson.

"This is Broken Arrow Leader, convoy halt at checkpoint alpha, out."

"It's about damn time," blurted Private Higgins, Cummings's alternate driver and personal tormentor for the previous forty-eight hours. Higgins, a native New Yorker from the Bronx, in addition to being a malingerer, was a constant complainer who never had anything good to say about anything.

"We been on the road eight bloody hours. If you ask me, this whole hushed-up, super-secret, need-to-know mission is the usual shit. I mean, who ever heard of leavin' one truck at a time, thirty minutes apart. And what was all them grunts we got in truck number two standin' there with all them automatic weapons when they was loadin' up them locked boxes? If it was somethin' really important, then we'd have had a whole bloody company as backup. Nobody's told us shit, how're we supposed to know what to expect?"

Young Corporal Cummings, a Midwest farmer's son by birth and a quiet and stable young man by nature, could only reply with, "I don't know, Higgins, maybe you ought to ask Wild Bill and see what he has to say."

"Hell, nobody can talk to that SOB, and by the way, what the hell is a full Bird Colonel doin' on a small detachment like this? Every time I been on one of their silly-assed missions, there's always been a Captain or maybe even a Major in command. If you ask me, there's somethin' damn strange goin' on."

"Well, Higgins, nobody asked you. All I know is that in three weeks I'm getting discharged. After that I don't have to worry about the Army, Wild Bill, or yourself."

Cummings knew as soon as he arrived in Panmujom that he would never want to leave any place as bad as he wanted to leave Korea, and the succeeding fourteen months had only strengthened his resolve. For a twenty-one year old man, away from home for the first time in his life, there could be no worse place on earth, or so Cummings thought.

Korea was not a pleasant place, especially with the extreme change of seasons. In winter temperatures could fall to thirty-five below zero with a wind blowing at forty miles an hour. And in summer the temperature could reach better than ninety-five degrees with a humidity of ninety percent.

Wild Bill leaned out the right side of the lead command jeep, the canvas and plastic door hanging open. He waved everyone to the left before his truck turned onto the obscure side road. The two six-by's in front of Cummings's truck followed suit. *Higgins—whatever he was or was not—did have a point*, Cummings thought. Since being in Korea for

Prologue

the last fourteen months as a driver—and he could drive anything—Cummings had been a part of so many fetch and carry assignments that they had become more than routine. Last July, when the monsoon had socked in all the airstrips, he had personally driven the Mercedes Benz that carried President Syngman Rhee from Seoul to Taegu. On another occasion he had driven one hundred and twenty miles with two fully armed platoons late one night to pick up fifty sirloin steaks and two cases of whiskey for a General's party. Even when he'd driven President Rhee, there was only a Major in charge, and on the "meat mission," there had been a Lieutenant Colonel in command. Now here was Wild Bill, a full Bird Colonel with two tours behind him, leading a no-name convoy up to Seoul to pick up twenty-five locked boxes and deliver them to God knows where.

Touching his left breast pocket, which contained his latest letter from his girl, Cummings thought, *three more weeks, just three more weeks—twenty-one days—and then discharge and back to Kansas, back to Margie.*

The lead truck came to a halt. It was snowing harder now, and the wind had picked up. Wild Bill jumped out of the lead jeep; walking past the two lead six-by drivers, he pointed his index finger to the sky repeatedly as he passed each driver, giving the signal to keep the engines running and stay in the vehicle. With his U.S. Army "horse blanket" draped over his shoulders and an olive drab scarf tied over his head with his fatigue cap underneath, he was quite a sight. Cummings could not decide if, in his six-foot five-inch frame, Wild Bill looked more like a grizzly bear with a nervous tic or an overgrown bag woman signaling the arrival of UFO's.

He walked on past Cummings's vehicle just as the corporal was chuckling at his analogy.

Commenting on Cummings's snicker, Higgins asked, "What's so frickin' funny? At least we get to stay warm for the next couple of minutes before Wild Bill makes us all get out and orders us to take a leak. Besides, this turnoff gives me the spooks. It's got too much cover. What the hell are we pullin' off on a road with all these trees around for?"

Good point, Cummings thought. This wasn't the perfect place for a convoy stop with all the cover, not to mention the fact that with the blowing snow you couldn't hear or see anything past the tree line at the edge of the road. After all, this was "Indian country," a term used to denote hostile territory. With the drop-off on the left and all the rocks and trees around, there was more than reasonable cover for an enemy ambush.

Anderson walked past Cummings's truck on his way back to his jeep. While Higgins was expounding on his feelings and thoughts about the U.S. Army in general and Korea in particular, Cummings's thoughts were on certain questions that were beginning to form in his mind.

Cummings's vehicle was sitting just off to the right, giving him a good view of Anderson opening the door to his jeep. *Radio call coming up to dismount the vehicles and take a break*, Cummings muttered. *God*, he thought, *it was going to be cold outside.* In the long ride the truck heater had just about gotten the cab reasonably warm. However, the need to stretch his legs and ease his bladder outweighed his distaste for the weather.

Just then Anderson brought out what appeared to be a two-way radio, but it seemed too small to Cummings. He saw Anderson take the radio in his left hand, and after extending the antenna with his right, he turned on a switch. Cummings knew what was coming next and anticipated the command to shutdown and dismount by placing his hand on the ignition keys. As he reached forward to the dashboard to turn off the engine, he heard a slight hiss coming from underneath the dashboard. An image formed in his mind of his radiator hose springing a leak, and he detected the faint scent of roses.

The deadly concentration of VX nerve gas quickly spread into the cabin of the six-by.

Why would I smell roses in a place like this? Cummings wondered. He began to feel nauseous and dizzy. But soon it was as if he was back in Kansas, walking through his mother's rose garden. He was ten years old again, savoring the smell of perhaps the most beautiful red rose he had ever seen. His mother had called it Marchioness of Londonderry, but Alan just knew it was the biggest and sweetest smelling rose he'd ever seen. That had been eleven years ago, and for corporal Alan Cummings, son of a Kansas farmer with three weeks until discharge, the sight and smell of that prize-winning rose was the last sensation he would ever experience.

Alan Cummings died while he was warm, his body inside the cab of a six-by truck on an obscure road in South Korea "Indian country." But his

Prologue

mind was thousands of miles and years away in his mother's rose garden in Kansas.

* * *

Friday, May 12, 1951
U.S. Army Geologic Survey Camp Thirteen
Great Smoky Mountains National Park

The three and a half pound rainbow trout hit the deep running jig like a juggernaut out of control. Captain George Jeffers, Chief Surveyor and Officer In Command at Camp Thirteen of the U.S. Army Corps of Engineers, let the hook set and then gave a firm snap on the eight-foot fly rod, pulling on the line with his left hand. It was his tenth catch of the day at the deep pool.

He'd been with the U.S. Army's Corps of Engineers for his entire fourteen-year career. The Second World War and action in Germany had provided him the opportunity to join the officer ranks. As part of Jeffers's distinguished career in combat, the army had rewarded him with the Silver Star, a Purple Heart, and this survey assignment. This was a cushy assignment, a phase-out for a career army officer who had started as a private.

He had been Survey Chief and commander of this camp for the past three years with the assigned tasks of surveying, mapping, bridge building, making soil studies, and numerous other duties associated with such a position.

The detachment of eight men that he supervised in Survey Camp Thirteen was not composed of misfits but rather with skilled geologists, surveyors, and mapmakers. It was a wonder to him why some had not elected to attend officer's candidate school. Maybe they'd had the foresight to sacrifice an extra year of service by volunteering for the privilege of practicing something interesting rather than being riflemen in Korea.

Jeffers picked up the trout net from the elastic line attached to his belt as he pulled the big rainbow closer in. With the trout thrashing in the net,

SmokeFire!

he laid down his fly rod, reached in the water and grabbed the fish by the bottom jaw. When the rainbow was safely in his creel, he picked up his fly rod, stepped down off the huge black rock beside the stream, stowed his gear in the Jeep and began the five-mile drive back to Camp Thirteen.

There had long been speculation about the location of "Jeffers's Hole," the name given to his secret fishing hole by the men of the camp. Out of respect—and the stoic George Jeffers had the respect of all of the men in Thirteen—none had ever followed him to Jeffers's Hole. Perhaps it was because if they violated "his hole," then they would no longer be able to partake in the fruits of his labor, as Jeffers had always shared his catches. Perhaps they adhered to the rule of good sportsmanship shared among fishermen that you do not trespass upon another man's secret fishing hole.

When he walked back into camp, the men had a fire going. It had become to be a kind of ritual in the last year: when Captain Jeffers went fishing on Friday afternoons, he always returned with enough rainbow and brook trout to feed the eight of them. In turn, they would build a fire, clean the fish, cook them, and clean up afterwards.

At the edge of camp, Jeffers met the Logistics and Administrative Clerk, Jim Simons. Their most recent cherry, or new recruit, greeted Jeffers with his usual exuberant and excited manner, something Jeffers couldn't help thinking was out of place in the army.

"Captain Jeffers, a shipment arrived this afternoon after you left. It's marked *'Seismic Explosives - To Be Opened By Capt. G. Jeffers Only.'*"

"Thanks, Jim, I'll get to it as soon as I get the guys started on supper."

One of the responsibilities of this detachment was to conduct geologic seismic studies in the national park. In these studies low yield seismic charges were placed in a drill hole and detonated while sensitive equipment measured the vibrations. This data was then recorded and analyzed to determine subsoil stability and fault detection for possible later construction projects. Although the devices were low yield, they were still dangerous, and Jeffers always oversaw to their unpacking, storage, and use.

"But, sir, there's a whole truck load of this stuff, enough to last us years! I'm a little concerned about all of it sitting in one place on that truck. Logistics guys who dropped it off said that after we'd unloaded it,

Prologue

somebody would be by to pick up the truck. Said it'd be sometime in the next couple of weeks or so."

"Okay, Jim, probably some kind of administrative screw up. I'll take a look at it later after these babies," he said holding up his creel. "Take 'em to Balisterros and tell him to do his thing. Also, I noticed some contraband someone left in the stream over by the big fir tree. Please get it and instruct Balisterros to prepare it for destruction," referring to the case of Falstaff beer he had picked up on his last trip into town to see his family, and which he had placed in the stream to cool several hours earlier.

Jeffers had long before learned that the way to earn respect from his men was to treat them as he'd like to be treated. Neither a stickler for army protocol, nor someone who disregarded the rules, Jeffers treated his men right. This was an unimportant survey camp, a relatively unimportant job, but he found it enjoyable and rewarding nonetheless. He treated his men like the professionals they were, not as Privates, Corporals, or any other subordinate rank.

After the "Fri-Fry," as Ballisterros called it, the men retired to the gray sheet metal Quonset huts, two of which were being utilized as barracks and the third as a mess hall and supply storage. Jeffers, in his usual routine, returned to his twelve by ten-foot log cabin to write a letter to his wife as he had done on each of the Tuesday and Friday nights for the last several years. After writing about his latest excursion to Jeffers's Hole, he remarked about the letter he had received only a week before from an old army acquaintance. Colonel Bill Anderson, who was stationed in Korea, had not written to him within the previous sixteen months.

He and Anderson had attended OCS together in 1945. While Anderson had an appetite for command, Jeffers had an appetite for solitude. Jeffers guessed they had both gotten what they wanted, as Anderson was in Korea on the line and Jeffers was in the mountains living the quiet life. He had never become really good friends with Anderson, but they had shared more than a passing relationship. Anderson and Jeffers enjoyed many of the same activities—fly fishing, an occasional canoe trip down a river on leave, and once, in their younger days they had shared a two-week trip up Mount McKinley.

However, there was something about Anderson that bothered Jeffers. Maybe his feelings came from Jeffers's own imagination or perhaps it was insecurity, caused by Anderson's success. Anderson was definitely a man

SmokeFire!

in control, and had risen through the ranks rapidly. Whatever it was, Jeffers somehow seemed to always get the feeling that he was being manipulated, that there was something more that Anderson was after.

Halfway through his letter to Mary, his wife, he decided to stop and check out the shipment that Simons had mentioned.

As he walked across the compound, he began to think of his and Mary's retirement. Mary had given birth to a daughter only one year ago, an 'accident' as it were. When they had discovered that Mary was pregnant, Jeffers was distraught. He was forty-five years old at the time, and they had been told that Mary could never have children. Their life-plan for after his retirement had not included any children, but since Ruth's birth Jeffers's feelings of anxiety about having children were replaced by something he had never expected—extreme pride and a feeling that he was truly needed. It had made him feel young again.

Walking across the compound, Jeffers unbuttoned the back pocket of his khaki trousers, removed his wallet, and looked once again at the picture of Mary holding Ruth's hand up as if in a wave to an unseen person. It was dark but Jeffers had looked at the photograph so often that he could see it as if in the light of day. *How things change*, Jeffers thought. He was going to retire from the army in six more months, and with the birth of Ruth, they needed to re-examine their plans for the future. Ruth had changed so much of his and Mary's life, and all for the better. Jeffers was very much looking forward to a future with his wife and new daughter.

Maybe they'd stay here, nice country and nice folks, he thought. He and Mary had casually discussed staying here; they had purchased a modest home last year as there was no army base in East Tennessee, and Jeffers wished to be near his family.

Jeffers untied and threw back the tarp leaf covers on the rear of the cargo truck, unlatched the tailgate and climbed in. Flashlight and screwdriver in hand, he stared at the twenty-five or so metal crates stacked and tied down in the forward portion of the truck. The crates were like none he had seen before. They were gunmetal gray and of heavy construction that looked as if they were intended to keep somebody out, not to keep something in. Upon examining the locks of a couple of the crates, he determined that more than a screwdriver would be required to open them. He'd expected wooden soft-packed crates, the kind in which

Prologue

chemical seismic explosives were usually shipped. Instead, these crates had flush-mounted key locks, and were stenciled with *Seismic Explosive Charges—Handle With EXTREME CARE.*

Jeffers returned to his cabin to check the paperwork that accompanied all shipments.

Lifting the manifest from his desk and looking through it, he noticed some oddities. Just about all of his regular equipment was shipped out of Fort Meade, but this shipment listed the point of origin as Fort Armstrong, California. Little else was detailed, except that twenty-five crates of various types of seismic charges (with detonators) was shipped as per his request. Jeffers knew that he had authorized no request for additional charges. He also knew that they had more than enough charges to satisfy their needs for the next six months. Conducting Seismic studies was only a very small part of their purpose here, and consequently they were required to keep only a relatively small amount of charges on hand. He decided he would check with Simons tomorrow to make sure that he hadn't inadvertently requested shipments that they didn't need when he was still a "cherry." In the meantime, the strange appearance of the crates got his curiosity up.

Armed this time with a hammer and crowbar, he returned to the truck and climbed in the tailgate. Again he examined the outer appearance of the crates. Indeed, they were stamped with the typical *DANGER EXPOSIVE* sign, but seismic charges were normally shipped in wooden crates much smaller than the two-by-two metal boxes and had wooden lids strapped on, not locked.

Knowing that it took quite a jolt to detonate a seismic type II detonator, Jeffers placed the screwdriver against the lock and struck full force with his hammer. The lock gave way, and Jeffers opened the lid on the strange gunmetal gray lock box, expecting to see his usual seismic charges delivered in some new type of container that the U.S. Army thought to be better, complete with straw packing.

Instead, as Jeffers scraped back the shredded wood wadding that comprised the top layer of the container, he was struck with awe.

There must have been some terrible mistake, was the first thought that occurred to him. Upon opening the second and third box, he discovered the same contents. "Sweet Mother of Jesus! Something is very, very wrong here!" he muttered to himself. Taking no chances, he took the only

SmokeFire!

appropriate action he could think of, as he must do something to safeguard this cargo.

Jeffers returned to his cabin five hours later after completing his task. Even though it was almost four a.m., he finished the letter to his wife, then walked to the end of the trail that led to the camp where there was a homemade 'mailbox' mounted on an old poplar tree. He placed the letter in the box and leaned a five-foot long branch against the side of the tree, a signal to Gus, the local postal carrier for this part of the area, that there was mail to be picked up.

After walking back to his cabin and retiring to his bunk, he stared up at the tin ceiling. He was worried, seriously worried. It was not uncommon for the army to foul up shipments. Sometimes when you ordered toilet paper, you got typing paper. Sometimes you got ten times more of what you really wanted; sometimes you didn't get anything at all.

However, this was a shipment that was extremely important to someone, someone who never intended it to be delivered to a nondescript survey camp, yet it had his detachment's delivery address stenciled on each crate, along with the standard seismic charge warning. *Did the shipper know what he was shipping? They must have known to whom they were shipping it, as it had their correct delivery address. But did the shipment get labeled incorrectly? How could they screw up something like this? The manifest showed that the cargo had left Fort Armstrong three weeks ago. How come there had been no inquiries when this cargo did not arrive at its intended destination?*

Just before five a.m. as Jeffers slipped off to sleep, a violent explosion ripped through his cabin. So violent that Captain George Jeffers was instantaneously vaporized.

Simultaneous explosions destroyed the three Quonset huts housing the remaining crew and supplies of Survey Camp Thirteen, including Simons, who was also lying awake in his bunk wondering about the gunmetal crates in the delivery truck.

Survey Camp Thirteen, along with its complement of talented geologists, map makers, surveyors, and newly arrived Administrative and Logistics Clerk, ceased to exist in the early morning hours of May 13, 1951.

Chapter One

**Monday, April 5, 1999
Knoxville, Tennessee**

The immaculately restored vintage, 1977 Datsun 280-Z was at a standstill in the eastbound lane of interstate 40, halted by bumper-to-bumper traffic. It was seven-thirty in the morning, and the rain was coming down so hard it sounded like pellets striking the roof of the bronze-colored car. The Z's windshield wipers could barely keep up, even at full speed.

"Hells Bells!" exclaimed the driver. Victor Scofield had become accustomed to the morning traffic jams, or as accustomed as one could be to traffic jams. The traffic report on WXKX was about to inform him of what he already knew, complete with one of the traffic reporter's manic episodes when he finally had something unique to talk about, when Victor inserted a cassette tape of Ronnie Jacobs' latest jazz release into the tape player. Victor thought it would be more appropriate to play Karen Carpenter's *Rainy Days and Mondays*.

Like most of the work force, Victor didn't particularly care for his job and cared even less for Mondays, especially when it was raining

SmokeFire!

As Vice-President of Second National Bank in charge of Information Technology—a euphemism for data processing—it was Victor's responsibility, at least as he saw it, to manage the 'nerve center' of the bank. *Vice-President*, Victor thought, *sounds impressive*. But any banking institution the size of SNB had more vice-presidents than they had tellers. It seemed that he was constantly at odds with the upper management of SNB, especially his immediate superior, Bill Vodeski, over the management of the computer center. They seemed to view his department as an expensive accessory, perhaps due to their lack of knowledge concerning computers and their own insecurities regarding technology. Or they saw it as 'a non-tangible asset,' an expression for something that you could not sell for a profit or at least sell to break even. Six months ago SNB had purchased, against Victor's objections, a new software package to manage SNB's demand deposit accounts—the checking and savings accounts, as well as all seventy-five of the twenty-four hour automated teller machines. The software package, which was unproven in the field, was purchased for the sum of 1.2 million dollars from a newly formed national accounting firm that ostensibly specialized in banking. Victor speculated wryly that the fact that a United States senator and two state senators from Tennessee controlled the majority of stock in the accounting firm had absolutely nothing to do with selecting Mitchelson, Langworthy & King as the vendor. Not to mention that the U.S. senator from Tennessee and one state senator sat on the board of SNB.

Victor had vehemently argued against purchasing an unproven software package for such an exorbitant sum. He agreed that having their computer programmers write such a package would take years, and suggested that they evaluate and purchase a package that had a proven track record. In the end he was overruled. Mitchelson, Langworthy, & King acquired 1.2 million dollars, and SNB acquired a software package which, in the last six months of running 'live', had proven to be a nightmare.

Ronnie Jacobs's jazz played on to the unhearing ears of Victor until he was jolted out of his reverie by the repetitive honking of a horn from the driver behind him. Traffic had already started to move again and Victor was just sitting there, contemplating why he subjected himself to such a thankless job.

Chapter One

At eight o'clock Victor drove into the subterranean executive parking lot of SNB and took the elevator to the third floor computer center. He was checking his mailbox when the nightshift supervisor appeared behind him.

"Mr. Scofield, Mr. Vodeski is already here and wants to see you in his office pronto!"

"Herb, is there some problem I should know about before I go to Vodeski's office?" Victor asked.

"Maybe. The share drafts blew up last night, and the ATM's are down."

"Why didn't you phone me at home, Herb? Then maybe I could have done something about it?"

"I tried, Mr. Scofield, but there was no answer. I even tried your cell phone but you didn't answer."

Fantastic, Victor thought. *Just what I need. A back stabbing nightshift supervisor, a computer illiterate Senior Vice-President, in a job which I have no control over, on a rainy Monday.* The nightshift supervisor stood looking at Victor as if he were expecting something more.

"Okay, Herb, message delivered. Don't you have something to do other than play hall monitor, like go home?" Herb swelled up and stormed off while Victor pretended to sort through his mail.

Great, Victor thought, *just great*. Vodeski was on the warpath again, spurred on by the nightshift supervisor, 'Herb the Turd,' as Victor had privately nicknamed him. Eight-to-five odds Herb had called Vodeski last night or, more accurately, early this morning, concerning the problems with the system, hence Vodeski's early arrival. *So be it!* Victor hadn't selected the software and his analysts and programmers were doing the best that they could to try to make the system work by putting in fourteen-hour days over the last five months.

Victor stopped off at his office to drop off his mail, intending to proceed to the fifth floor 'glass house' to meet with Vodeski. With his back to the door he was startled by "Dammit, Scofield, didn't Moyers tell you that I wanted to see you ASAP?"

Turning around, Victor saw Vodeski standing in his office doorway with his hands on his hips.

"Yes, Bill, Herb just informed me and I was dropping off my mail before I came up to see you."

"Next time someone tells you I want to see you immediately you get your ass up to my office *immediately*, understand?"

You poor bastard, Victor thought. *I wonder what kind of relationship you have with your wife and kids.*

"Do you understand, Scofield?" Vodeski exclaimed as Victor stared at him, contemplating his last thought concerning Vodeski's interpersonal relationships.

"Yes, Bill, I understand," Victor said as he turned and put the mail on his desk.

"I've told you before, don't call me Bill. It's Mr. Vodeski to you, Scofield. The system's all screwed up, as usual. The share drafts haven't been transferred and a huge load of the ATM's all over town are spitting customer cards back out without a *How do you do?*. I want to know what's going on and what's being done."

"Mr. Vodeski, I had my cell phone with me last evening until ten o'clock and after that I was at home. I was never contacted, and at this point you probably know more about what's going on than I do. I can't give you any answers until I have an opportunity to assess the damage and have my analysts explore the possible causes. When they arrive this morning, that is."

"Scofield, your department's on thin ice. The new system is damaging the bank's reputation and hurting our customers. It's one problem after another," he said, with exasperation.

"I've got a meeting scheduled at ten o'clock, so call me before then and give me an update, okay?"

"Yes, Mr. Vodeski, I understand and I'll take care of it."

Great, another rock-and-roll Monday at SNB, Victor thought as Vodeski walked out of Scofield's office. *Business as usual. This has got to end.*

Vodeski, although a Senior Vice-President who held a seat on the loan committee, had nothing to do with overall banking policy, nor was he in a position to significantly influence any major strategic business decisions.

He had been hired two years previously, when Victor's previous boss retired, and though he was not cordial during the early tenure of his

Chapter One

position, he had at least been civil. Over the past year, however, his behavior had seemed to deteriorate to that of increasing intolerance and irritability. Victor had heard rumors of problems in his personal life with his family, and perhaps this, coupled with his apparent insecurity and lack of knowledge about technology, had taken its toll.

The Chairman, Brad Herron, seemed to be a reasonable man, but gave Victor the impression of being weak and indecisive. He tended to rely heavily on his senior VP's, with the possible exception of Vodeski. Victor hadn't had many occasions to talk with Herron, but it seemed that if he could approach the man on some logical basis, between the two of them they could find solutions to SNB's computer system problems, and perhaps even get Vodeski out of the management of the computer center. He would have to think that over.

Meanwhile, he had to schedule a meeting with his senior systems analysts to ascertain some solution to their present problems. Victor had about fifteen minutes to get his thoughts together before his analysis and programming staff was scheduled to report for work. Instead of thinking about the current system problems, Victor found himself thinking about his and the Tippins' annual excursion into the Great Smoky Mountains National Park next week.

Since moving to Tennessee six years ago after his wife's death, he and Buddy Tippins, along with Buddy's wife Donna, had scheduled their vacations to coincide so that they could take a hike into the backcountry of the Smoky Mountains.

During 1968 and 1969, Victor and Buddy had been in the same unit in Vietnam, through a tour on Long Range Reconnaissance Patrol (LRRP's). Victor had been a captain, since he had a Bachelor of Computer Science degree from Cal Tech after graduating in 1967, while Buddy was an E-6. Upon arriving in-country and being attached to Buddy's unit, Victor quickly learned that Buddy—who was beginning his second tour of duty—was an experienced and resourceful combat soldier. In fact, although Victor was Officer-In-Charge, Buddy had saved his life on no less than three occasions during their tour together.

Like most officers, Victor had been acutely aware that the backbone of the United States Army was its NCO's, not its officers or enlisted men. Buddy, with his extensive combat experience and concern about the well-being of the men under his charge, reinforced this fact. This,

SmokeFire!

coupled with his more than considerable backcountry experience in the Smokies before joining the army, made him extremely competent in the jungles of Vietnam.

Yes, the trip into the 'non-hostile bush', as Buddy had come to call their hiking terrain, would be a welcome relief. Victor smiled to himself as he thought about being with Buddy and Donna, his only family now.

* * *

Victor met with his senior systems staff at eight-thirty and by nine forty-five, the programmers had discovered and corrected yet another of the seemingly endless software bugs that caused Victor and his staff to lose sleep many nights. The ATM's were now working properly, and the share draft processing had been restarted. It was time to go up to Vodeski's office and give him the news.

When Victor entered the outer vestibule of Vodeski's plush office, he was greeted by Brenda Haskins, Vodeski's Administrative Assistant for the last four months.

Brenda always seemed to be in a cheerful mood, which Victor thought to be quite an accomplishment considering the temperament of her boss. Her predecessor had lasted for only two months before storming out in a rage, vowing never to return, as Vodeski's verbal abuse just got to be too much for her.

One month after coming on board as Vodeski's assistant, Brenda had come to Victor's office in tears after a tongue-lashing by Vodeski over some petty administrative error. Victor had listened and tried to console her, explaining that in the previous two years he had observed, and been the recipient of many of Vodeski's outbursts. He counseled her to try to not take it personally, as some people were self-made assholes. She had laughed at that, and ever since that day she and Victor had been friends.

"Hi Victor, what brings you to the lion's den?" Brenda asked with a smile.

"Oh, not much, just thought I'd drop by and ask Vodeski if I could buy him lunch at Deluca's since he's always so kind to everyone. You know, as a token of our appreciation for having such a generous and understanding boss."

Chapter One

"So right you are, Victor. Be sure to express my appreciation as well, right after you dump his lunch over his head," she said with a smirk.

"Actually, I'm here to give his Highness the update on our problems of last evening. Is he free?" Victor asked.

"Yeah, he's sitting in his office. Probably practicing tying a hangman's knot. Go on in and good luck."

Victor smiled at Brenda, knocked and opened one of the eight-paneled double walnut doors before walking into Vodeski's office.

After two years Victor was still somewhat overcome by the opulence of Vodeski's office. The floor was covered with a deep pile dark red carpet that Victor thought was softer than his bed. Around two walls were inset walnut bookshelves lined with volumes pertaining to banking regulations, taxation, and a full set of the Tennessee Code Annotated, as Vodeski was also an attorney. Interspersed among the books were quite a number of expensive knick-knacks. *Probably paid for by SNB*, Victor speculated.

From behind his massive mahogany desk, Vodeski looked up and glared at Victor.

"Scofield! You've got three minutes before I have to leave. I hope you're here to tell me your problem is solved!"

Your problem, Scofield thought. *Not our problem, but your problem.*

"Yes, sir, the staff uncovered another software bug in the share draft processing module, as well as a communications protocol bug in the software that drives the ATM's."

"Don't try to razzle-dazzle me with any computerese vernacular, Scofield, it doesn't impress me. Is the problem solved or not?"

"Yes, the share draft update has been restarted and all the ATM's are back up."

Standing up, Vodeski unzipped his leather valise and, while placing a file folder inside, asked, "Why wasn't this discovered during the testing of the system?"

"It was an error in the original software we purchased from ML&K. It wouldn't have shown up in our initial testing, but only when there was a peak load on our ATM's. I'll prepare a full report and submit it to you by tomorrow," Victor said.

"Today, Scofield! I want the report today, got it? I've got some explaining to do, and I need that report ASAP!"

SmokeFire!

Zipping the valise closed, Vodeski stepped around his desk and said, "Now, if you don't have anything else, I've got to get upstairs."

"As a matter of fact, Mr. Vodeski, there is one more thing. As you know, I've had my annual vacation scheduled for next week. I just wanted to..."

"No vacations, Scofield! Not for you and not for your staff. Not until all these computer problems are straightened out."

"Mr. Vodeski, I'm the only member of my department with any scheduled time off next week. I have several very competent people who can handle any problems that might come up. I cleared this with you late last year, and I've made plans. Plans which involve people other than myself."

"I know about your plans, Scofield, playing Boy Scout in the woods. It's not like you've rented a condo in Bermuda, and it wouldn't make any difference if you had. I repeat, no time off for you or any of your people and that's final."

Victor turned without saying another word and walked out of Vodeski's office. *What a prick,* he thought. *I'll bet if we didn't have any computer problems, his attitude wouldn't be any different.*

Reading his mood as he walked from Vodeski's office, Brenda asked, "Hey, Victor, what about an early lunch with a friendly face?"

"Sorry, Brenda, I'd really like that but I have to prepare a report about last night's problems and have it to Vodeski by this afternoon. How about a rain check? It seems that I'll have plenty of time next week."

"I thought you were going up to the Smokies with Buddy and Donna next week."

"Not any more. Vodeski made short work of that."

Sensing the disappointment in his voice, Brenda said, "I'm sorry, Victor, I know you look forward to your trips with Buddy. Maybe you guys could postpone it until Vodeski's in a better mood."

"That would mean postponing it until Vodeski's retirement, and I'm not sure I can wait that long, but I'll call Buddy and see what we can do."

Garnering her courage, Brenda was just about to ask Victor to come over to her apartment for dinner that night when Vodeski came out of his office and glared at the both of them. He tossed a file folder into Brenda's 'in' basket and walked toward the elevator.

Chapter One

Brenda knew the moment was lost, and the sight of Vodeski had weakened her courage. Victor said he would see her later and then he was gone.

Ever since her conversation with Victor several months ago, after Vodeski had reduced her to tears, she had wanted to get to know him better. She was twenty-eight, many years younger than Victor, but that didn't make any difference to her. Victor seemed like an intelligent and sensitive man. Not especially macho, Victor was only about five-feet eight-inches tall, clean-shaven with short cropped black/brown hair that was beginning to turn gray at the temples. At forty-nine-years-old, he wasn't one of those men whom women turned to look at, just slightly better than average looking. But the more Brenda talked with Victor, the more she was attracted to him, and Brenda wasn't attracted to many men.

Over the last couple of months they'd had casual lunches together several times and Brenda wanted more. She didn't delude herself into thinking that Victor was 'Mr. Right,' and wasn't in love with him or anything like that. She just wanted to get to know him better. Although she had hoped Victor would ask her out, he had never intimated that he was interested in anything more than a casual friendship.

Brenda had learned from Victor's secretary that his wife had died of leukemia about six years ago. Although she had never experienced the death of anyone close to her, she imagined it must be extremely traumatic. She didn't want to force anything on Victor, not so much from fear of rejection or that her intentions would be misinterpreted, but she suspected that Victor had loved his wife very much and that he was still grieving. There was an aloofness about Victor, like he was standing on the outside and was observing everyone else. Victor was always cool and calm and always seemed to say the right thing at the right time. When he spoke to anyone, he looked him straight in the eye, and Brenda got the impression that Victor, with his bright blue eyes, was looking right into her soul when she talked to him. It seemed that any relationship with Victor would have to be in his own time and probably on his own terms. She could wait and hope that someday he would notice her.

In point of fact, Victor had noticed Brenda. As he was walking back down the stairs to his office, he reflected on her offer of lunch and was touched. Brenda was a nice girl, Victor thought. She'd make somebody a good wife. She had a kindness about her that he found attractive, and a good sense of humor that he appreciated in anyone, especially women.

He was aware that Brenda was interested in him, but he just couldn't bring himself to become involved with anyone since Cathy's death. It wasn't out of respect for Cathy, for she would want him to be happy and he knew that. But when Cathy died, a part of Victor died too. He had seen much death in Vietnam and had lost many friends there, but that pain was nothing when compared to losing Cathy.

Shaking his head to ward off unpleasant thoughts, Victor punched in the code key for access to the computer center and entered his small glassed-in office. Before preparing his report for Vodeski, which would probably go unread, he would call Buddy and cancel out on the trip. *Sometimes life really sucks*, Victor thought, not knowing how bad things could really get.

Chapter Two

Friday, April 9, 1999
Knoxville, Tennessee

The rest of the week at SNB was uneventful. The problems with the computer center settled down thanks to Victor's competent staff. He had called Buddy the previous Monday and explained the situation, and as he had expected, Buddy was pissed.

"Come on, Vick, why don't you tell Vodeski you're going anyway? Better yet, why don't you tell him to kiss off and leave those ingrates to their own devices? God knows you can afford it."

While driving home Victor contemplated Buddy's comment. He had thought of quitting on more than one occasion, and Buddy did have a point. Victor's salary was one hundred thousand dollars a year, and he lived a relatively frugal lifestyle. In the six years since moving to Knoxville, he had managed to save over two hundred and fifty thousand dollars, and that, coupled with Cathy's life insurance benefit and some wise investments, had resulted in an investment portfolio of approximately three-quarters of a million dollars. More than enough to allow him to quit work for several years.

SmokeFire!

He had once heard the term 'go to hell money,' and he guessed that's what he had, but Victor wasn't ready to pull the plug on SNB yet. Maybe Vodeski would make a serious error in the future, serious enough to make Brad Herron fire him, and maybe Herron would replace him with someone who was a professional, thus making Victor's job easier. *A lot of maybes*, Victor thought, *but then again, you never know what is going to happen next.*

Victor pulled into the driveway of his modest little English Tudor house in west Knoxville, activated the electronic garage door opener and pulled in. After pressing the button on the remote that closed the garage door, he walked into his kitchen, retrieved a Glorsch beer from the refrigerator, popped the snap cap, and took a large swallow. Setting the beer on the kitchen table and taking his coat and tie off, he sat down and wondered what he was going to do this weekend.

Buddy and Donna would be preparing to leave for the trip and would probably be busy packing up. Buddy was meticulous in his packing—never taking too much, but always seeming to have what was needed. Once, a couple of years prior, they had been on the trail for several hours on a hot summer afternoon. While they were taking a break, Donna had said, "Boy, something cold would really be good right now," and Victor had agreed. Buddy added, "Yeah, how about a cold glass of Chablis?"

Victor had replied with, "Buddy, you'd have to be crazy to haul a cold bottle of wine into the backcountry." And Buddy had remarked, "You're right! That's why you're carrying it." Sure enough, Buddy had somehow slipped a bottle of California Chablis, complete with cold packs, into Victor's backpack.

They had all had a good laugh over that, and, of course, each of them had consumed several cups of Chablis. Victor had made them drink it all so he wouldn't have to carry it any farther.

Victor smiled when he recalled the image of the three of them sitting along the trail drinking cold Chablis. He remembered criticizing Buddy for having to drink it out of a paper cup.

"Figured you'd get suspicious if I'd packed three stem glasses in your pack, but I considered it."

Yes, Buddy was always ready, ready for just about anything that came along, and always ready with his quick wit and practical jokes.

Chapter Two

The thought of another lonely weekend loomed in Victor's mind. Maybe he would go down to the video store and pick up some movies, order a pizza, and have a quiet weekend.

Finishing off his beer he got up to get another and decided to call Buddy and Donna and wish them well on their trip. Maybe they would invite him over tonight, Victor hoped. He was feeling lonely and could use some company, and it was Buddy and Donna or nobody, since Victor had many acquaintances but only two real friends.

Snapping off the rubber cap of another Glorsch, he dialed Buddy's number. Donna answered on the second ring.

"Hello?"

"Hi, Donna, it's Vick."

"Vick! I've told you it's not necessary to identify yourself when you call. Stop being the banker." Donna knew Victor hated being called a banker, but she couldn't resist. Every time Victor called, he identified himself as if she wouldn't recognize his voice. After all, she'd only known him for thirty-plus years.

"I'm not a banker," Victor said, recognizing the old jibe. "What are you guys doing?"

"Buddy's down in the den repacking our packs for the umpteenth time and I'm here in the kitchen feeding Jennifer," she said, referring to Buddy and Donna's two-year-old daughter whom Victor adored.

Every time he saw Jennifer, Victor wondered what his and Cathy's life would have been like if she hadn't gotten sick. They'd talked about kids and had decided that after Victor had gotten his Master's degree in computer science, they'd buy a house and Cathy could quit her job and get pregnant. Victor remembered joking that after that they could get a station wagon, a sheep dog, and that he could build a white picket fence around the front lawn and go bowling every Wednesday night with the boys.

Watch it, Vick, he thought, *that's in the past.*

"What are you doing, Vick, trying to decide what movies to go rent and whether or not you're going to have pepperoni on your pizza?"

She knows me too well, Victor thought.

"Not really, I just got in from work and thought I'd give you guys a call to wish you a good trip," Victor responded, trying to evade the truth.

"Victor, don't lie to me. I know you're depressed about not going with us, but Buddy just couldn't change his vacation time. I also know you're

SmokeFire!

sitting there thinking about what you're going to do this weekend while drinking one of those horrid green beers, and that you've already checked the TV guide to see what's on the tube tonight."

Got her, Victor thought, smiling into the mouthpiece. *I haven't checked the TV guide yet—and she thinks she's so smart.* Thank God they didn't have phones connected to video cameras. Donna knew Victor better than anyone else, except for Cathy. Buddy and Victor were best friends, but Donna had that special insight that only some women seemed to have. While Buddy could sense Victor's moods and what motivated him, Donna sensed his feelings and how they affected him. Sometimes, it was as if she could read his mind, or his heart, as the case may be. Some men might find that trait uncomfortable; however, Victor prized it as a special quality that strengthened relationships and allowed for more intimacy. Cathy had possessed it, and when Donna showed those flashes of insight, it often saddened him, reminding him of how Cathy had sometimes given him a special smile, as she looked into his heart.

Buddy is a very lucky man. I was a lucky man once, Victor thought.

"No, Donna, you're wrong again. I just wanted to wish you good weather and good fishing."

"Listen Victor, I've got to get all of Jennifer's things together to take to Mom's in the morning, so I'm going to be pretty busy. You know how Buddy gets before these trips and he needs some company. Why don't you come over and get him out of my hair? He's driving me batty!"

Beautiful, Victor thought, *just beautiful*. Donna knew how to care without putting someone in an uncomfortable position; there was that flash of insight again. Accepting her subtle offer, Victor said he'd be glad to help and would be over in about thirty minutes.

Buddy and Donna lived in a small split foyer over in Crestwood Hills, about a ten-minute drive from Victor's house. He had time to take a quick shower and stop off at the package store for a bottle of Chablis. Maybe he'd get two bottles, and if Buddy left him alone with his pack long enough, he'd be able to obtain some payback.

* * *

Chapter Two

Victor returned home from Buddy and Donna's about eleven o'clock feeling much better for having been with them. They'd talked mostly about the trip.

Several months previously they'd grilled some steaks and then gotten out a detailed map of the Great Smoky Mountains National Park to plan their next excursion into the non-hostile bush. Over the years they had hiked almost all of the main trails, but they preferred the less crowded primitive backcountry campsites where most tourists dared not venture. They would typically start out at some point on one end of the Park, and over a week's time would hike quite a number of miles to another exit point where they had left a second automobile for the return trip. This allowed them to explore trails and campsites that they had never been to before.

Sometimes, if the campsite was 'primo,' as Buddy called it, and if the trout fishing was good, they would stay there and then hike back out to their point of origin. Mainly they had no hard and fast plan, but preferred to be flexible and take advantage of whatever was offered along the way.

On this particular trip they planned to start at the Deep Creek trail and proceed up towards Clingman's Dome. Instead of climbing to the top of the sixty-six-hundred foot peak of Clingman's Dome, they planned to intercept the Nolan Divide Trail and move across the mid-point of the Dome, then descend back into the valley along Panther Creek, and exit at a point near Fontana Lake.

Buddy, having been raised in the foothills of the Smoky Mountains in the little town of Maryville, was the one most familiar with the mountains and its trails and acted as their guide. On this particular trip he said they would enjoy some excellent trout fishing, view some of the oldest trees in the Park, and even pass through an old survey camp that was established in the late forties. The camp had been destroyed by a fire in the early fifties that had also claimed a number of lives. "Thus," as Buddy had stated, "providing some excellent ghost story material." Telling ghost stories was one of Buddy's favorite campsite pastimes. *Probably*, Victor speculated, *because it scared the hell out of Donna.*

However, Victor would miss out on all this since Buddy couldn't reschedule his vacation time and Victor couldn't get any time off. So, Buddy and Donna had decided to go it alone, and Victor had made them promise that they would take many pictures. When they returned the

SmokeFire!

following Saturday, he expected to hear every detail, including stories of hundred pound fish that Buddy had landed—with one arm! When Victor left their house, Buddy promised that he'd take some time off without pay later in the late spring or summer, so Victor could have an opportunity to go into the non-hostile bush with him. Donna gave him a hug and a kiss on the cheek, and putting her lips close to his ear said, "Remember, Vick, we love you, and we'll be back soon," which embarrassed Victor somewhat but also touched him deeply.

Victor drove out of the driveway, smiling to himself over how fortunate he was to have such good friends, and also much pleased by the thought of Buddy's discovering a bottle of French Chablis in his backpack, albeit hot, with a note attached stating, "Not with you in body, but in 'spirit'."

Chapter Three

Saturday night, April 10, 1999
Great Smoky Mountains National Park
Four miles due west of Mt. Lanier

Buddy and Donna finished setting up camp. It had started raining late in the afternoon and hadn't stopped yet. It wasn't a thunderstorm but a warm and steady rain. The temperature was fifty-two, warm for this time of year, but it would cool off considerably by early morning, perhaps even dropping down to freezing.

We're not getting off to a good start, Donna thought. The rain, coupled with the ordeal at Park Headquarters, had slowed down their progress considerably, and they had reached the campsite just as the sun was going down.

They had arrived at Park Headquarters early that morning in order to obtain their backcountry permit. The park ranger issuing permits was a petite young blond and she stood behind a long counter. When Buddy had requested a permit for the areas in which they would be hiking,

SmokeFire!

she had informed him that permits were not issued for their requested jump off point. There were no primitive campsites in that area nor were there any improved trails.

Buddy had explained that they were experienced hikers, had shown her their itinerary, and had pointed out the unimproved trails they would use on a map underneath a piece of plastic on the counter.

"Sir, your experience as a hiker doesn't matter. Permits are not issued for that area, so you'll have to choose another point of origin," she had said.

"I don't want to choose another point of origin, I want to start there." He tapped his finger twice on the map, indicating a point about five miles south of the Abrams Creek ranger station. "We'll only be in that area for one night, then we'll be moving on, intercepting the Gregory Bald trail here," he had said, his finger following a small line on the map. "And later, tomorrow afternoon, we'll make camp here, at site number fourteen."

The ranger had been adamant, and Buddy had become disgusted, stating that the National Park belonged to the taxpayers and not the park rangers and that he could hike any damn place he wanted to. About that time another ranger, a large man, appeared and had asked if he could be of service.

"Sir, this gentleman wants to hike in an area where there are no trails and to make camp. I've told him we don't issue permits for the area," she had said rather snootily, Donna thought, to the large ranger who she thought closely resembled 'Smoky The Bear.'

"My name is Harrison Pike. I'm the Chief Ranger," he had said, turning his six-foot five-inch frame towards Buddy. "Where is it you're wanting to go?"

"We want to start here," once again indicating a point on the map just south of the Abrams Creek Ranger Station, "and work our way up the stream. We'll make camp tonight here, in this small valley, continuing on tomorrow where we'll pick up the Gregory Bald trail, about right here," he said confidently, while moving his finger along their intended course.

"Sorry, the young lady's right. We don't issue permits for that area. In the first place, that's where we place rogue bears. Besides that, y'all get back in there, fall and break a leg or get snake bit, and we'd have a helluva time gettin' you out with no trails and all."

Chapter Three

Buddy had attempted to argue the point, but the Chief Ranger wouldn't budge, simply stating that it was Park policy and not his.

In the end they had issued a permit for them to camp on the Rabbit Creek trail, far from their intended route.

Buddy had seemingly acquiesced and accepted the permit, but when they had gotten back into the car, he had said, "Screw that, the fishing's terrible on Rabbit Creek. We're sticking to our original plan. Those idiots'll never know the difference."

Donna had not felt comfortable deceiving the rangers, especially the Chief Ranger, but she trusted Buddy's skills in the bush. He had a point, she had thought, when he said those trails were for pilgrims, his term for amateurs, and that they would have to share the campsite with other hikers, which neither of them wanted to do.

They had parked Donna's Toyota on the gravel road that led from Chilhowee Lake to the Abrams Creek Ranger Station; Buddy fly fished as they hiked up the creek, catching several respectably sized rainbow trout, especially at one deep pool.

After making camp, the rain showed no promise of slacking off, so they crawled into the small mountain tent for shelter. Buddy pumped up and lit the small backpack Coleman lantern, and the interior of the tent glowed as if in the light of day.

"Good thing we wrapped these bags," Buddy said as he unrolled the sleeping bags from dry cleaning cellophane, "or we'd be wringin' 'em out about now. That's the only thing I don't like about hiking in the Smokies in the spring—the rain."

"Oh I don't know, it's kind of romantic. Sitting here in the tent, just the two of us, listening to the rain fall on the roof."

"You want romance? I could have packed Jennifer's battery-powered record player and a couple of Johnny Mathis albums in Vick's pack if he had come along," he said with a laugh.

"I wish Vick was here. He was pretty depressed about not being able to come along."

"Yeah, I noticed that too. It's not just that, though, it's that crappy job of his. And the anniversary of Cathy's death is coming up soon too. Guess it's all weighing pretty heavy on his mind."

"Does he talk very much to you about Cathy? You being his best friend and all?" Donna had asked.

SmokeFire!

"Sometimes, not so much anymore, though. He still misses her a lot and I don't think he's quite ready to let her go. They had made a lot of plans after he got out of graduate school, and all that went down the drain when she died. It's taken its toll on him, but he does pretty well with it, better than I would have probably," Buddy said, looking at Donna while raising his eyebrows and tightening his lower lip.

"I hope neither one of us has to ever face that Buddy, I know I couldn't do it."

"Well, I guess one of us is going to have to face it sooner or later, and none of us knows what we're capable of dealing with until it happens. Anyway, speaking of romanticism, how about a glass of Chablis."

"Buddy, if you packed a bottle of wine in my backpack, I'm going to drink it all myself and put the empty bottle, with the cork stuck in the top with the corkscrew, in one of your anatomical orifices."

Donna really didn't care whether or not Buddy had put it in her pack or his. The sound of the rain coming down on the top of the tent and knowing they were probably more alone than anyone else in the Smokies, at least in terms of distance, made her feel very romantic. But she couldn't resist giving Buddy a hard time about the 'shill wine,' as Vick had called it on one of their previous trips.

She knew that after supper and a couple of glasses of Chablis, Buddy would proceed to relate some fabricated ghost story about this particular campsite and how previous campers here had come to some mysterious and hideous end.

"No, this time believe it or not, I lugged it in myself. Actually Vick slipped it into my pack last night when I went to the bathroom—he thought I wouldn't know. Not only that, but I put two, yes count em' two, of our "T" glasses in my sleeping bag when I rolled it up," he said, referring to two of the four Waterford wine glasses engraved with a gothic capital "T" that Victor had given to them the previous Christmas.

"Why don't you unpack the rucks," pointing to their backpacks, "and figure out something to go with these rainbows while I go get some firewood. After supper I'll tell you about what really killed the men in the army survey camp near this area over forty years ago."

"Buddy, let's lose the ghost stories for tonight, okay? You can tell me all about the Monster of Gregory's Bald tomorrow night when we make camp at fourteen, and how it's eaten numerous boy scouts over the

Chapter Three

years," Donna said as she turned to the corner of the tent, untied the hold-down elastic straps on her backpack, and tossed back the top shield.

"No, this story's kind of a legend, not something I just made up," Buddy said. "It really happened around 1951. Some Army Corps of Engineers camp was totally destroyed. They never really did find out what happened..." His voice trailed off dramatically and then he began again with enthusiasm. "But I'll tell you another one tomorrow night about the 'little people' of the Chimneys. It was passed down by the Cherokee Indians and is obscurely referred to in some of their history when they roamed the area now called the Smoky Mountains. It's kind of interesting in a way, as..."

Interrupting, Donna announced with an inflection that said that she meant business, "Buddy, cut it out! You're ruining my mood and making me wonder what's outside the walls of this tent. Don't do this tonight! Let's just build a fire, fix some supper, and enjoy the serenity of being here together. Don't spoil it by making me afraid of the dark!"

"I'm sorry, I didn't mean to scare you. I just read this article a few months ago in Archeology Today, which focused on the Cherokee's lifestyles, and some of their superstitious beliefs. It made reference to a 'spirit' which the Cherokee's believed..."

"Buddy!" Donna exclaimed as she pointed her finger towards him.

Holding his hands up as if surrendering, Buddy said, "Okay, Okay! I'm going to set up the lean-to, and then go get some firewood. You get out the stuff and I'll be back in about twenty minutes. I'll build a fire and cook supper while you open up the Chablis. After that maybe we can figure out something else to do!" He winked, unzipped the mosquito netting on the tent door, threw the flap back, and was out before she could respond.

Most people would have believed that it was impossible to start a fire in such a steady rain, much less gather any kind of dry firewood. However, Donna had known Buddy long enough to know that there wasn't much that he could not do in the forest—in the bush, as he referred to it.

Many years before, he had shown her that the correct way to start a fire in the rain was to gather as much dry wood as was possible. While it had been raining, they had walked just outside the perimeter of their campsite, and Buddy had looked up into the trees.

SmokeFire!

"When it's raining you won't find any dry firewood on the ground, it's water-logged," he had explained. "You got to get a lot of small dry stuff off of the dead trees. The small branches on dead trees don't hold water very well, especially on their underside, so it'll be drier than any you'll ever get off the ground." He then went through the area pulling limbs of assorted sizes off of dead trees. As he held one out to Donna, she was amazed at how dry it was, considering how long it had been raining.

"That's where you'll find the dry stuff, still on the trees. Only pilgrims try to dry out wet wood when starting a fire, which is okay if you happen to have forty pounds of dry newspaper available. Remember, start with a lot of small stuff off the branches. If you don't have half a bushel of sticks the diameter of matchsticks, then you don't have enough. Work your way up to the larger sticks—all of them off the trees, not on the ground. Once you got it going good, you can put the waterlogged big stuff on and the coals will dry it out before it burns. You don't have to worry about keeping the rain off your fire. Unless it's a real 'gully washer' it won't put your fire out. Contrary to what most people think, it takes a lot of water to put out a fire, more than you'll get in the average rainstorm if you keep it going good."

She'd been amazed at the fire he had built in that rain. She had never thought it possible.

She looked out of the netting through the thick fog that had formed in the steady rain. Buddy was just completing setting up a lean-to that would keep their equipment dry. Later he would raise the backpacks up into a tree with a rope to prevent any wildlife from breaking into their quarters while they slept and tearing open the packs.

With his hooded poncho strings tied tightly around his chin, he gave a wave and went off in search of firewood. The fog was becoming so thick Donna could barely make out his features even though he was only ten feet away, and soon he disappeared into the trees at the edge of the campsite.

After unpacking the items that they would require for supper, Donna found a corkscrew in the side pocket of Buddy's backpack along with the bottle of Chablis and Vick's note.

Smiling as she read Victor's note, Donna again found herself wishing that Vick were here with them, with her. She always felt safer with Vick around. Not that she didn't feel safe with Buddy, because she did. It was

Chapter Three

just that Vick seemed always to be in control—Vick with all the answers—always making her feel comfortable, like nothing bad was going to happen to anybody as long as he was around.

Donna would never share her feelings about Vick to anyone else, as these were her private thoughts. She loved Vick, not in the sense of romantic love but a love that was different. A love of friendship, maybe even something more than that, she thought. She did not deceive herself in that if it weren't for Buddy, and all things being equal, she could fall for Vick.

These thoughts, as they had before, made her feel a little guilty since Donna and Cathy had been good friends, and she sometimes felt like she was betraying Cathy, and Buddy, for that matter, when she looked at Vick and had a feeling that she understood him.

Shrugging off her thoughts she spread a white towel between their two sleeping bags and smoothed it out with her hands, creating a makeshift dinner table. She set the two Waterford glasses on each corner.

Searching further in Buddy's pack, she found a small candle, and ripping off a small square of aluminum foil to catch the wax, she set it on the center of the towel.

Buddy wouldn't ever admit it, she thought, but at heart he was a romantic too. Otherwise he wouldn't have packed the candle.

Buddy had now been gone for about thirty minutes, and during that time the rain had stopped. Donna wondered what was keeping him, as it usually didn't take that long for him to gather firewood, even in the rain.

Taking up her flashlight and switching it on, she threw back the inner mosquito net of the tent and the outer nylon flaps and stepped out.

Such a clean and fresh smell, *kind of makes you feel on the inside what you feel on the outside after taking a shower*, she thought.

She walked to the edge of the campsite, which was just a small clearing of about twenty feet in diameter, and shone her flashlight into the lingering dense fog. She called out to Buddy and when he didn't answer, she called out again.

"Buddy, where are you? Please don't try to scare me." But something inside said that Buddy wasn't trying to scare her, and she began to feel uneasy. This was a really primitive area, and the terrain was rough. Maybe Buddy had fallen and hit his head, and couldn't answer. *Okay*, she thought, *get a grip! Buddy's probably just getting the driest wood*

SmokeFire!

obtainable in the National Park and has wandered farther away from the campsite than he'd intended. He'll be back any minute.

Just then she heard a sound off to the right, like a stick breaking when stepped on. Swinging her flashlight, she called out. "Buddy, get in here and start the fire, I'm getting cold!" But there was no answer. There was only the glistening reflection of the flashlight beam on the rain-soaked bark of the trees at the edge of the campsite and the impenetrable fog beyond. The flashlight's beam suddenly seemed painfully inadequate. She swung the flashlight left and then right again, scanning the tree line. *God, it's dark*, she thought.

"Damn this fog, if I didn't know better, I'd think it was getting thicker!" she said out loud, as the flashlight could hardly penetrate more than ten feet now.

There was a sound behind her, something moving in the thick rhododendron! She swirled around and shone the flashlight's beam in the direction of the sound.

"I can't see anything in this fog," she muttered to herself in a panic. She wanted to call out to Buddy, but her mouth and throat were so dry and she was breathing so fast that she couldn't speak.

If this is one of Buddy's ghost story tricks, she thought, *I'll kill him!*

Off to her right a twig snapped. Without swinging the flashlight around, she looked in the direction of the sound. Something was there! *Where was Buddy—was it Buddy?* she asked herself. She could hear her heartbeat in her ears, like a bass drum growing louder with each beat.

Just then the rhododendron moved, and she saw the brightest, reddest eye she had ever seen. By now her fear had reached such a peak that she just let the flashlight's beam fall to the ground beside her feet as she looked at the beaming red eye staring back at her. Just as she was about to scream, she was knocked to the ground with a tremendous blow.

Lying on her back she could see some stars through the breaking clouds and the early leaves of the trees. She felt very dizzy and sleepy. There was a spreading warmth over her chest and shoulder and a numbness in her neck. She felt no pain, but when she tried to move her arms and legs, they wouldn't respond.

What is happening? Donna felt more than thought.

Chapter Three

Still looking up, she saw the branch of a birch tree sway in the gentle breeze, and a bright star shone overhead through a little break in the clouds.

How clear the image. I wonder what star that is? Donna asked herself, and then she thought, *Why would I think about that at a time like this? What's happening?*

Donna Tippins knew with a certainty that she was about to die. She did not know why or how, but she knew. She tried to speak, but there was only a bubbling sound emanating from what was left of her throat.

In the thick fog she saw something very large, something very dark moving through the rhododendron, coming towards her. She could now see the one large red eye as it approached her.

By now almost all rationale and sanity had left her, as her mind, confronted by such extreme terror, began to shut down.

Again Donna tried to speak, but the words only echoed in her mind. She tried to raise her right arm up, as if reaching for something, but it would not move. Using all her strength, she was able to raise her right hand about one inch off the ground just as the giant figure with the bright red eye seemed to reach towards her.

Thinking of her daughter, she tried to scream, but the sound existed only in her mind.

Oh, God, Jennifer... Suddenly for Donna Tippins there was nothing, nothing at all.

Chapter Four

10:30 a.m. Monday, April 19, 1999
Knoxville, Tennessee

In his glass fronted office in the computer room, Victor sat in his Steel Case desk chair with his feet propped on the corner of his desk. He flipped idly through a technical journal, unable to concentrate.

Dammit, something's wrong, he thought to himself. Buddy and Donna were supposed to be back by last Saturday night, at the latest.

He had expected a phone call from Buddy sometime late Saturday night, regaling him with prevarications about enormous prehistoric rainbow trout hooked but not landed, of dubious intrusions of black bears and mountain lions into their campsites, and of incredible events befalling him and Donna while in the non-hostile bush. But there had been no call.

Sunday he had passed the time by sleeping until nine-thirty. He had called Buddy's about eleven that morning, giving them time to sleep in. He figured they had probably returned late the previous evening, and he had not wanted to disturb them by calling too early, but there had been no answer.

SmokeFire!

He had passed the time yesterday afternoon by playing a Star Trek fest on his VCR, and calling Buddy every hour or so. Listening to the endless ringing of their telephone, his uneasiness had continued to grow.

All right, time to take ball in hand, he thought, throwing the technical journal onto his credenza and swinging his feet off his desk onto the floor.

Victor had debated about calling Donna's mother and unduly worrying her. But if anybody knew the status of Buddy and Donna, it would be Mae, as Mae was babysitting Jennifer while they were away.

Victor picked up the telephone receiver and dialed nine for an outside line. Once he heard the second dial tone, he dialed Mae's number and waited for her to answer. She picked up on the second ring.

"Hello!"

"Mae, this is Victor Scofield. I was calling to see if maybe you had heard anything from Buddy and Donna."

Before Victor finished his statement, sensing the meaning in her pause, he knew that he had made a mistake, that Mae had heard nothing from them. *Damn*, he thought.

"No, Victor, and I'm very worried and you must be too if you're calling me. I expected them back late Saturday night and Donna said that they would be by to pick up Jennifer around lunch yesterday."

Trapped, Victor thought, *I'm trapped. How do I alleviate this woman's fears without alarming her?*

"I'm not worried, Mae, just curious. I heard from the park ranger that the trout were really hitting up on Panther and Rabbit Creek, and I thought that Buddy might have called in and said they were staying a couple of extra days since he's probably hauling them in. You know how Buddy is when it comes to trout," Victor said, trying to sound casual.

"Victor, I'm well aware of how Buddy is when it comes to trout, or for that matter anything else! I'm also aware of how responsible my daughter is when it comes to worrying her mother unnecessarily. God knows her husband doesn't give a Gabrials horn about what I think, he only cares about himself!"

I should have known better, Victor thought. Mae had never liked Buddy and had always felt that Donna had married beneath herself, and she had never let Buddy—or anyone else for that matter—forget it. *Her and her proud religion*, Victor thought. Always belittling Buddy, always

Chapter Four

attempting to demean him to anyone who would listen. Her truth—the truth—one and the same. Deprecating the finest man that Victor had ever known. Once again he bit his tongue.

"Okay, Mae, I just wondered if Donna had called in saying they were staying a couple of extra days. I'm sure they are. You know telephones aren't too handy in that area. When I hear from them, I'll call you. Goodbye," Victor said, placing the phone gently in the cradle, not waiting for a response, and resisting the temptation to slam it down. *Okay*, he thought, *next step*.

Victor inserted the small key into the lock of his center desk drawer and, pushing the drawer in, locked his desk. He walked out of his office, passing the system console where his senior analyst was examining the screen with one of the computer operators. Victor said he had an appointment and would have his cell phone if they needed him.

Victor had thought of phoning the park headquarters to see if they had any information about Buddy and Donna, but he thought he would get better results by making his inquiry in person. He didn't know the procedure for reporting lost persons, if in fact they were lost. It seemed logical that someone would have to report that two hikers had not returned before the park service would initiate any kind of investigation as to their whereabouts, since backcountry hikers were not required to report in at the completion of their hike.

Victor waited for the wooden gate at the exit of the underground parking lot to open, then pulled out and turned left onto Gay Street heading south. Since he was already downtown, he decided to take highway 441 south through Pigeon Forge and on into Gatlinburg rather than taking the circuitous route of Interstate 40 and going through Sevierville.

Crossing the Gay Street Bridge, Victor wondered if he was overreacting. The thought of Buddy, and, for that matter, Donna, becoming lost in the Smokies was ludicrous. Buddy had grown up in East Tennessee and had been in the Boy Scouts from age nine until he was seventeen, finally achieving the rank of Eagle. Much of his eight years in scouting had been spent in the backcountry of the Smokies. Buddy had often remarked that he had learned more about survival in the Boy Scouts than he had ever learned in Ranger School at Fort Gordon, and Victor had believed him.

SmokeFire!

If they're not lost, Victor thought, *then there must be some other reason as to why they are two days late.* Even if the fishing had been extraordinarily good, Donna would not have conceded to staying a couple of extra days without calling her mom and letting her know their plans. Since there were no phones in the backcountry, Donna would have insisted that they leave, and that he and Victor could return the next weekend for a short fishing trip.

The more he went over it, the more he was convinced that something must have happened. Given that Buddy would not—could not—become lost, something else must have happened. Maybe one of them had fallen and broken a leg and was unable to walk out. The thought of Buddy or Donna pulling the other on a litter formed in his mind. No, they would not do that. If someone were injured in the backcountry, the priority would be to get the injured person stabilized and comfortable, and then go for help. With both of them being familiar with the geography, either one of them could walk out without a pack in less than a day, as he or she would be moving fast. So that scenario didn't make sense either, he thought.

What if something happened to both of them? Victor visualized Buddy with his fly rod standing in the middle of Panther Creek while Donna lay on the side of the stream getting some sun or reading, when a wall of water from rains in the high country rushed through sweeping both of them downstream.

No, Victor thought. *Flash floods do occur in the mountains but they're extremely rare, as the streams tend to swell gradually over a period of several hours rather than instantly flooding.* He also knew that even with flooding being a rarity that Buddy would be on the alert. That couldn't be it either.

The traffic was bumper-to-bumper through Pigeon Forge, which was usual for that time of year. The tourist season was just getting underway, and before Labor Day fifteen million people would have passed through the area.

Pigeon Forge is a community located near the famous resort town of Gatlinburg, which is nestled on the boundary of the National Park. It had cultivated a tourist attraction of its own within the past decade, capitalizing on the Smokies and Gatlinburg attractions. He passed new hotels, restaurants, and amusement parks. It had been a couple of years

Chapter Four

since he had driven this route, and he was amazed at the rate of growth, which was evidenced by the congested traffic.

Victor downshifted the 'Z' and pulled up behind a large Airstream trailer with Ohio tags. It was useless to speculate, he thought, and the best course of action was to alert the park personnel and let them handle it. He retrieved a Grover Washington tape from the cassette caddy and inserted it into the tape player, hoping it would ease his anxiety and keep his imagination from running wild.

He pulled into the park headquarters building outside of Gatlinburg at twelve-fifteen. Getting out of his car, he wondered what he was going to say to the ranger on duty.

He opened the door to the headquarters building, an older wood structure, and walked up to the counter. A young man dressed in a park service uniform was talking to a young couple about the particulars of the Alum Cave Bluff trail, a short trail of about two and one-half miles that was on the way to Mount LeConte. Their questions about the danger from bears and mountain lions revealed that they were obviously inexperienced hikers.

The ranger explained patiently that there was certainly no danger from bears in that part of the park; and as far as mountain lions were concerned, there had been few sightings over the last ten years; and, further, if they encountered any wildlife of the four-legged variety, it would probably be deer. He assured them that it was a very scenic trail that could be hiked in a few hours and encouraged them to be sure to take their camera.

Seemingly reassured by the ranger's encouragement, the couple thanked the ranger for his advice and walked past Victor on their way out.

Victor approached the counter as the ranger was refolding a trail map.

"Can I help you?"

"My name is Victor Scofield. I'm from Knoxville," Victor said, hoping that would give him some credibility, "and I'm concerned about two friends of mine who went into the backcountry over a week ago. They were scheduled to return last Saturday but we haven't heard from them. They're both experienced hikers and it's unlike them to be overdue, and I'm concerned that something might have happened."

"What area were they hiking in, Mr. Scofield?"

SmokeFire!

"They started off at the Abrams Creek Bridge on Highway 129 and were going up Panther Creek, intercepting Parson's Branch Road, over to Gregory's Bald to Shuckstack, and exiting at Fontana Dam."

"Well, they wouldn't have gone up Panther Creek, as that's a restricted area where camping is not permitted. We use that area to relocate rogue black bears, and besides, there's no trails there. If that was their intended route, then the ranger on duty at the time they obtained their backcountry permit would have insisted on another point of origin. What are their names and what was their departure date, Mr. Scofield?" His forehead was wrinkled with concern and he held his pencil ready.

"Tippins, Buddy and Donna, and they departed a week ago Saturday, April the tenth." Victor felt a small sense of relief at being able to share his fears, but at the same time, hearing himself tell of his lost friends made his worries seem more real.

Advising Victor to wait, the ranger turned and exited through a door behind the counter. As Victor turned around, leaning on the counter, he noticed a couple in their early forties and their teenage daughter standing right behind him. By the look on their faces, they had overheard most of Victor's conversation with the ranger. Startled, as Victor had thought he was alone at the counter, his eyes met those of the mother.

Turning to her husband, she announced rather than said, "Oh Harold, I told you we should have gone to the beach instead of coming here. Two people are lost in the mountains, probably eaten by bears or God knows what. If you want to go on one of these *nature trails*, be my guest, but Kimberly and I are going shopping in Gatlinburg." The term "nature trails" seemed to be fired at the husband.

"Emily, please don't start again. This is a national park, not Central Park, and bears don't attack and eat people. It's beautiful, safe country, not anything like we could see in New York."

Turning to Victor, the woman stated, rather than asked, "Didn't you just tell the ranger that two friends of yours had disappeared here? You must think they're either lost or dead or you wouldn't be here, right?"

Her question and its abruptness caught Victor by surprise. Not wanting to become involved in their dispute and not liking her nagging attitude, Victor said without thinking, something quite out of character for him, "Madam, right now I don't know jack!"

Chapter Four

The ranger returned, and with a somewhat disdainful look at Victor, said, "Mr. Scofield, if you'll follow Ranger Teasley," pointing to a young woman who had appeared on Victor's side of the counter, "she will be glad to assist you."

The young, blonde-haired girl, who looked to Victor as if she would be more at home as a cashier at a K-Mart checkout lane than a national park ranger, waved her right hand, motioning Victor to follow her.

As Victor fell in behind her, he was struck by the thought that this was not going as well as he had hoped. He had already embarrassed himself and had the feeling that the rangers seemed to look upon him as some kind of intruder.

Once through the door from the main lobby and into the back offices, Ranger Teasley pointed to a chair next to a dilapidated gray steel desk. It was one of those desks one would expect to find in a U.S. government facility—rubber top, steel frame, and so on, and it looked like it had seen better days.

"If you'll wait here, the Chief Ranger will be with you in a moment," she said, and without another word she turned and walked out the same door by which they had entered.

Victor leaned over, resting his elbows on his thighs, and looked straight ahead. He asked himself if he was doing the right thing.

Before he could answer his own rhetorical question, a large man with two silver stars on his left collar entered the office, carrying a one-page printout from a computer.

Victor was struck by the very size of the man. At over six feet tall—at minimum six-five—muscular, and with the traditional military crew-cut hairstyle, he reminded Victor of drill instructors from his days at Fort Bragg. Although he was probably only a couple of years older than Victor, he gave the impression that he was more seasoned. He was intimidating, to say the least, but this was probably due more to his physical stature than his position.

Strictly a no-nonsense kind of guy, this one, Victor thought. *He's been in the 'business'.* He had seen the look—the 'thousand yard stare' as the grunts used to call it—too many times in 'Nam. *This man could be an ally*, Victor thought, *just the kind of man I need.*

"Mr. Scofield, I'm Harrison Pike, Chief Ranger of the park. I understand that you're inquiring about some friends of yours."

SmokeFire!

"Yes, sir, my friends..."

"I know about your friends, Mr. Scofield," Pike interrupted. "I was here when they requested their backcountry permit. I'll have to say, Mr. Scofield, Mr. Tippins' attitude was quite argumentative and combative when I denied him permission to enter the Panther Creek area. I explained to him that the Panther Creek area was restricted and that camping was not permitted. To make a long story short, I finally issued him a permit to start at the Abrams Creek area and proceed along the Rabbit Creek trail to campsite seventeen at Flint Gap."

Victor immediately disliked Pike's attitude. *This is a man used to using his authority to intimidate people*, he thought. Undaunted, Victor asked "What do you mean 'to make a long story short,' Chief?"

"As I said, when I told your friend he could not go into the Panther Creek area, he advised me that I did not own the Park, that in fact he owned the Park! He further advised me that he could hike, as he phrased it, any damn place he pleased in the Park! His wife finally settled him down enough to accept a permit to enter at Abrams Creek."

It sounds like he's met Buddy, Victor thought.

Victor knew the fishing along Rabbit Creek was not good. There would be many tourist campers at the Abrams Creek Campground, and if Buddy were lucky, he might catch a few trout well below the size limit of six inches. Buddy would have put up a fight, Victor thought.

"So, between Mr. Tippins's wife and myself, we talked him into entering at the Abrams Creek area," Pike said.

Feeling somewhat angry, Victor said firmly, "Be that as it may, Chief, the Tippins are way overdue and that's very unlike them. I don't know what the procedure is here, but I'm advising you that you've got two hikers in the backcountry who are two days overdue. It is possible that they could have originated at Abrams Creek as you suggest, and it is also possible that they could have disregarded your instructions and originated their hike at Panther Creek. I'm not here to discuss the legalities of hiking and camping in a restricted area. I'm here to advise the park service that two people are missing. I want to know what's going to be done."

"Mr. Scofield, what's going to be done is that I'm going to send an experienced ranger to the Rabbit Creek area and have him proceed along the trails to see if he can locate your friends."

Chapter Four

"Chief, Buddy Tippins and his wife are experienced hikers. Do you think that having one person walk along well-traveled trails will actually locate any trace? I suggest..."

"Mr. Scofield, there are certain procedures which I must follow in attempting to locate lost persons, the first of which is not to send in a team of personnel to obliterate the path of the people we are searching for. More often than not, the people we search for who have become lost have become disoriented and panic, and many times we find them just sitting down on the main trails. Regardless of a hiker's experience in the backcountry, becoming lost can cause many of them to become frightened and confused. I will dispatch a searcher immediately, and if you will give me a phone number where I can reach you, I will notify you of our results."

"Here's my business card, with my home and cell phone numbers on the back," Victor said, writing the numbers on the back of the card.

"I don't mean to tell you how to do your job, Chief, I'm just a little upset and concerned about my friends. I hope you understand."

"I do understand, Mr. Scofield, and if you can become upset sitting here in this office, think about how upset and confused your friends might feel in the backcountry if they have become disoriented. I assure you that we'll locate your friends safe and sound, and that I will personally contact you as soon as I have any news, okay?"

Victor didn't like Pike's patronizing tone, but the ranger had promised to do his best to find his friends. Victor wanted to keep Pike on his side, regardless of his personal feeling for the man. "All right, Chief, I appreciate your consideration and your time. I apologize again for becoming upset, and please keep me advised as to any progress."

"No problem, Mr. Scofield, in my years here at the Park, I've helped locate many lost persons, and I understand your concern. I'll be sure to contact you personally of any changes in the situation. Also, if you hear from your friends, please let us know."

Pike then stood up from the chair next to the desk, indicating the end of the conversation.

Victor took the cue and stood up himself, extending his hand to Pike, and said, "Okay, Chief, I appreciate your taking the time to listen to me, and if there's anything I can do to help—anything which I can do to add something to this investigation—please call me. You have my numbers."

With more than a firm grasp, Pike returned Victor's handshake. It was not exactly a crushing wrestler's handshake, but certainly more than a casual business associate's grip. For a moment Victor felt that Pike could, and would, crush his fingers. Pike's handshake was firm, lasted just long enough, and then was over.

Pike smiled as he released Victor's hand, and said, "We'll find 'em, Mr. Scofield, and it'll be okay."

Leaving the park headquarters, Victor felt somewhat better now that something was being done. It had not gone quite like he had expected it, but then again he had not known what to expect. Pike certainly seemed confident, *and he is a professional*, he thought. If Buddy and Donna did not turn up soon, then one of Pike's rangers would surely find them.

Unlocking his car door, Victor wondered if Buddy and Donna had returned while he was sounding the alarm. That would undoubtedly make him look the fool, he thought. He decided he would use his cell phone on the way back to call the bank for messages and then call Buddy's home. Buddy was probably cleaning trout on his back deck right now and would invite him over for a fish fry this evening. When Victor told Buddy and Donna what he had done this afternoon, they would probably laugh their butts off.

* * *

Before Victor had driven out of the parking lot at Park headquarters, Pike was dialing the Abrams Creek Ranger station to speak with Steve Russell, the ranger responsible for that area, to begin the initial search. After the sixth ring, Pike was thinking he would have to hang up and call Steve on the radio and have him call back by telephone. Pike did not wish to advise Russell of the situation over the radio where there could be too many other ears listening—amateurs who, upon hearing of lost persons on their scanner and seeking glory and adventure, might enter the area and possibly disrupt their search efforts.

Just as he was removing the phone from his ear, Russell answered.

"Abrams Creek Ranger Station. Ranger Steve Russell speaking."

"Steve, this is Chief Pike."

"Hello, Chief, sorry it took me so long to get to the phone but I just drove in from morning rounds," Russell said between deep breaths.

Chapter Four

Pike envisioned the zealous ranger running from his four-wheel drive truck, unlocking the door to the Abrams Creek Ranger Station and sprinting to the phone.

"Listen, Steve, I've got a report of two backpackers overdue in your area. They filed permits and entered the Abrams Creek area a week ago Saturday and were due back last Saturday. They're from Knoxville, and a friend of theirs just left, stating that they had not returned home yet, and no one's heard from them since they went in. They're described as a Caucasian male, aged forty-nine, and a Caucasian female, aged forty-eight. The permit was filed under the name of Mr. and Mrs. Buddy Tippins. I want you to saddle up your horse and ride in and find 'em. Be advised that they're supposed to be experienced hikers, so they may have left the trail thinking they wouldn't get lost. Be sure to take your radio and report any developments to me immediately."

"Okay, Chief, I'll leave right now," Russell said somewhat excitedly, obviously welcoming the challenge and responsibility.

"Okay, get to it," Pike said, and hung up the phone without farewell as is customary with most para-military personnel.

Russell replaced the phone on the receiver and noticed a slight tremor in his right hand. *A Search!*

Russell had been at the Great Smoky Mountains National Park for only two years, both of which were spent at the Abrams Creek Ranger Station. Before that his only other post had been at Yosemite National Park, where he had been stationed for four years, after receiving his Bachelor's degree in Forestry from Colorado State. At twenty-nine years of age, and although having been a professional park ranger for six years, the most important task he had ever performed in a crisis was that of managing a medic phone bank in Yosemite three years ago during a major forest fire. There had been a few injuries to the firefighting personnel at the time, all of which had been minor. The task had held some degree of moderate importance, but Russell had yearned to be on the fire line. While waiting for the phone to ring at medic HQ, he fantasized about burning Douglas firs tumbling to the ground in a thundering crash only a few feet from him while he barked orders over a 'Handi-Talkie' two-way radio. He imagined directing firefighting operations among yellow-suited firefighters while wearing a mask, shield, and oxygen tank. The bright colors of yellow, blue, and orange—

SmokeFire!

the smell of smoke and the feel of heat, the only entities his sense receptors realized.

His daydream never came to fruition, and his only injury during the crisis had been that of a sore ear and a stiff neck from having cradled a telephone during the operation.

This is my chance! Not one, but two lost persons. And in my area!

He would be the initial search probe! He had mental visions of applying tourniquets to stem the bleeding of ruptured arteries due to broken femurs. Fantasies of saving lives, of newspaper write-ups, raced through his imagination as he hurried to the garage to retrieve bridle, saddle, saddlebags, and all the other necessary equipment required to conduct his initial search from horseback.

This could be the chance he'd been waiting for. If he could find these lost folks safe and sound, he thought, maybe the Chief Ranger would take notice of his skills and he would be moved to a more prestigious area of the Park, like Cades Cove or Smokemont, where there was always something going on.

Russell walked to his stable where Old Spotty, his mount for the previous two years, lived. Old Spotty was a Palomino that had been at Abrams Creek for the last twelve years. He'd been acquired and given the name by perhaps the most famous Ranger of the Park, Quince Haskell, who had found and guided more lost persons to safety than any other Ranger in the Park's history.

Russell did not know much about horses, but he knew that Old Spotty was gentle, intelligent and obedient. He had never attempted to bite Russell—as had more than one mount in Yosemite—and it could be safely said that Russell was not an equine enthusiast. That didn't matter since Haskell had stated to Russell, when he assumed this post, that this horse had found more lost persons in his years of service than he had, although Haskell had been allowed to take the credit.

After putting the tack to his mount, he gathered the necessary supplies for a possible overnight excursion, and opened the wooden gate to the stable. He led Old Spotty outside the split rail fence—which was more in keeping with the motif of the Smokies than a barbed wire fence—and latched the gate behind him.

Saddling up and gathering the reins in his left hand, he remembered the words of Quince Haskell—words which Quince had told Steve would

Chapter Four

induce Spot to search. Russell bent down to Spot's right ear. "Okay, Spot, we got people lost," he whispered, gently while smelling the musky odor of horse, of fur, and of adventure. He patted Spot softly on the right shoulder and said in a trusty voice, "Let's ride—let's find 'em, Spot!"

Old Spotty snorted as if in understanding. He lowered his head, took a step forward, and trotted down the dirt driveway onto the gravel road, hooves crunching on the gravel. His gait had a sense of purpose, almost like a person who had places to go, people to see, things to do, and the young rider in uniform sitting stiffly upon his back with a Smokey The Bear hat atop his head couldn't have been more proud. Park Ranger Steven Russell—conscientious, daydreamer, fighter of fires, finder of lost persons, stemmer of blood flows, saver of lives—rode his mount down the gravel road that led from his small frame house.

Underneath the budding trees, which were welcoming the season of spring, the thought of *be careful what you wish for, for you just might get it,* never crossed his mind.

Stephen Russell, atop a true finder, turned his horse into the trail that led to the exit of Abrams Creek.

* * *

Victor turned onto I-40 west at the Sevierville exit and put the 'Z' to eighty. No radio or cassette played this time, as he was lost in his own thoughts, with eyes that did not see.

He had placed two calls from his cell phone, the first to SNB and the second to Buddy's home. No messages at the first and no answer at the second. His anxiety was reaching new heights, perhaps due to his visit to Park Headquarters. This, coupled with the lack of contact from Buddy, fed his increasing uneasiness. Something was wrong. Something was terribly wrong!

Victor looked down at the speedometer and saw that he was doing eighty-five.

Better get a grip, Vick, we got enough problems without accidents or traffic tickets, he thought. He slowed the 'Z' to seventy and switched on the radio, hoping some white noise would help to calm him.

The clock on the 'Z's dashboard told him it was two-thirty. He wasn't in the mood to return to SNB but couldn't think of anything else to do.

SmokeFire!

Go home and do what? Wait for a phone call from Pike? Go to Donna's mom's and try to explain what was going on and what was being done? He was tempted to call SNB and tell Vodeski to go screw himself, then go home and get his backpacking equipment together, and conduct his own search.

"Shit!" he growled, gritting his teeth as he slammed his right palm against the padded steering wheel. Thinking it was best to let the professionals handle it, Victor decided to return to SNB, as maybe a little work would take his mind off of the situation. He would need to call Donna's mom sometime this afternoon or tonight and bring her up-to-date. It was a call that he did not look forward to. Whatever she was or was not, Victor felt that she deserved to know the truth, as he was sure that she had, by this time, worked herself into a frenzy over worrying about Donna. Victor could envision her doing the 'Tackie Lordies' as Buddy called them, going from room to room saying to no one in particular, "Lordie, Lordie, Lordie, oh merciful Lordie."

Victor took the business-loop exit and returned to SNB, parked the car, and went to his office. Fortunately, neither Vodeski nor anyone else, it seemed, had noticed his absence. The last thing he needed now, he thought, was for Vodeski to dress him down for taking a long lunch hour.

He worked the rest of the afternoon answering memos via electronic mail and reviewing status reports from the systems staff concerning the seemingly never-ending problems with the DDA software. Strictly no brainer stuff, but he didn't feel like even starting on the upcoming year's budget (which was due in less than five weeks) as he was finding it difficult to concentrate. At five o'clock Victor took the elevator down to the subterranean parking lot, got into his car and drove onto Gay Street.

The rush hour was going full blast, and Victor cursed himself for not having left a few minutes earlier or later.

He turned right onto Gay Street, intending to head west and go home, when he was struck by a sudden feeling of guilt. He had not called Donna's mother to let her know what was going on.

What the hell is *going on*, he thought, *What can I tell her?* He didn't know, but knew he had to tell her something. Long ago, Victor had learned that telling someone the truth was the best course of action.

Chapter Four

He took the on-ramp to eastbound I-40 towards Donna's mom's house instead of turning west towards his own. He must tell her the truth, no matter how painful.

While Victor had been attending graduate school and was facing final exams, a Catholic priest whom Victor had been extremely close to had died. Cathy, knowing how stressed Victor already was about exams, had elected not to tell him of Father Ballinger's death until he was through his tests.

After Victor had taken his exams, they had gone to a moderately expensive restaurant to celebrate, and Cathy had decided to tell him that evening of Father Ballinger's passing. Victor had been feeling the post exams high, as he called it, and had been ready for a good time.

Over dinner Cathy had told Victor of Father Ballinger's death the previous week, and he had been furious.

Cathy had understood his anger, had expected it, and had been willing to take the brunt of it. Victor had been very close to Father Ballinger, and she had insight enough to know that with Victor, death always brought on anger.

She had endured his anger, explaining that she felt that he had had enough stress upon him at the time, that she knew how hard he had studied, and that she had not wished to introduce any additional emotional stresses.

Victor had understood this, even through his anger, and they had left the restaurant and their half-finished meals in silence.

On the way home Victor had reached across the car seat, and taking Cathy's hand, he said he understood and appreciated what she had done, although he did not agree with it.

She had cried and told him that she had not intended to deceive him, that she loved him and was only trying to protect him. She had said that she was sorry and that she was wrong, and Victor had pulled over to the side of the road and said that he was sorry for being so abrupt and that she hadn't been wrong.

They had embraced and cried together—Victor for the death of Father Ballinger, for the memories it brought back, for being insensitive to the perspectives and feelings of his wife, and Cathy for hurting Victor, and in empathy for his pain, which ran so deep.

SmokeFire!

They had made an agreement that night, as they held each other in the car on the side of the road, that they would never keep the truth from each other again, no matter the circumstance. It was an agreement that had had its own rewards and its own pain.

When Cathy had been diagnosed with leukemia, she had told Victor right away after visiting the clinic, when the doctor had revealed the conclusive results of her tests.

They had cried and held each other, each trying to be strong for the other, each facing their own pain and fear, and they had faced it together that night and in the days and nights to come. They had stayed up most of that night talking, crying, and holding each other so tightly that it seemed their hearts would break from the pressure.

In retrospect, hearts had been broken—Cathy's from disease, and Victor's from helplessness, from anger at God and himself, from longing, from loneliness, and for a love lost forever.

They had kept their agreement, made upon the side of the road that night. Victor had known the truth, and had felt the pain of that truth. It had not set him free but had captured and tortured him like a prisoner of war, but at least he had known the truth.

The truth shall set you free. He had never really understood exactly what that phrase meant. Perhaps it was just some platitude that sounded good, or maybe there was something to it. Regardless, Victor knew one thing: truths will often hit you in the face like a cold bucket of water, and more often than not, they will be painful.

He took the Broadway exit off of I-40 and turned onto Chicago Street where Mae lived.

Driving up the hill on Chicago, he thought to himself that instead of flashing to the past, he should have been planning on what he was going to say. He thought of driving around the block a few times or pulling over and gathering his thoughts, but before he could make some decision as to what to do, he was turning into Mae's driveway. *Too late now,* he thought, *gonna have to wing it.*

Before he cut the engine off, Mae had pulled the curtains back and was peeping out the front window. Victor pretended that he didn't see her, turned the ignition off, pulled the hand brake on, unbuckled his seat belt, and got out.

Chapter Four

Facing away from the window and shutting the door of the car, he thought, *Showtime! I hope I'm not screwing up!* As he turned from the car, he heard the wooden front door open and the old storm door squeak on its rusted actuator. Mae stepped onto the porch.

"Victor, what a surprise!"

Victor tried to smile and to return her greeting, but the seriousness of his errand showed on his face. He was totally honest with Mae and related the events to date, his concerns, and his conversations with Pike. To say that Mae was distraught would be an understatement. She was utterly devastated.

"Oh sweet Lordie Jesus! What am I to do?"

Victor had given this some thought and said, "Mae, the best thing that you can do now is to pray for Buddy and Donna, and look after Jennifer until we know something more."

"Oh, Victor, do you think that they have gone to meet the Lord or has that boy just kept my daughter up in that horrible place so he can fish or what?"

Victor explained that at this point he really didn't know any more than what he had told her already. He did say that he wasn't giving up hope and that she should not either. He further explained that he was going to keep in close contact with the authorities at the Park and that he would keep Mae updated on any news. At this point, he said, it was best to let them handle it.

"Oh, I just know that the worst has happened! I just know that my Donna is gone. What's going to become of little Jennifer?"

Victor encouraged her to keep hoping, that there might be a logical explanation for everything. He didn't want to give her false hopes, but at this point he felt it would serve no purpose to relate his fears to her.

He told her of a housewife who wandered off the trail while hiking with her family several years ago. The park rangers had looked for her for three days, and after the search was called off, the woman wandered onto a paved highway on the North Carolina side of the Park. She was hungry and scared, but otherwise all right.

"Mae, I remember this story and everyone had given up hope. The weather was warm in the Park then, just like it is now and she just kept walking until she finally found this road. She flagged down a car and everything turned out all right. This woman had absolutely no

SmokeFire!

backcountry hiking experience and she survived. Buddy and Donna have a lot of backcountry experience, and I have hiked with them many times. If something has happened, I feel sure that either one of them will know what to do. We cannot give up hope! What you have to do now is look after Jennifer until they get back."

Victor stayed and talked with her for a while longer, hoping to get her calmed down. Donna's father had died many years ago, and Victor was deeply concerned about whether Mae would be okay staying alone.

He wrote down his telephone numbers, and put the paper under a little angel magnet on the refrigerator. He told her that she could call him anytime day or night, and that he would keep in close contact with her as well.

On the drive home he reflected on Mae's question of what would happen to little Jennifer. Assuming the worst, Jennifer would be an orphan. Mae was too old to take care of her, and neither Buddy nor Donna had any siblings. Further, they had no close friends who might be able, or willing, for that matter, to take on such a huge responsibility.

Certainly he could not take care of Jennifer. He lived alone and knew absolutely nothing of children other than that they were a tremendous responsibility. He loved and adored Jennifer and wanted only the best for her. But what could *he* do?

Easy, Vick, you're starting to sound like Mae now, he thought to himself. *One step at a time—now is a time for cool heads and clear thinking.* The best plan now was to let the Park Service handle it and keep out of their way.

Driving along the interstate he remembered something Buddy had said to him about planning before going out on their first patrol in Vietnam.

Victor, and the fire base commander, along with an intelligence officer, had developed a plan for a reconnaissance patrol insertion near the Ho Chi Minh trail.

While going over the plan with his NCO, who had been in Vietnam on a previous tour, Buddy had said, "Sir, with all due respect this plan ain't good! Let me tell you about planning in the bush, sir. Plan for something, maybe everything to go wrong. If you don't, then we ain't

Chapter Four

gonna be ready when the bad stuff comes down, and if we ain't ready, then Mr. Charles," referring to the Viet Cong, "bounces us!"

Victor, recognizing that Buddy's experience was extremely valuable, had asked what was wrong with the plan. How could they, he asked, plan for something, maybe everything to go wrong?

"Well sir, it's tough to plan when you're traveling light like us in the Land of Bad Things, but I know one thing this plan hasn't got. It hasn't got a backup plan, and a backup plan is what you use when everything turns to crap. We need at least one backup plan, if not two. Now here's what I suggest we do..."

Buddy had then laid out alternate evacuation routes and pinpointed no less than ten possible extraction points along the backup routes where helicopters could make a pickup. In addition, he laid out escape routes to forward fire bases in the event that the weather would be too bad for helicopter extraction.

Driving along, Victor thought about that. Maybe the best plan right now was to let the Park Service handle it. *But I need a backup plan if they are unsuccessful, maybe even two backup plans*, he thought.

SmokeFire!

Ideas were beginning to form in his mind. *Okay,* he said to himself, *let's devise a plan.*

* * *

When Victor got home, he went into his home office, which was actually a second bedroom. Its furniture was comprised of a large inexpensive oak desk, two bookcases, and a large work table he had found while accompanying Buddy and Donna on one of their garage sale excursions.

The oak desk was undoubtedly his most prized possession. He and Cathy had purchased it just after they were married. Cathy had refinished it, and although it was now in bad need of a new refinishing, Victor could not bring himself to sand down all of Cathy's hard work. When he worked on it, he felt as if Cathy was near. Sometimes late at night when he was working, he would stare into the desktop and run his hand along it, touching the same wood that Cathy had so patiently sanded and stained. And although it brought that now-familiar pain in his chest, he would smile and remember.

He walked in and cleared all of the SNB papers from off the desk and work table, and turned on his computer.

While the computer was powering up, he went into the kitchen, fixed a sandwich and retrieved a beer from the refrigerator.

Sitting down at the desk in front of the computer, he brought up the word processor. First he made a bullet list of possible alternatives should he need to take over the search on his own. *What equipment would he require? What resources? What kind of information was needed? What contacts? What would the timing be? Where would he start? How would he start?*

He worked on into the night, and by three a.m. had a rough draft of what was necessary and what his course of action would be. He would refine the plan in the next couple of days while the Park Service continued their search, and if they failed to turn up anything by Thursday, he would put his plan into action.

Chapter Five

11:00 a.m. Wednesday, April 21, 1999
Great Smoky Mountains National Park

Harrison Pike tossed the Handi-Talkie two-way radio onto the front seat of the Land Rover, which sat two miles up the dirt road that served as the Rabbit Creek Trail.

The Tippins' car, a 1990 Toyota Corolla, had been previously found in the parking lot at the trailhead of the Abrams Falls Trail.

Thirty-two Park Rangers had just completed a thorough grid search of the entire Abrams Creek area, and no trace of the Tippinses had been found. Hikers in the area had been interviewed, off-trail areas had been systematically searched by horseback, and over seventy-five square miles of the Rabbit Creek area had been scoured over the previous forty-eight hours. No information about the Tippinses had been obtained; there had been no sightings of them by other hikers and there were no clues as to where they had been or where they might be going.

SmokeFire!

"Two days, two whole damn days, Russell. There's going to be hell to pay for this!" Pike said to Steve Russell, as he ran his right hand over his short-cropped scalp and down the back of his neck.

"It doesn't seem possible, Chief," Russell said. "Someone had to see them, there's a lot of backcountry campers in this area and only one trail. I don't get it, even if they drifted off the trail, there would have been some sign of their passing, and after all this searching we would have seen it, or maybe heard of it!"

"Well Russell, it obviously is possible as we found their car on this trailhead, at the parking lot, and we haven't found jack in two days. There's only so much money in the budget to continue a search of this magnitude, and we got to find these people. We've got to find them soon or call off the organized search. And, if we call off the organized search without results, then there'll be hell to pay with the publicity! The rest of the Park is going to hell in a hand basket while all this manpower is concentrated here! The Superintendent's going to have a feast, with me as the main course, before this is over! Two pilgrims, Russell! We gotta find 'em, and find 'em quick!"

Russell was somewhat taken aback by Pike's frustration, and he was obviously frustrated. Russell's visions of rescue had been squelched after completing his initial search of the Abrams Creek area and finding nothing. He desperately wanted to contribute, but did not know what to do next. He wanted to make a suggestion, but was afraid of being rejected by Pike. Finally, he decided that the cause was worth the risk.

"Chief, my grandmother used to say when I was a kid, that when I lost something and couldn't find it, then I must be looking in the wrong place. Maybe we should split our search force and move to another area."

"Not a bad idea, Russell, I was thinking the same thing," Pike said.

Russell fairly beamed, and with renewed courage said, "I was thinking that maybe I could take, say ten guys, and search the Coopers Road area north of here, and that Jenkins could take the other guys and search the Hannah Mountain area to the south."

"The Coopers Road area is our next best bet," Pike said. "Hannah Mountain would take a hundred guys a month to search. With its dense contours it is dangerous terrain, and I don't think they would have drifted into that area. If it had been just a couple of guys, I might consider that area as a possibility, but no experienced hiker in his right mind would

Chapter Five

take his wife into that area. Besides, why would they have left their car at Abrams Falls if they were going to Hannah Mountain?"

Pike's reasoning was good, and Russell said as much. Pike retrieved the Handi-Talkie from the front seat and instructed the searchers to rendezvous at area number sixteen on the Little Bottoms Trail. Turning to Russell, Pike said, "You take Spot and ride over to sixteen. Send half of them up Beard Cane Trail and have them disperse and move west toward the Park boundary. Disperse the other half along the Little Bottom trail to the west and have them move north. That way they'll overlap each other. It shouldn't take 'em more than six hours to do that area. Have everyone converge at the Cane Gap trailhead late this afternoon. I've got a feeling that we'll get lucky. If we don't, then we'll resume the search tomorrow at daybreak and move east all the way to Cades Cove. If they're not in either of those areas, then it's my guess they were never in the Park and we're dealing with something else entirely. I'm going back to Park Headquarters and talk with the Superintendent. Keep me advised, Russell!"

"Yes, sir," Russell said as he put his foot in the stirrup of Spot's saddle, climbed up, and reined around. Never, even in his wildest dreams, had he envisioned assuming the responsibility of taking command of a search. He rode off at a fast trot, never looking back, even as the engine of the Land Rover cranked to life and Pike backed up, turned around on the narrow trail, and drove off.

"This is going to be it, Spot! They're there and I can feel it, and I know you feel it too!" Russell said as he ducked under a low hanging branch.

If Russell had known anything about Spot, he would have surely known that Spot did not share his sentiment. Spot seemed to balk at turning north as he sidestepped along the trail.

"Come on, Spot, this is no time to think about going back to the station, let's go!"

Like all animals, Spot relied solely upon instinct, not reasoning—as he knew nothing of reasoning—he just *knew*. Spot, who knew nothing about points of the compass, the sun setting in the west or rising in the east, of moss on the north side of the trees, *knew, felt,* that whatever was to be found was to the south.

SmokeFire!

"South," echoed into the mind of Spot. "It is that way, not this way! South!"

Horse and rider rode north towards Coopers Road.

* * *

6:30 a.m. Thursday, April 22, 1999
Great Smoky Mountains National Park

Harrison Pike lay on the canvas fold-out cot in his office, covered by an unzipped sleeping bag, soundly sleeping when the wrist watch alarm on his left arm sounded at six-thirty.

He had been asleep only three hours, which was all the sleep he had been able to manage in the past forty-eight hours.

Being a light sleeper, even in his state of fatigue, the chime woke him immediately. The night before he had been up until two-thirty a.m., helping to coordinate the search, which had yielded absolutely nothing.

The entire area north of Rabbit Creek had been thoroughly searched by yesterday morning. Thirty-six thousand dollars in personnel costs, the Superintendent had informed him, had already been expended in the search effort, and the budget had all but run out. He had been forced to send many of the rangers back to their respective areas of responsibility throughout the Park.

The searchers had found no trace of any hikers, much less the Tippins, and at two o'clock in the morning Pike canceled the search effort, convinced that they would never find the lost hikers.

His conversation with the Superintendent on the previous Monday had been less than pleasant. The 'Super' had given Pike another forty-eight hours, after which all efforts would be terminated, as there were simply no funds left to continue the search.

Already there had been several articles in the local and surrounding county newspapers concerning the disappearance of the Tippinses. Pike had refused numerous requests for interviews in an attempt to 'minimize the damage,' as per the Superintendent's orders.

In their conversation the previous evening, Pike had given the Superintendent a detailed account of the search efforts thus far. The Superintendent, a reasonable man, had not criticized Pike or the other

Chapter Five

rangers with regard to their search tactics, nor their lack of success. It was a tragedy, he agreed, but there was little else that they could do. With that, he had instructed Pike to cancel the search. Maybe something would turn up later, he said, meaning discovery of the bodies.

* * *

6:45 a.m. Thursday, April 22, 1999
Knoxville, Tennessee

Victor had finally began to sleep soundly around four a.m., after worrying all night about Buddy and Donna as he worked on his "operational plan." He was awakened by what he thought to be the alarm clock but, instead, turned out to be the phone. Thinking it was the computer center's third shift operator 'Herb The Turd,' Victor rolled over, picked up the phone and said, "What?" in a somewhat less than congenial intonation.

"Mr. Scofield?"

"Yes," Victor responded, recognizing the unmistakable deep voice of Harrison Pike.

"Mr. Scofield, this is Chief Ranger Pike. I'm calling to bring you up-to-date on the search for the Tippinses, if you have a moment," he asked.

"Sure, Chief," he said, quickly sitting up on the edge of the bed. "What have you found?"

"We have conducted a thorough search of the Abrams Creek area, the Rabbit Creek area, and Hannah Mountain and unfortunately have been unable to locate your friends. I met with the Park Superintendent last night, and he instructed me to terminate the search. I regret that I don't have better news."

Victor felt a wave of nausea and despair wash over him. Running his hand through his hair, he replied, "Terminate the search! Chief, if the search is called off, then there's absolutely no hope of finding the Tippinses! It's only been..."

Interrupting Victor, Pike continued by saying, "I hope you understand that we have limited funds to conduct searches of this magnitude on an indefinite basis."

"I understand that, but two people have vanished up there and..."

SmokeFire!

"Now, that is my official statement as set forth by the Superintendent, but I want to tell you that I am not giving up the effort. I am going to instruct my rangers to continue the search on a more limited basis in hopes of finding your friends, but I have to be honest by saying that it doesn't look good."

"Chief, I appreciate your calling me," Victor said, now fully coming out of his sleep, "and all that you're doing, but I must say that I am extremely disappointed in the fact that your personnel have turned up absolutely nothing after such an intensive effort! My friends are up there somewhere! It's not such a large area, I mean, it's not like we're looking for them someplace in Kansas or anything!"

Victor felt himself rising to anger and he put it in check, as he knew he was only taking out his frustration on Pike. But there was something more, something intangible, something filtered—just out of reach—thoughts—old feelings from Vietnam?

"Mr. Scofield, as I said to you when this all started, I am sympathetic to your concern for your friends, and I share in the loss," he said sincerely. "Also, as Chief Ranger of the Park, it doesn't do my reputation any good to lose two hikers without a trace, much less one of them a young woman, and I assure you that we are going to continue to do all that we can to locate them. But I must operate within the limits as set forth by the Park Superintendent and by the Department of the Interior. I hope you understand my position as well as I understand yours."

Taking his voice down a notch, Victor said, "I'm terribly afraid for my friends and feel helpless and frustrated, and I know you understand my concern for them."

"I wish I had some better news for you, but I don't. I'm sorry."

"You said your people searched the Rabbit Creek and Hannah Mountain areas, but did you search Panther Creek and the Noland Divide trail areas as well?"

"Mr. Scofield, we sent a team along the Noland Divide trail and searched as well as we could," Pike explained, "but as you know that is some rough terrain and we only searched the trail areas. As far as the Panther Creek area is concerned, no, we did not search it. As you know, there are no trails there, and it would not be practical to search that area for several reasons."

"What reasons?" Victor asked.

Chapter Five

"The Tippinses permit was issued for Rabbit Creek, which is a long way from Panther Creek, towards the north side of the Park. Also, since there are no trails there, we wouldn't know where to begin. Searching it would take a hundred men over a month. Even then, with no trails and dense forest, it's unlikely we would find them, even if they did go there, which they did not."

"How do you know they didn't, Chief?" Victor asked.

"Because we found their car at the Abrams Falls trailhead. They couldn't have hiked from Abrams Falls trail to Panther Creek. It's too far, there are no trails, and the contour is to severe."

In a solemn voice, Victor said, "Chief, let me ask you a question, off the record. Do you think my friends are dead, and if so, what chance would you give of their bodies being recovered?"

Victor knew that Pike had his own ideas as to what was going on here, and that he would probably keep those ideas to himself, as Pike seemed to be the kind of person who played his cards close to his chest. Victor felt that he had to bring this out, but he didn't know exactly why or how, at least not yet.

"Mr. Scofield, I'll be completely candid with you. I must act upon what I know as fact, and that is that the Tippinses sought a permit into the Panther Creek area, were denied, and ultimately obtained a permit into the Abrams Creek area. These are the facts. Further, no other hikers observed them in any of these areas, which is highly unusual, to say the least, given that these trails are relatively well-traveled and that we had issued no less than twenty-four permits for those areas within a two-day period prior to their departure." He continued by saying, "Those facts, plus Mr. Tippins' knowledge of wilderness and survival and, by the way, I have taken the liberty to look into his service record, which is rather impressive—lead me to believe that there is little chance of such a man becoming lost in the backcountry. So, we are assuming that some tragedy befell both of them."

"That's possible, but I don't know..."

"Please, Mr. Scofield, all that I'm saying is that an accident of some sort is possible. It would explain a lot. To answer your question, if that is the case, then it's likely that they will eventually be found."

Victor had seen this type of bureaucratic behavior from the senior faculty at the university, the management at SNB, and, last but not least,

SmokeFire!

numerous company commanders and officers in Vietnam—washing their hands of any unpleasantness.

Pike seemed to express concern not only for Buddy and Donna but for his reputation and position as well. Nonetheless, something nagged at Victor's subconscious, something that he could not dismiss. Was Pike being too political, saying something without really saying anything? Was he threatened by what was happening here? Was Pike's job on the line because of Buddy and Donna's disappearance? Was there more, or was it just his imagination?

Time to be cool, act uninformed, act naïve, the thoughts echoed in Victor's mind.

"I understand, Chief, and I respect your candor. You have given me your honest assessment and I appreciate that, I really do! I know that you are doing all that you can. So, what's the next step? Where do we go from here?"

"Where we go, Mr. Scofield, is that myself and my rangers will continue the search, albeit on a somewhat limited and discreet basis, as the search has been officially called off, and I will keep you advised. If the Tippinses are up here, then we will eventually find them."

"I really have to go," Pike said, "but please keep me updated on any information you come across, and I'll keep you posted if we find out anything, all right?"

This was not going as Victor had expected, if he had had any expectations at all. Pike was bailing out, that much was evident. But it was no longer in Pike's hands, as far as Victor was concerned. *So be it!*

"Chief, if I hear from them or come across anything that might help, I'll get in touch with you immediately. Again, thanks for your help."

"It's my job, Mr. Scofield, and again I'm sorry that I didn't have better news."

Victor bid Pike goodbye, hung up the phone, and rolled over onto his back, staring at the ceiling. With the possible exception of when Cathy had died, he had never felt so alone and so helpless.

* * *

Chapter Five

Victor took a shower, got dressed and went into his home office. He had been working on his plan all week, and he would now put it into action. It was time, and he had been sitting on the sidelines too long.

His thoughts now turned to how he would handle some time off from SNB. This had been in the back of his mind while he had been conceiving his plan. Vodeski would not be pleased, even though Victor's friends were either dead or in very serious trouble.

Victor had arrived at one key thought. He must have the time to conduct his search his way, and this could not be done while he was required to be at the bank. Therefore, the question was how to get some time off without jeopardizing his job.

The idea had broken itself down into two courses of action. One, to feign illness, and secondly, to be honest with Vodeski and request a temporary leave of absence.

While Victor did not wish to lie, he also felt that Vodeski would not care about the truth. If he requested a temporary leave of absence and Vodeski blew up and denied it, then Victor would have no alternative but to resign, which was something he was not prepared to do right now.

After some thought, he decided on the first course of action. He would call Vodeski this morning from his cell phone and tell him that he had a flu bug and would not be in. That would give him today, all day Friday and the weekend to implement the first phase of his plan. He rationalized it with something his mother had said long ago. "There are some people who will not accept the truth and deserve a lie. When confronted with it, give them one!"

He went into the third bedroom and retrieved a canvas zippered satchel from the spare closet along with his camera equipment bag. He carried both into the living room and set them down on the carpet. Next, he went into his office, opened his briefcase and got a small minirecorder, which he used to record notes on while driving, and several blank tapes. He also got a pair of binoculars, which he had purchased several years before, and carried them into the living room and set them beside the other items.

Looking at the bullet list from his plan, he double checked the inventory items. The only thing missing was cash. He would stop by a

SNB branch in the morning, withdraw five thousand dollars, and be on his way.

Victor then cleaned and loaded the camera equipment with high-speed film. He transferred several camera lenses and extra film canisters into the canvas satchel along with the binoculars, mini-recorder, and several blank tapes. Then he replaced the batteries in the camera's motor drive and placed it in the satchel. He spent the rest of the day going over the map—the 'area of operations' as he called it—and making notes.

At eleven o'clock that night, he folded the map and placed it with his notepad in the canvas satchel and went to bed.

Lying awake, he said a prayer that Buddy and Donna were safe, and asked God to guide him no matter what he might find. Although he had never been much of a religious man, he knew that this was one thing he couldn't face alone. *Please, God, help me to find some answers.*

Chapter Six

Friday morning, April 23, 1999
Highway 441, Pigeon Forge, Tennessee
Fifteen miles outside of the Great Smoky Mountains National Park

Victor had awakened at seven a.m., dressed, placed the canvas satchel in the 'Z' and driven towards Pigeon Forge. The morning was clear and crisp, an essential element for 'phase one' of his plan.

He stopped by an SNB branch at nine a.m. and withdrew five thousand dollars in cash in various denominations. While in the parking lot of SNB, he placed two thousand dollars in his wallet and the remaining amount in his canvas satchel. He got into the 'Z' and turned onto Interstate 40 East before taking Exit 403, the most common tourist route to the Park and Gatlinburg.

While driving through Pigeon Forge, Victor passed a large miniature golf course with a dinosaur motif. He recalled driving down a similar highway in California many years ago with Cathy. At her insistence they

SmokeFire!

had stopped at a miniature golf course as she exclaimed, "Oh Vick, it'll be fun! Come on, you don't have to plan *everything*, let's be spontaneous!" He recalled how Cathy had putted the ball, sending it bouncing off the sideboard and into a small pool to the side of the "fairway."

"What's that club those golfers use, a wedge? Well, I need one 'cause I'm going to play the lie."

He remembered Cathy taking off her sneakers and socks, and stepping into the shallow water with the putter.

"Watch this, Vick! A chip shot with the putter!"

And to his total amazement, as well as to the amazement of other bystanders, she had taken a slow practice swing, the club head crossing just above the water, and then deftly chipped out the ball from the two-inch water to within one foot of the cup. The splash soaked Victor's pant legs.

He still remembered her jumping up in the water laughing and saying, "Yo! She's gotta be pleased with that one!" like some sports announcer at the U.S. Open.

That night at dinner it had been necessary to relive the shot to the accompaniment of several glasses of Chablis. They had laughed, not so much about the golf shot as from sheer happiness.

Vick, it's been a long time and you have to give it up, he thought. *Cathy's gone, and for all we know, so are Buddy and Donna.* However, it was a great chip shot, and it was funny—really funny—and he smiled at the thought.

Just outside of Pigeon Forge, Victor found what he was looking for. He had read several newspaper articles over the past few years about the local merchants and homeowners complaining about the noise from tourist helicopter rides, and there had even been some civil suits filed in hopes of shutting them down.

Fortunately, the injunctions were evidently still tied up in court as there were several locations that had signs stating 'Scenic Helicopter Rides - $10.'

He made a pass up the divided highway, surveying the aircraft at several establishments in order to select one that was best suited for his requirements. He passed some which used the old Bell 47G's, like on the television program M*A*S*H. These probably didn't get the

Chapter Six

maintenance they deserved and, further, would be too slow and have too limited a range for his purposes.

Just before entering the Pigeon Forge commercial district, he saw a sign stating 'Helicopter rides - $25,' and on the grass pads sat two modern Bell Jet Ranger Model III helicopters.

He would try this place first. He made a U-turn through the divided highway and drove onto the gravel lot.

It was still early, and there were two men sitting under a wooden awning attached to a small block building, drinking coffee, waiting for the tourists. Retrieving his satchel from the passenger seat and locking the car, Victor approached the two men.

"Hello! I'm from Knoxville, name's Victor Scofield. That's some fine equipment you guys got here! Can I buy some of your time?"

"Sure, fifteen minute ride is twenty-five dollars," the older of the two, said. "Thirty minute ride is forty dollars. But you'll have to wait until we get a couple more riders at that price."

"Well, I have some specific needs. What would be the rate for, say, a four-hour ride with just me?"

"Four hours! Partner, that's gonna be pretty expensive. Maybe you should think about the bus tour they got on up the road."

"Well, as I said I've got some specific needs. See, I'm a graduate geology student from the University of Tennessee, and I really need to do some aerial research over the southwest corner of the Park. Guys, I'm really in a bind here, 'cause my research papers are due next month and frankly I've been putting this off because I'm scared of flying. Surely you could help me out for a fee, I mean it's grant money from UT, so it's not like it's mine. What do you say?"

"Well, four hours is going to be about a thousand bucks, cash!"

Opening his wallet Victor pulled out ten one-hundred dollar bills and laid them on the table. "Sounds fair to me, let's go!"

The two pilots looked at each other, and the older one got up and shook Victor's hand. He was about Victor's age and had the seasoned look that a lot of pilots possess.

"I'm Wally McAllister and I'll be your pilot. Where do you want to go, Mr. Scofield?"

SmokeFire!

Victor opened his satchel and spread the map out on the table. "I have a couple of areas I need to survey and photograph. These are the routes and areas I'm interested in."

For the next few minutes Victor briefed the pilot on his required flight plan. They discussed altitudes, course headings, and 'time on station' over the target areas.

"It's a calm morning so there should be no downdrafts, which would adversely affect us doing some low level overflights or hovering," Victor said. "There will be areas where I want to get down on the deck and take some photographs, and other areas which I would like to see from an altitude of five hundred to one thousand feet, and I don't expect to land anywhere."

The pilot didn't have any problems with the flight plan, so they went out to a black and red Jet Ranger. The pilot opened the left copilot's door, and Victor climbed in.

By the time the pilot climbed into the right seat, Victor had already secured himself in the four-point harness belt and donned the headset for intercommunications between himself and the pilot.

As McAllister climbed into the pilot's seat, he looked at Victor, holding his gaze for several seconds. Then he started the turbine engine, engaged the rotor, and lifted off.

The first target area Victor had selected was the Abrams Creek Trail. They would start at the Abrams Falls Trailhead then continue west along the trail until they reached the Abrams Creek Ranger Station. The trailhead was about twenty-three miles from the takeoff point, and with the Jet Ranger's high performance, Victor figured they should be over the area in about twelve minutes.

As the pilot climbed to cruising altitude and turned on a southwest heading, Victor picked up his canvas satchel from behind his seat and took out his camera. He had already mounted the wide-angle twenty-eight millimeter lens and had a full two-hundred shot bulk roll of high-speed 400 ASA film loaded.

He wanted to make a total of four passes across the entire Abrams Creek Trail area. They would fly almost due west along the meandering north side of the trail at a high altitude, and he would photograph the trail and river with the wide-angle lens for maximum coverage. After about ten miles they would turn on a reciprocal heading after about ten

Chapter Six

miles and fly east along the south side of the river where he would continue his photography. Finally, they would repeat this route at a low level and slower airspeed, and he would photograph it with a zoom lens.

The only concern Victor had at this point was being able to shoot the pictures and perform visual observation simultaneously.

"On these passes I need to photograph as much of the area as I can. I also need to make some notes on my tape recorder and get first hand visuals, so I'll need you to slow the airspeed," Victor said as he keyed the button on the headset's wire.

"No problem. I'll slow up when we reach the trailhead. If I get going too fast for you, just yell and I'll slow her down. We should be over it in about five more minutes."

They flew over Cades Cove, a National Historic Site and one of the most beautiful places in the Park. The lush meadows in the Cove encompass 5,000 acres, and from the valley floor at 1,900 feet above sea level, the mountain vistas climb 5,500 feet high into the sky. Victor recalled that settlers first came to Cades Cove in 1819 and farmed the rich land until the Park was formed in the 1930's.

As they flew over the Cove, Victor could see the pioneer log cabins, the mill, and churches with their old cemeteries. Looking down it was easy to see why it was the most visited location within the Park, but Victor knew it was even more beautiful from the Loop Road that encircled the Cove. He saw families with picnic blankets in the open meadows, and even saw two deer at the edge of the forest.

"Okay, Cable Mill coming up, but we probably ought to keep the altitude up until we exit the perimeter of the Cove. Wouldn't want the Park Rangers getting pissed at us for low level flying here—they're kinda sensitive about that," McAllister said through the headset.

"Understood. Let's not drop down until we're a mile or so from the trailhead. That should be okay, and there's not much in the way of any geologic anomalies here anyway."

About a mile past the Cable Mill, McAllister dropped the Jet Ranger to about five hundred feet and slowed the airspeed to about thirty knots.

"This too high or too fast, Mr. Scofield?"

"This should be about perfect. I may need to open the door and lean out to get some good shots. Is that okay?"

"No problem, just keep the harness buckled."

As they flew down the north side of the trail, Victor noticed several hikers along the way. *No way Buddy would want to be here—too crowded*, he thought to himself, *but I need to stick to the plan.*

They flew a winding route along the trail and stream, and McAllister was doing an excellent job of positioning the helicopter to give Victor maximum advantage. As they flew along, Victor took photographs, looked through the binoculars, and made notes on both the map and the tape recorder. Occasionally, when a large rock outcropping would become visible, Victor would make some remarks like: "Large limestone pinnacle exposed by runoff from the river at location such and such—appears to be Pennsylvanian Period," into the tape recorder, thus giving credence to his 'geologic survey.'

Back at Cal Tech, Victor had taken a geology course as a technical elective. He thought it would be an easy grade, but to his surprise, it was a difficult course and an interesting subject. Thereafter, when a technical elective was required, he continued with various geology courses, never imagining the knowledge would be useful in any way.

They continued up and down the trail and river according to the flight plan, and as time passed Victor became more convinced that Buddy would not have chosen this area to spend the week in.

"Let's head southwest from the Ranger Station at Abrams Creek toward Chilhowee, and follow the river before we move into the next area."

This was near where Buddy and Donna's car had been located, and he wanted to check out this lesser traveled area more closely, as it was theoretically possible that Buddy had used the permit and entered at Abrams Creek. But he doubted it.

They had been in the air about an hour and a half, and Victor wanted to spend the majority of his time in the southwest portion of Abrams Creek and Panther Creek, his second and main area of interest. He had about two and a half hours of air time left, but he felt sure he could convince McAllister to stay up longer with the promise of additional payment.

Chapter Six

They spent the next hour flying pretty much the same flight plan south of the Abrams Creek Ranger Station as Victor took pictures, reloaded the camera, and made more notes.

Once, when they were flying down near Chilhowee, Victor made another note into the tape recorder regarding a large brown outcropping of rock.

"Appears to be Chapman Ridge sandstone, worth further investigation and study." He made a point of speaking loudly so McAllister would hear him over the drone of the helicopter.

"Okay, now let's head over towards the south side of Hannah Mountain and work the Panther Creek area. I want to spend some time over there as that is a primitive area of the Park with rough terrain."

"The contours are gonna make it a little tougher, Mr. Scofield, that's some pretty rough country up there."

"Yes, but if we stay over the creek, the overgrowth should be at its minimum allowing me a good view of the banks and surrounding areas. I'm especially interested in the deep pool areas where there are better chances of rock extrusions. I want us to work those especially slowly, okay?"

"No problem, but we are kinda running out of time."

It was now eleven-thirty and Victor wanted at least two more hours to work this area. Feeling that this would come up sooner or later anyway, he made his proposal.

"It is taking a little longer than I expected, but this is really important to me and I'm under the gun. What would you say to another thousand dollars for the rest of the day, and if we get back earlier you can keep the money?"

"Mr. Scofield, you just bought yourself a pilot for a day!"

"Great! Follow highway 129 southeast towards Fontana and stay on the north side. I want to get a look at the physical geologic characteristics above Calderwood Lake. Then when we get to the point where Panther Creek flows into the lake, turn northeast and follow it. I want to do the same type of passes we did over at Abrams Creek, but I want to go slower on the low level passes."

With Calderwood Lake to the south, he had a good view of the lake shore that ran parallel to the curvy two-lane Highway 129. This was actually Cherokee National Forest, which bordered the Park on the

SmokeFire!

south side. He was not particularly interested, as this area was not within the search zone, but he made a show of taking some pictures and making notes into the tape recorder.

He saw weekend travelers driving along 129 towards Fontana Village, a very small resort community on the banks of Fontana Lake in the foothills of the Smokies.

Formed by the Fontana Dam, the lake catches the runoff from many of the streams and rivers of the Park on the south side. It is a beautiful and primitive area and, aside from fisherman, out-of-state tourists rarely visit it.

They passed over Fontana Dam where Victor saw a tiny "marina" on the river with small fishing boats for rent and a little store. As they were nearing the entrance of Panther Creek, he saw a large limestone quarry on the opposite bank of the river.

"What quarry is that, Wally? Looks like they've got a pretty big operation going there."

"Appalachia Stone. Opened it about five years ago. They're taking limestone out of the cliff face. I hear people around these parts are a little upset, though, 'cause they don't hire much local help. Guess they can get those foreigners to work cheaper."

Victor could see the crushers and conveyors working, while dump trucks were being loaded with gravel and 'rip rap,' the grapefruit-sized rock chunks most commonly used to control erosion.

"Panther Creek. I'll get us some altitude for our first two passes up and down the river," McAllister said through the intercom.

"Good. Be sure to take it slow, Wally, this area is really important to my work."

It was an extremely primitive area, with no visible trails and very dense undergrowth. Panther Creek was much larger than Victor had imagined, spanning up to sixty feet or more at the low end. As they flew up the creek, Victor noticed some very old and rusty abandoned rail cars in a flat area near the creek, just barely visible through an open space in the forest.

"Wally, hold up! Swing the ship around this area again, over to the right. Did you see those old rail cars in that overgrown area?"

"Nope. Didn't see it, but I'll come back around."

Chapter Six

As McAllister turned the helicopter around, the rail cars became visible. There seemed to be three of them from what Victor could see, although they were overgrown with vines and weeds. Upon closer inspection they appeared much like a typical railroad car, only considerably smaller. Whereas today's rail cars—the 'hopper' types used to haul coal—can hold one hundred tons or more—these would do well to hold ten or twenty tons.

The cars sat on a section of mine gauge track that was narrower than standard railroad tracks and had considerably smaller railroad ties.

"Wow! Those babies look pretty old. Wonder how long they've been here," McAllister said.

"Difficult to say," Victor replied while looking through the binoculars, "but judging by the corrosion and undergrowth, I'd say at least fifty years, maybe much longer."

Looking through the binoculars, Victor could see more details. There was no ballast, the small egg-sized rock used on commercial railroad tracks to keep fires from being started by sparks from the car's wheels. Also, there was a lot of rusting junk lying haphazardly around—pieces of wheels, axles, even an old wheelbarrow made from wood and with an iron wheel.

As McAllister held the helicopter in a hover about one hundred feet over the site, Victor lowered the binoculars and scanned the region. Only about seventy-five feet of track was visible through the weeds in the center of the site, and there were rising hills all around that were densely covered by forest. Because of the extreme contours, it would have been nearly impossible to lay track all the way to the main river, and even if they had, the cuts into the hillside should still be visible at least in some spots.

"Judging by the fact that there's no rail cuts beyond the site, I'd say they were mining ore out of that escarpment behind us, bringing it out by these rail cars, then taking it out on horseback or mules. If so, then the site would be much older than fifty years, maybe dating back to the Civil War," Victor said.

"Hold this hover for a couple of minutes and let me take some shots with the zoom lens, then take a slow swing down and back up while maintaining this altitude."

SmokeFire!

Victor continually shot the site with the lens zoomed to about eighty millimeters. As McAllister slowly circled the site, Victor let the motor drive on the camera do the work, shooting about one shot per second.

McAllister circled back to the original northeast heading, and Victor said, "Very interesting. No visible trails in or out. Wonder how many people know it's here?"

"No telling, Mr. Scofield. This is one of the most primitive areas in the Park. There's no trails here and no backcountry camping sites. Could've been years since someone was here, maybe decades."

As they flew further northeast, the mountainside got steeper and McAllister had to keep the helicopter over the creek for Victor to get the visibility he needed.

They continued with the flight plan, repeating the procedures used over at Abrams Creek, and saw nothing of interest other than a wild, primitive area with old growth forest.

By about two o'clock, they had made several passes up and down Panther Creek at various altitudes, and Victor had taken about another two hundred shots or so of film.

"Okay, Wally, that's about it. I think I've gotten what I came for," Victor said.

McAllister nodded his head, and they flew back towards Pigeon Forge.

On the way back Victor said, "Wally, I thought all helicopters had dual controls. How come this one's only got a single control?"

"Insurance company won't let us have dual controls. When we fly the tourists around, we might have four or five people in here, so we let someone sit on the left side so they can get a good view. With a single stick there's no possibility of some tourist accidentally interfering with the controls."

"Makes sense, now that I think about it," Victor said.

They approached the landing area and McAllister descended, flared the helicopter, and set it gently down on the flat grassy pad.

As McAllister shut down the engine, Victor took off the headset and unbuckled the harness. Reaching into his wallet, he pulled out the money he had promised.

McAllister opened his door, but before getting out he said, "Hold on just a sec Mr. Scofield. Open your door so it'll cool off in here."

Chapter Six

Victor opened the door and was about to hand the money to McAllister when the pilot turned sideways in the seat and said, "It's none of my business, Mr. Scofield, but I've noticed several things today. First, you seem a little old to be attending graduate school. Second, I don't think you're too much afraid of flying 'cause I suspect you've been in a helicopter before by the way you put on that headset and got into the harness, not to mention leaning out the door. You might even have had some flying experience judging by the aviation terms you've used today. Third, I noticed you making notations on the map and taking pictures when there were no rocks in sight. Fourth, there's no sandstone of which I'm aware of in the high country. Sandstone is generally found in more low-lying areas. Fifth, I don't know of any graduate program that would let some student spend two thousand dollars on aerial photography for a research paper."

Victor looked at McAllister through his sunglasses as if seeing him for the first time. *Had it been that obvious?* he wondered.

"So, I don't know what it is you're lookin' for, but it ain't rocks. I flew Medevac's in Vietnam back in the early seventies, and I've noticed you're about the right age to have been there, too. You pretty much used some of the same techniques we used there when trying to locate troops in the jungles, so I think it's some*thing* or some*body* you're lookin' for. But it ain't rocks!"

"I'll bet you were one helluva dust-off pilot, Wally!" Victor said with a laugh, referring to the slang term used for Medevac. "I am looking for something, and without going into any details, let me assure you my search in no way has to do with anything remotely illegal or even unethical—in fact, just the opposite."

As Victor handed the money across the console, McAllister said, "Why don't you just give me three hundred, Mr. Scofield, just to cover the extra fuel we used today."

"Wally, our deal was for an extra thousand, and believe me you've been of great help already and you don't need to..."

"I insist, Mr. Scofield," McAllister interrupted. "And good luck with whatever it is you're looking for!"

McAllister then pulled three one hundred dollar bills from Victor's hand, stepped out of the helicopter and walked towards the little building without saying another word.

SmokeFire!

Victor gathered up his satchel, stepped down from the helicopter, and walked towards his car. He unlocked it and dropped the satchel on the passenger seat. He started the car, and when he looked up to back the car out, he saw McAllister bending down to get a can from the soft drink machine. As McAllister looked back at him, the pilot gave him a casual salute with his right hand and smiled. Victor returned his 'salute,' backed the 'Z' out, and drove away.

Three o'clock—just enough time to drive back to Knoxville and stop by the One Hour Photo Shop to have the film developed, he thought.

He had not really noticed anything during his reconnaissance, but then again he hadn't expected to. The intelligence-gathering portion of his plan was going well. He wanted to go home and review his notes and photographs from today so he could get started early tomorrow on the next phase.

During the drive back, his thoughts turned to Buddy and Donna. He was now almost totally convinced that a serious tragedy had befallen them and that they were in all likelihood no longer among the living. Whether they were alive or dead, he was not about to abandon them; he would not give up until he had some answers.

Chapter Seven

Friday evening, April 23, 1999
Knoxville, Tennessee

Victor dropped off the film at the One-Hour Photo, and waited in his car going over his notes while it was developed. He also transcribed the remarks from his recorder and made additional notations from the marks he had made on the map.

Upon arriving at home he spread the map out on the table in his office and separated the pictures into groups according to area. The camera had a databack, so each picture had the date, the time, and a sequential number stamped on the lower left hand corner. This made the separation easier as he had made notes each time he had moved from one area to the next.

Although the Park Service had located Buddy and Donna's car in the parking lot at the Abrams Falls Trail near Cades Cove, he felt that this information was of little use. They had left on Saturday and were not scheduled to return until the following Saturday, so if whatever had happened to them had not occurred early in the hike, they could be far away from that area.

SmokeFire!

An average hiker could travel approximately twenty miles in one day, depending upon terrain and if they moved fast. On previous trips he and Buddy had selected sites along the trail for possible camping and fishing, carefully measuring the distances between each point to give them plenty of time to set up camp, do some fishing and relax. He recalled that when he had been with Buddy last Friday, Buddy had told him his intention was to start about five miles south of the Abrams Creek ranger station, then continue along the Hannah Mountain Trail.

While sorting the photographs, he was bothered by something, but he couldn't exactly define what it was. He stared down at the map and traced what he thought to be their route, which would have led them to the Panther Creek area, and then along Hannah Mountain. *What was it that was nagging at him?*

Sometimes, when he was working on a technical problem and couldn't seem to find the answer, he would get away from it, hoping that the distance would give him perspective. Often this had proved to be a successful strategy, so he decided to take a break.

He went to the refrigerator, got a beer and some crackers and went out to his little patio. Sitting down, he opened the beer and tried to clear his mind. Some unconscious thought had been triggered when he recalled being at Buddy's last Friday. *What could it be? The route, it was something about the route, but what?* Then he had it: *Buddy had not given him his itinerary!*

"Plan for something, maybe everything to go wrong," Buddy used to say. For just that reason, Buddy would not have overlooked giving him his itinerary.

He would drive over to Buddy's and see if he had left it where Victor could find it. He bolted from the lawn chair, grabbed his car keys off the kitchen counter, and went to his car.

* * *

During the ten-minute drive to Buddy and Donna's, Victor began to have additional questions that led to doubts.

Even if he did find an itinerary, how would this help him? Buddy could have changed his mind at the last minute and decided to take

Chapter Seven

another route into a completely different area for a number of reasons, or he could have deviated from the intended route.

You're letting your imagination get away from you, he thought. *First things first—see if we can locate an itinerary and go from there.*

He pulled into Buddy's driveway and parked the car around the back near the garage entrance. It, like Victor's, was a modest house. From the front the living area was at ground level, and the driveway sloped downward and circled around to the back where there was a garage entrance into the basement and den.

He climbed the stairs to the deck and, using his keys, let himself in the back door, which opened up into the kitchen.

The house smelled slightly musty from not being lived in for two weeks. Standing just inside the door, Victor looked around the kitchen. As usual, everything was neat and orderly as Donna was a good housekeeper.

He looked around the kitchen for the itinerary, hoping to see it on the countertop or the kitchen table. Not finding it, he walked from the kitchen into the small dining area, and then looked in the living room. Surely if Buddy had left the itinerary, he would have left it in plain sight where it would be easy to find. But there was nothing.

He continued into Buddy and Donna's bedroom, looking on the dresser and the chest of drawers without success.

A sense of despair and sadness began to take hold of him. All around were reminders of his two best friends.

In the dining room, stored in the china breakfront, were the dishes Donna was so proud of that had been wedding gifts—her 'good china,' which was reserved for special occasions. On the dresser were several photographs of various sizes. A younger Buddy and Donna eating wedding cake. Buddy, Donna, and Victor at a neighborhood block party two years ago, smiling, with their arms draped over each other's shoulders. His eyes fell on Donna's jewelry box, which Victor had given her last Christmas. Opening it, he saw various earrings, necklaces, and the small sapphire ring that Buddy had given to her on her last birthday. She wouldn't wear it because she was always afraid of losing it. Victor picked up the ring and looked at it closely, then placed it on his little finger.

SmokeFire!

Sitting down on their bed, he looked at the ring and thought, *Where are you, Donna? Talk to me? What happened?* He put his head into his hands and began to cry silently.

After a few minutes he composed himself, put the ring back in the jewelry box, and continued his search for the itinerary in Jennifer's room and the spare bedroom. Still nothing. It was inconceivable to him that Buddy would have overlooked something so important as leaving his itinerary. But, then again, perhaps in the excitement or due to running late, he had. Buddy so rarely made a mistake, and perhaps this one would prove to be fatal.

The itinerary had seemed such a likely prospect, and now he was back to square one. He left a couple of lights on in the house, got into his car, and left.

It was now after ten o'clock, and he realized that he hadn't eaten all day. Stopping at an all-night deli, he picked up a sandwich and a six pack of beer and headed home.

When he got home, he put the sandwich on the kitchen table, opened a beer, and got out the photographs he had taken earlier. Scanning through them while he ate his sandwich, Victor began to wonder if taking them had been a stupid idea. They all kind of resembled each other, lots of trees, streams, and even a few hikers on the trails.

While looking through the next batch that were of the Hannah Mountain and Panther Creek area, Buddy's choice of route, he came across the pictures of the abandoned rail cars.

Interesting, he thought, and wondered what the history was. There were many things in the Park that were unknown to tourists, and to the local population itself, for that matter. For instance, many aircraft had crashed in the mountains, and several of them had simply been left behind, because dismantling and removing them would be extremely difficult in the harsh terrain. They had been marked with paint so a pilot flying over them at a future time would realize that this was a previously located crash site. Some of them dated back to the nineteen forties.

The remaining photographs revealed absolutely nothing. Bundling the pictures up with a sigh, Victor took them back into his office. He

Chapter Seven

got another beer and went out to his patio to formulate his thoughts in the quiet night air.

Okay, he thought, *let's look at this logically and consider all possibilities, starting at the beginning.* As he sat down, he mentally enumerated these possibilities.

One, they either went into the mountains or they did not. Chief Pike confirmed the unpleasant exchange that took place while Buddy was seeking a permit. Conclusion—they went into the mountains.

Two, they were missing. They had either had an accident or they had not. If they had had an accident, almost certainly the Park Service or other hikers would have found them, although it was possible that their bodies had been overlooked. Most hikers who got lost in the high country and lost their lives did so while attempting to cross streams. Although the streams looked small, shallow and easy to wade across, they were highly deceptive as the current was usually swift and the rocky bottom very slippery. The bodies of these lost hikers were sometimes found several miles downstream from where they had slipped and fallen, their deaths due to being knocked unconscious and drowning. An accident in which more than one hiker lost his or her life was very uncommon and almost totally relegated to the winter months, Victor recalled. Given Buddy and Donna's backcountry experience, coupled with the fact that the weather was good, a double accident seemed very unlikely.

If they had not had an accident, then that left two possibilities: either they were missing by choice or they were not.

If they were missing by choice, what could possibly be the reason? They had nothing to run from, and Victor would most certainly have known if they had any serious problems. Secondly, it was absolutely unimaginable that they would leave their child behind. Conclusion—they were not missing by choice.

Considering the other possibility, that they were missing against their wills, what did that leave? Abduction of adults in the United States was an almost unheard of crime, and most child abductions were related to custody battles between divorced parents. Second, abducting two adults in the Smokies would be extremely difficult, as getting them out without drawing attention would be almost impossible. Third, there was no logical motive for abduction. There had been a couple of instances that Buddy had related on one of their back country trips in which he suspected that abduction had been a possibility, but these had involved children many years ago. Conclusion—abduction seemed unlikely.

That left only one remaining possibility, that they had been murdered. *Murdered in the Smokies?* Victor thought. Contrary to popular belief, the high country was one of the safest places to be, provided one used good judgment and had the necessary experience. As Buddy had once said, "There isn't anything up there to be afraid of, except falling or animals of the two-legged variety."

Victor went in and got another beer while contemplating the latter possibility. Murder in the Smokies was extremely rare; however, a couple of years ago two people had been murdered on the Appalachian Trail, Victor remembered. The perpetrator was later apprehended and turned out to be a psychopath. He also remembered a situation back in 1998 when a fugitive had escaped into the Cherokee National Forest mountains bordering the Park, eluding the authorities, and was never found.

If they were murdered, what would be the motive? Theft seemed unlikely, as hikers rarely carried anything of value. Victor had heard of no reports of fugitives on the loose up there, nor was he aware of any other problems. Surely if there had been, Chief Pike would have mentioned it. *What if Buddy and Donna had come across a rapist or psycho killer?* Victor thought. Someone clever could kill them and bury the bodies where no one would find them.

What was the saying? Victor wondered. W*hen you eliminate all that is possible, whatever remains, however impossible, must be the truth.* Conclusion—they must have been murdered.

Okay, if they were murdered, then his approach to the problem would have to be totally different. He didn't know what that approach would be, but everything that had been done so far had been ineffectual.

Somehow Victor felt that if he discussed this possibility with Chief Pike, Pike would immediately dismiss it out of hand for a number of reasons. First, Victor had no evidence. Second, Pike would not wish to admit it was even a possibility for fear of negative publicity. Third,

Chapter Seven

Victor was convinced that Pike felt that he had done all he could and had pretty much put the whole incident behind him.

He determined that he must approach someone else—someone within the Park Service who was both knowledgeable and was willing to help, but who?

It was now nearly midnight and rain was beginning to fall, and Victor went in and cleaned up the kitchen while he thought of whom he might contact.

Lying in bed and listening to the rain, he thought of one possibility. He would consider it more in the morning. Sometime later he dropped off to sleep, dreaming of himself and Buddy back in Vietnam, and of Cathy.

Chapter Eight

Saturday morning, April 24, 1999
Knoxville, Tennessee

Victor awoke early with a slight headache, probably from the five beers he had drunk the night before, he thought. After a long shower and some aspirin, he felt better.

He repacked his camera with some extra film, put his map, binoculars and compass into the canvas satchel and headed out.

He intended to speak directly with the Park Ranger responsible for the Abrams Creek area. He had thought about calling ahead for an appointment, but felt that it might be difficult to get the phone number of the Ranger's in-park residence, and secondly, that the Ranger might be compelled to contact Chief Pike about his visit. Victor's relationship with Pike was barely a cordial one, and he preferred to keep him out of it, at least for the time being.

On the map, the Abrams Creek Ranger Station was located on the western boundary of the Park. Victor felt that the best route would be to

SmokeFire!

Maryville, then highway 321 to Walland, across the Foothills Parkway to Chilhowee, and finally back up to the Ranger Station. A trip of about fifty miles, it should take just over an hour. It was now eight o'clock, and that would put him there just after nine. Hopefully, since it was a Saturday, he could find the Ranger at his in-park residence.

During the drive he reflected upon his idea that Buddy and Donna had been victims of some kind of foul play. Although the idea seemed unlikely at first, the more he thought about it, the more he felt that it would explain a lot of the facts.

He did not know the name of the Abrams Creek Ranger, and hoped that it wasn't another 'Pike' who gave the impression that you were interfering in his day anytime you spoke with him.

The drive along the Foothills Parkway was absolutely beautiful during the early morning hours. He passed by Look Rock, where the view over the west end of the Park was breathtaking. The early morning mist was settled into the valleys, and the sun made the mountain peaks glow. *Such a beautiful place, and such a sad time*, Victor thought. He popped a tape into the cassette player, rolled both windows down, and let the fresh early morning air of the high country blow through the car, in hopes that it would improve his spirits.

He turned left at Chilhowee and was now nearing the Abrams Creek area. Up ahead he noticed a small store and decided to stop and ask directions to the Ranger Station.

When he opened the door to the store, a bell rang and the middle-aged woman behind the register looked up.

"Good morning! I'm looking for the Abrams Creek Ranger Station and I wondered if you could give me directions."

"Be glad to. It's just up the road a piece. 'Bout three miles on the right. You can't miss it."

"Do you happen to know if the Ranger's residence is near the station?"

"Yep, it's 'bout two miles into the Park past the Ranger Station. Stay on the gravel road when you pass the station and it's a dark green house up on the right."

"I appreciate it. Hope you have a nice day," Victor said, and the woman wished him the same.

Chapter Eight

Just as he was opening the door to leave, another thought struck him, and he turned and asked, "By any chance do you know the Ranger's name?"

"Sure do, name's Steve Russell. Nice fella."

"Thanks for your help," he replied, and got back into the car.

He then drove on until he came to a small wooden sign upon which were carved the words "Ranger Station" in white letters. Turning onto the gravel road, he decided to stop at the Station first and see if Russell was there. The door to the small wood building was closed, and when Victor turned the knob, he found it locked. He knocked on the door and waited a couple of minutes, but when there was no answer, he decided to try the residence.

He drove on up the narrow gravel road and came to an older small frame house painted dark green. Turning into the driveway, he hoped that Russell would still be home as it was only nine-thirty. He hadn't really thought about what he was going to say, so he decided he would have to wing it when he met Russell.

Opening the screen door he knocked on the front door and waited. In a minute he heard the lock being thrown and the door opened.

A lean young man in his late-twenties standing just under six feet tall greeted Victor. He wore Park Service uniform pants and a T-shirt. His face projected a friendliness and affability that Victor didn't expect from someone who had been disturbed so early on a Saturday morning.

"Can I help you?"

"I hope so. My name is Victor Scofield, from Knoxville. Are you Steve Russell?" Victor asked.

"Yes, I am. What can I do for, you Mr. Scofield?"

"I'd like a few minutes of your time. Some friends of mine got lost up here a while ago, and were never found and I'd like to get your opinion."

"You mean the married couple named Tippins, right?"

"Exactly. Do you have a few minutes to talk about it?"

"Sure, come on in. Want some coffee? I just made a fresh pot," Russell said as he opened the door for Victor to enter.

"That would be great!" Victor replied.

"Have a seat and I'll get us a couple of cups. How do you like yours?" he asked, as he turned and walked into the small kitchen.

"Cream and sugar please, if it's not too much trouble."

"No trouble at all, that's how I like mine too."

As Russell made the coffee, Victor looked around the small living room. It looked to be a two-bedroom home, and it appeared that Russell lived alone. The furniture was old and inexpensive, and there were no decorations that hinted at a woman's touch.

Buddy had told Victor that the Park Service furnished these homes for the rangers who worked in different areas. They weren't considered so much a perk as a convenience to allow the rangers to live within close proximity to their stations.

Russell came back into the living room and handed Victor a cup, saying "Watch it, it's hot!"

Taking a sip of the coffee, Victor said, "Where did you learn to make coffee? This is great!"

"My mom taught me. I come from a long line of coffee connoisseurs."

"I hope I'm not inconveniencing you, Mr. Russell."

"Not a bit. I'm usually off on Saturdays this early in the season, but I like to get down to the station before lunch just in case someone needs me. Besides, I really don't have anything else to do. How can I help you?"

The more Russell talked, the more Victor liked him. He was very friendly in a boyish sort of way, and seemed to take pride in his job. Victor decided to be candid with Russell and see where this approach took him.

"Well, this might sound a little crazy. The Tippinses are my closest friends, and Buddy Tippins was an experienced backcountry hiker in the Smokies. I've been on many backcountry trips with them, and Buddy was the finest woodsman I've ever seen. He once said that they could drop him anywhere in the Park blindfolded and without a compass, and it would take him no longer than three days to walk out after removing the blindfold. So, the idea of him getting lost is inconceivable to me."

"You know, it is a strange case," Russell agreed as he took a sip of his coffee. "I've only been in this park for two years and before that I was at Yosemite for about four. People do get lost in the National Parks, and some of them are never found, but it's pretty rare. I was in on the

Chapter Eight

search for the Tippinses and knew that he had some experience, which makes it strange."

"What makes it even stranger to me," Victor said, "is the fact that both of them disappeared. I mean it would be easier to understand if it was only one person, but two? And she had experience, too, just not as much as Buddy."

"I know what you mean. I've thought about this a lot myself. I love the parks, helping the visitors and hikers and all, and it's always really bothered me when someone gets lost. Most of the time we find them before anything bad happens, except in the winter months when their chances aren't as good. It's almost like something happened to both of them at the same time. About the only way I know of that happening is if they both fell, either off a cliff or into a river. But Abrams Creek is not really a dangerous stream, and if they had fallen off a cliff or something, we would have found them for sure."

"That's what I mean," Victor said. "You said you were in on the search. What area did you search?"

"Their permit was for the Rabbit Creek trail and the search teams covered the entire region. I guess you know that Mr. Tippins wanted a permit to jump off just south of here and move up Panther Creek. That's some pretty rough country even for an experienced hiker. I heard that he and the Chief got into an argument over it before they left."

Russell took another drink of his coffee and thought for a minute.

"You mind if I smoke, Mr. Scofield?"

"Please call me, Victor, and not a bit."

"Okay, then call me Steve."

Russell got up, picked up both cups and went into the kitchen. He returned with two refills and a pack of Marlboro Lights. Setting the coffee down on the table, he shook out a cigarette and lit it, then took a drink of coffee.

"Victor, you said that something might sound a little crazy. What did you mean?"

"I've given this a lot of thought, Steve, and I figure there's only two likely possibilities. First, your search area was in the wrong place, or, second, they didn't get lost, but something happened to them."

SmokeFire!

"I thought of that, too," Russell said. "As to searching in the wrong place, I thought the same thing. But their car was found at the parking lot at the trailhead of the Abrams Falls Trail that leads to Rabbit Creek. As to your second idea, I thought of that too. It has happened in this park, and others, too, that hikers sometimes meet up with some bad people, but that doesn't happen very often in any park. There was a couple killed up on the Appalachian Trail just before I came to the Smokies, but that's the only incident I know of."

"I heard something about that from Buddy sometime back," Victor said.

"Yeah, it was some bad guy who had a long record. They found him a couple of days later when he tried to kill another hiker, but the hiker got away. Since he committed the murders on federal property, he got locked up in the Atlanta federal penitentiary for about a zillion years."

"What if they had really gone to the Panther Creek area instead of to Rabbit Creek, Steve? Did you all search that area?"

"Since their car was found at the parking lot at the trailhead of the Abrams Falls Trail, Chief Pike concentrated the search to that region. It didn't make any sense to search anywhere else."

Taking his time as if thinking, Russell lit up another cigarette and said "Victor, I'm gonna tell you something, but I'd like to keep it just between us, okay?"

"My word on it, Steve."

"I thought the same thing. The Rabbit Creek and Abrams Creek areas are pretty tame. Lots of hikers on the trails, and the terrain's not very severe. I think if they'd gone in there and gotten lost, we'd have found 'em. Even though the search has been called off, I've decided to kinda conduct my own search of the Panther Creek area. If Chief Pike finds out, he'll be pissed 'cause there's really no reason for me to be back in there since there's no backcountry campsites and all. Not even any trails really. In fact, that's why I was getting dressed today. I was gonna take Old Spot and head over there and start up the river."

"Old Spot?" Victor asked.

"Yeah, he's my horse. I kinda inherited him when I took this post. He's pretty old, but he's a damn good horse." He looked down at his coffee for a moment and then looked Victor in the eyes. "You think they went into Panther Creek?"

Chapter Eight

"Yes, I do. Buddy liked his fly fishing and liked the more out-of-the-way places in the Smokies. Last hike I did with them we went down the Noland Divide Trail to Steel Trap for a week."

"That's some pretty country down there, rough contours, though," Russell said, referring to the steep inclines and valleys. "But if they did go into Panther Creek, why was their car found at the Abrams Falls Trail?"

"I know," Victor said, "that would imply something entirely different since it's such a long way away from Panther Creek."

"If they did go into Panther Creek, maybe they hired someone to take the car over to Abrams Creek where they were gonna come out. Lots of people do that," Russell said.

Sharp kid, Victor thought, *I hadn't thought of that. That's exactly something Buddy would do.*

"But if he hired someone to take the car over, where would he have found him, Steve?"

"Oh, I dunno know, there's lotsa places around here where you could hire someone for twenty bucks to drop a car off."

"So you're going to start searching the Panther Creek area today, huh?" Victor asked.

"Yeah, was gonna pack me up a lunch, saddle up Spot and head on up."

"Need some company, Steve?"

"Well, Victor, I only got one horse and to do it on foot would take too long. Why don't you let me go in over the next couple of days and then we'll see, okay?"

"Sounds good to me. Is there anything I can do to help?"

"Not really. Let's exchange phone numbers and I'll give you a call tonight after I get back."

"If you find anything I'd like to be the first to know, if that's okay," Victor said.

"No problem, my word on it, Victor. The Tippinses are mighty fortunate to have a friend like you. Most people would've just given up."

"They're really the only friends I got, to tell you the truth. Buddy and I go back a long way. In fact, he's the reason I moved to Knoxville, since he was from here and all."

SmokeFire!

"Let me ask you something, Steve, off the record as well. If you don't find anything, then that could mean that something happened to them. I mean, what if they were murdered?"

"I've thought of that, too, and if that happened, then the bad guy could've buried 'em where nobody would ever find 'em. Unless he tried to kill again like that other guy a couple of years ago, then we'd never know what happened," Russell said.

"If I wanted to look into people who have gotten lost up here and were never found, who could I talk to that would know about it?" Victor asked.

"There are a couple of people that I know of. First, I'd start with the Park Archivist, her name's Marsha Benton. She's down at Park Headquarters. She's probably there today. Marsha's only been here a little less than a year and she's usually in on Saturdays," Russell said. "You might head on down there and talk to her. There's a ton of records that she could let you look at. Tell her I sent you—we're, ah, kinda friends," he said rather sheepishly.

"The other guy you might wanna talk to is Smoky Tobias. Old hermit and kind of a legend around here. Lives alone not too far from here, in fact. Got himself a little cabin over near Chilhowee. He's in a wheelchair now, but I hear that he used to hike all over the high country, especially in the southwest region. Used to pan for a little gold and collect rocks."

"Smoky Tobias, huh?" Victor said. "What makes him a legend?"

Lighting up another cigarette, Russell explained, "A retired Park Ranger named Haskell told me about him when I came here. Said the guy's been here as long as anybody can remember and knows the region like the back of his hand. Also supposed to be some kind of expert on local folklore."

"Could be somebody I might need to talk to," Victor said, making a mental note of the name.

"Could be. Marsha can tell you how to get there. I've only met him once and he's a cranky old guy, but I hear he knows his stuff about the Park."

"Sounds good. I'll go down and talk with Marsha while you and Spot head up Panther. Give me a call when you get in tonight. Here are my numbers," Victor said, handing him a piece of paper on which he'd written his home, cell, and office number at SNB.

Chapter Eight

"Listen, Steve, I really appreciate what you've told me today and what you're doing. I don't know how I can repay the favor, but I'll try."

As Russell handed Victor his phone numbers, he said, "Don't worry about that. Let's just find 'em, or at least find out what happened."

As Victor got up to leave, he shook Russell's hand; covering Russell's outstretched hand with both of his, he said, "You be careful back there, Steve. Good luck and thanks again. I know Buddy and Donna would appreciate what you're doing. And by the way, next time I see you, you've got to teach me how you make coffee. It really was great!"

"I'll do both. If you don't mind, tell Marsha I'll call her tonight. I enjoyed talking with you too, Victor."

As Victor drove down the narrow gravel road, he reflected upon his visit with Steve. He really liked the guy. He was easy to get to know, friendly, intelligent, and even though he was probably only in his late-twenties, there was a sense of enthusiasm about him. *Maybe I've met a new friend,* Victor thought, as he headed toward Park Headquarters.

Russell stood at the open door and watched Victor drive away. *Nice old 'Z', and in mint condition, too. Looks like its been professionally restored. Scofield seems to be a pretty classy guy. I wonder what he does for a living,* he thought. *Obviously a professional of some kind—seems like a technical guy. Definitely not a salesman or a lawyer.*

Maybe when all this settled down he, Marsha, and Scofield could get together.

Closing the door he went to his bedroom and finished dressing. He and Spot had a mission!

* * *

It was now eleven-thirty, and Victor doubted he would get to talk with Archivist Marsha Benton before she went to lunch. The Abrams Creek Ranger Station was on the west side of the Park, and he would have to drive back over the Foothills Parkway to Walland, and then take the Little River Road to the Park Headquarters, which was just outside of Gatlinburg.

The temperature had risen to about sixty degrees, and the sun was burning off the mist that he had seen in the valleys on the trip over.

SmokeFire!

He wondered if he was going on a wild goose chase, looking into past occurrences of lost persons, as he did not really know who he was looking for or what he was hoping to find. Perhaps he would get some perspective and ideas about what to do next while Russell was looking into the Panther Creek area.

It was nearing one o'clock when he pulled into the Park Headquarters Building. He parked in the small parking lot, went inside, and approached the reception counter.

The young man behind the counter was the same one to whom Victor had spoken on his first trip.

"Hi! Victor Scofield, remember me?"

"Hello, Mr. Scofield," he said, in a less-than-happy-to-see-you tone. "What can I do for you?"

"I'd like to speak to your archivist, Marsha Benton. I've spoken with Steve Russell, one of your rangers, and he said she was in today."

"She was in earlier, but I haven't seen her since lunch. Saturday's not a work day for her, and she may have left."

"Steve mentioned that, but said she would probably be in most of the day. If it wouldn't be too much trouble, could you check and see if she's still here? I'd appreciate it."

"Just a minute," he said as he turned and went through the door back into the main offices.

Every time Victor came to Headquarters, he received the same cool reception, like the personnel here felt that everything that had happened was his fault.

He stood looking at the map of the Park on the counter, which was matted beneath a piece of plastic. The ranger came back out followed by a young woman in civilian attire. She was short, a little overweight, and had deep red hair that she wore long.

As the ranger went back behind the counter, the woman came up with her hand outstretched and said, "Mr. Scofield, I'm Marsha Benton. Steve called ahead and said you might be dropping by. Would you like to come back to my office where we can talk?"

Victor shook hands with her and said he was glad to meet her, and that yes, he would love to talk if she had a few minutes. She led him back through the hallway and turned into a small office near the back of the building.

Chapter Eight

"I really appreciate your taking the time to see me, Ms. Benton."

"It's Marsha, and it's no problem. Steve told me about talking with you, and I'm really sorry about your friends." When she made the last remark, she gave the impression that she was genuinely sorry and not just going through the motions. He was beginning to see why Steve liked her, and although he didn't know either of them, they seemed alike in their friendly attitudes.

"Thank you. I guess Steve told you that I wanted to look into some past occurrences of lost persons, but I'll have to be honest and say I really don't know why I'm doing it. I guess maybe to feel like I'm doing *something* to figure out what has happened."

"I understand. Please have a seat," she said, indicating the chair near her desk. "Can I get you a cup of coffee or something?"

"No thanks, it's a little late in the day for me, and I had plenty up at Steve's."

"Doesn't he make the most wonderful coffee? He's tried to teach me, but mine's just not as good as his."

"He certainly does," Victor said, wondering about the depth of their relationship.

"I haven't been here at the Park very long, and the previous archivist's record keeping was good if a little unorganized, if you know what I mean. I did go ahead and pull the records you're interested in. I'm trying to get the records computerized, but I think it's going to take me until I retire to do it," she said, smiling.

"The records are on what we call incident reports. As I said, my predecessor was good at record keeping, and I managed to locate the files. They were stored in a box in the file storeroom."

Pointing to a box sitting beside the desk, she said, "I figured you'd want a copy of them, so I've photocopied them for you. They are public knowledge so there's no problem with anything proprietary. Let me show you how they're organized," she said as she bent down and removed the lid from the box.

Inside were many sheets of papers and forms, separated from each other by bundles and bound together with rubber bands. All in all, it looked like there were about twenty pounds of the stuff. Russell must have called before Victor even got out of his driveway, as copying that many forms would have taken a while.

Picking up a bundle from the top, she removed the rubber band and laid the stack on Victor's side of the desk.

"All the files have the Incident Report as the cover sheet. It gives the basic particulars of each event. I've only included the ones which relate to lost persons because I didn't think you'd be interested in the rest, which are car vandalisms, petty crimes and such, of which there's a ton," she said, picking up the cover sheet.

"They have the date, time, location, and a description of the incident up here on the top," she said, indicating the boxes on the form with the point of a wooden pencil.

"On the bottom portion of the cover sheet is the final disposition. In other words, how the incident was resolved or ended up. Before the incident is closed, the Park Superintendent and Chief Ranger must give the final sign off," she said, pointing to signature areas on the bottom of the form.

"I'm afraid some of them are a little difficult to read. They date back to when the Park was formed and some of the papers were in rough shape."

"I really didn't mean for you to go to all this trouble, Marsha. I don't know what I expected, but I had no idea there was this volume of data," he said apologetically.

"It was no trouble really. We purchased a new copier this year and it runs them through pretty fast. Now these other papers behind the cover sheet are supporting documents. They go into more detail about the people who were lost, the search efforts, and any notes that might be relevant. The report of your friends' disappearance is also in the box," she said gently.

"Can you tell me something before I go?" Victor asked. "Do you know how many people have been lost up here who were never found?"

"Well, like I said, I've only been here less than a year and with all the other stuff I've got going on, I'm not really up-to-date on any statistics pertaining to lost persons. I understand it's pretty uncommon, though, not only in this park but the others as well. I'd be interested to hear what you find out after you review the files—might be interesting to know."

"I'll let you know, but by the looks of it, it's going to take me a while to digest it all," he said, nodding towards the box of files.

"Is there anything else I can do for you, Mr. Scofield?" she asked.

Chapter Eight

"Please call me Victor, and thank you but no, I've taken enough of your time with the copying and all. I really appreciate your efforts."

"Well, don't hesitate to call me if you need anything else. Let me give you my phone number," she said as she wrote it down on a pink Post-It note, pulled it from the pad, and handed it to Victor.

"Do I owe you anything for the supplies?" Victor asked, "The copies took a lot of paper."

"Don't worry about it, I'm just glad I could do something. I really hate to see something like this happen. I know you must be very sad as well."

As he stood up, Victor offered Marsha his hand and said again how much he appreciated her help and her sympathy, and how nice it was to meet her.

Picking up the box of files, which was heavier than he expected, he walked to her office door and turned around.

"One more thing, Marsha. This might sound a little crazy, but please tell Steve to be careful up there. I don't know what happened to my friends, and maybe I never will, but until I do, I think he should be extra cautious."

"That doesn't sound crazy at all and I'll be sure to tell him. Let me know what you find out after you go through those," she said, pointing to the box. "I'm really interested."

"I'll be sure to."

Victor walked to his car, opened the hatch on the back, set the box down, closed it, and walked around to the driver's side.

As he was unlocking the door, a green Park Service pickup truck pulled into the parking lot, and Victor recognized Pike behind the wheel. He didn't know if Pike saw him or not, and given their previous encounters, he wasn't about to go over and talk with him. Certainly nothing good would come of that. Also, Pike would undoubtedly ask what Victor was doing, and he didn't want to draw any attention to Marsha. He could easily envision Pike giving her a hard time about giving him the files, even though they were public knowledge.

He drove out of the parking lot and headed home, thinking of how best to go about reviewing the files. Maybe this is just like the helicopter trip, he thought, time-consuming and yielding little of value, but he knew he had to do something. He had considered going into the Panther Creek

SmokeFire!

area himself, but Steve was up there on horseback and could cover a lot more ground than he could on foot. Better to let a professional handle it.

He stopped off at the grocery store on his way home and picked up a few items, then at the package store where he bought a bottle of merlot wine. He would go home, unpack the files and scan through the cover sheets, and then throw a steak on the grill.

He also thought he'd better call Donna's mom to see how she and Jennifer were doing. There were probably going to be some legal issues to deal with concerning Buddy and Donna's estate, and Victor would have to help her through it. Just the thought of this gave him a sense of deep despair. On any other Saturday night he'd probably be over at Buddy and Donna's throwing a steak on their grill.

Drop it, Vick, he thought, *that's not going to help.* But that didn't shake his feeling of loneliness.

Pulling into his driveway, he remembered Steve's comment about Smoky Tobias, and that he had forgotten to ask Marsha for directions to his cabin. Sometimes you could get some good information from a local 'expert,' and although he did not know if he would learn anything of value, he figured a visit couldn't hurt. There was also one other agency with whom he wished to speak, and he would do that on Monday.

He had also thought about SNB on the drive home. Calling in Thursday morning, he had told Brenda that he had a flu bug and asked if she could please tell Vodeski that he wouldn't be in. She had suggested that Victor come to Vodeski's office and give him a kiss; if they were lucky, he'd catch the bug too.

Now, though, he had decided that he would request either his vacation time to continue his 'investigation' or a leave of absence. It would not be a pleasant conversation, and he wasn't looking forward to making the request.

It took two trips to the car to unload the groceries, the wine, and the box of files. He set the box down in the living room, put the groceries away, and got a beer from the refrigerator.

Victor decided that if Russell didn't call, he would call him at his Park residence. He found himself looking forward with anticipation to Russell's call that evening and hoping he had some news—any news.

Opening the box he took out the files and laid them on the living room floor, sorting them by the incident date on the cover sheets.

Chapter Eight

Looking down at them, he counted eighty-five file bundles. He had had no idea that there would be so many when he had thought of this, but he wasn't surprised, knowing that the Park had been open since the mid-thirties.

The file at the top of the pile, of course, was Buddy and Donna's. He set it aside as he wasn't ready to look at it yet. He picked up the next one, and taking it and his beer, he went out to the patio. This was going to take a while.

Chapter Nine

**Saturday night, April 24, 1999
Knoxville, Tennessee**

Victor, having long since consumed his steak, sat on the floor among the files.

He had begun reviewing them starting with the most recent—except Buddy and Donna's, which he would look at when he thought he could do it without bringing on the associated pang of despair.

Around nine o'clock Russell called, saying that he had gone up Panther Creek about four miles and had found nothing of interest. Since it wasn't a well-traveled backcountry trail and the undergrowth was thick, he said, the going had been slow and he had been forced to turn back in order to get home by dark. He had found no signs of recent campsites, the telltale indication of which would be extinguished campfires, chopped wood, or any other remnants that backcountry campers would leave behind.

Before getting off the phone, Steve gave Victor directions to Tobias's cabin. He said he was going to get up early and go back in, in hopes of going nearly all the way to the headwaters of Panther Creek, which was near Hannah Mountain, a distance of about twelve to fifteen miles.

Victor reiterated the comment he had made to Marsha encouraging Russell to be careful. Steve agreed and reassured him that he would call him back around the same time the next night.

After the call, Victor went back to the files, cursorily scanning through each file, as he had all evening. He made notes on each incident, copying down the date, trail area, number of persons lost, their ages, and any other particulars that he felt might be salient. So far, the only facts which he had found of interest were those he didn't find.

The first thing he noticed was that there had been no hikers who had vanished without their bodies ever being found, with two exceptions, both of which were children. The latest disappearance happened over ten years ago and the previous one was during the mid nineteen-sixties. Both disappearances had occurred on day hikes along well-marked trails.

The second point of interest was that no experienced hikers had been lost who were never found. The only instances in which the lost persons had died had occurred during the winter months, when the hikers had fallen victim to hypothermia.

In reviewing the files, he had also discovered that the searches had generally lasted no longer than two weeks before being called off, which was consistent with the search for Buddy and Donna. The only exception was in the searches for the two missing children, of which one had lasted almost a month. Probably because they were children, Victor thought, and the searchers' emotions identified with such a loss.

He had seen several files detailing cases in which a single person had gotten lost and had been found alive, sometimes several days later. In one particularly interesting case an inexperienced middle-aged woman had been hiking with some friends on a day hike and had fallen behind the group. Taking the wrong turn on the trail, she had been lost for five days.

The searchers had almost given up—he could tell from the notes—when the woman emerged thirty miles away at a paved highway in North Carolina, unhurt. This was the story he had related to Mae earlier last week.

Chapter Nine

The notes taken by one of the searchers during an interview with this woman showed that she had not really panicked, as many lost persons do, but had maintained some degree of composure and had followed a small river downstream until she walked out. *Impressive*, Victor thought. *Her survival was probably also due to the fact that this occurred during the summer months, where there is little risk of hypothermia.*

He was reviewing files dating back to the early sixties when he noticed a rather large file near the bottom. Picking it up and removing the rubber band, he immediately noticed that it was different from the other files—significantly larger.

Dated May 13, 1951, it was difficult to read in some places, probably because the originals were old. Also, it did not have the usual Incident Report cover sheet, because it was a report from the United States Army. Reading curiously, Victor discovered that a U.S. Army Corps of Engineers encampment, entitled Camp Thirteen, had been stationed in the Park.

A geologic survey detachment tasked with mapping the Park, it had been destroyed by a mysterious explosion and eight U.S. service personnel had died. The file gave the names, rank, serial numbers, and so on, of the personnel killed. Flipping though the pages Victor came across the investigative team's conclusion:

"*Simultaneous explosions of unknown cause - possibly due to improper storage/handling of seismic charges.*"

Going back through the file, Victor learned that the camp had existed for three years and was under the command of a Captain George Jeffers. He found a sheet outlining Jeffers's military experience and began reading. Jeffers had been a career soldier, highly decorated in combat.

Strange, Victor thought. *This guy was experienced and yet his entire encampment had been blown up due to improper storage or handling of seismic charges?*

Victor did not know a lot about explosives, but during his tour in Vietnam, he had had the opportunity to become somewhat familiar with their handling and storage. He knew that the ordinance personnel had always stored the explosives where, if they unintentionally detonated, they would do minimal harm.

SmokeFire!

The file stated that Captain Jeffers's lodging cabin and three Quonset huts were destroyed. *Simultaneous explosions in four buildings?* he wondered. *Or one large explosion?* But the report stated, *"Simultaneous explosions."* Victor didn't know anything about seismic charges, but he assumed that they were less powerful than regular military ordinance such as bombs or claymore mines.

Why would they store the charges in or near their living quarters? he asked himself. *That wouldn't make any sense. And how could they have simultaneously exploded? Why would they have such a quantity that it would result in such devastation?*

He flipped through each person's service record and noted nothing remarkable other than that Jeffers's family had lived in Knoxville, which only caught his eye since he, too, lived in Knoxville.

He restacked the pages, replaced the rubber band around the file, and put it back into the box.

Another wasted effort, he thought wearily. It seemed pointless to continue to review the files, so he gathered them up and put them in the box with the file from Camp Thirteen. He laid Buddy and Donna's on top and then he replaced the lid.

Tomorrow he would get up early and drive up to see Tobias, in all likelihood another wasted effort, he thought. He took the box of files into his home office, placed it in the corner, and went to bed.

Before he drifted off to sleep, he thought back over his review of the files. *Eighty-five files*, he thought—*over sixty deaths*. He also wondered about that U.S. Army survey camp. Something just didn't feel right about it.

* * *

The alarm woke Victor at seven-thirty. He rolled out of bed, placing his feet on the floor. His head was pounding from a headache, no doubt from the three beers and the bottle of wine that he had drunk last night while he ate dinner and looked at the files.

This stress is causing me to drink too much, he thought; *I've got to get a better grip on this!*

He packed up his usual gear and was on the road at eight-thirty. Smoky Tobias's cabin, Russell had said, was near Chilhowee, just

Chapter Nine

outside the Park, less than ten miles from the Abrams Creek Ranger Station.

He retraced his drive of the previous morning when he had gone to see Russell, taking the route over the Foothills Parkway. The vista was just as beautiful today. Driving along, he remembered that over sixty people had lost their lives in those mountains. It hardly seemed possible just looking at it, he thought, so beautiful, so peaceful.

He drove into Chilhowee—which was really just composed of a gas station, a general store, and a few other small businesses—and found the turnoff that Russell had told him led to Tobias's cabin.

Russell had warned him again when they spoke last night that Tobias was a pretty cantankerous old guy—almost a hermit. Russell never mentioned if Tobias had a telephone, and Victor had forgotten to ask. By the time he thought of it this morning, he figured Russell had already left to go back up to Panther Creek, so it would be pointless to call him and ask. He hoped Tobias would agree to see him, as it was a long drive from his house all the way over here.

The paved road turned to gravel after about three miles in. A rusted metal sign stating 'No Trespassing' in bold red letters was nailed onto a tree.

This is the place, Victor thought, and drove on until he came to a cabin, an old white frame house in desperate need of repair, situated among several old oak trees.

An old Ford pickup truck that looked like it had seen better days was parked underneath one of the trees. Victor pulled up next to it and got out.

"Hope he doesn't shoot me," Victor muttered as he approached the house. He walked up the stairs to the front porch, which extended the full length of the house, and knocked on the door. After a few minutes he heard a lock being turned, and an old man in a wheelchair opened the door.

"Mr. Tobias?" Victor asked.

"Yeah, whaddya want? You ain't no salesman, are ya?" he growled. Turning his wheelchair with his right hand, he swung it slightly to his left, blocking the entrance.

"No, sir, my name's Victor Scofield. I'm from Knoxville, and I've heard from the Park Service that you're the local authority around here

SmokeFire!

on the Smokies. I'm doing some research and hoped you would give me some of your insight. I'd be glad to pay you for a few minutes of your time," Victor said.

"Don't need no money! Got nothin' to spend it on up here! Far as my time goes, got plenty of that too," he said as he backed up the wheelchair, swiveling it to the right, and fully opening the door.

"Come on in an we'll talk."

"I really appreciate it," Victor said as he stepped into the house, "I hope I'm not inconveniencing you. I would have called, but the park ranger who gave me directions to your place neglected to give me your phone number."

"Don't matter none, damn phone company cut it off couple of years ago. Don't have no need for one anyways, got nobody to call!" he said with a grin that was more of a grimace, as he wheeled over next to a small wood burning stove.

Victor immediately felt sorry for him. He was at least eighty years old, in a wheelchair, living back in the sticks in this old house. The furniture, what there was of it, was threadbare and worn, and the house had the distinct odor associated with old people who lived alone—musty and closed up.

"Have a seat, young feller, and tell me what you're lookin' for. You some college boy writin' some paper on the Smokies? Come to ask Ole Smoky so's you can say you 'enteviewed some local folk?" he said, as he wheeled the chair around facing Victor.

"No, sir, I'm not in college," Victor said, and thought he should probably not admit to having earned his Master's degree in computer science, as he felt that 'Ole Smoky' would definitely not approve of that.

As he walked across the small living room, he said, "I wanted to talk to you about people getting lost up in the mountains. Earlier this month, two good friends of mine got lost up there and have never been found—man and his wife. They've searched all over and no trace of them ever turned up. They were both experienced hikers, and quite frankly, I just don't see how it could have happened."

"Happens, damn it! Stupid pilgrims go up there and git all twisted 'round. End up dead in some river in summer, or froze to death in winter. If you don't mind, how's 'bout grabbin' a log and throwin' it in this here

Chapter Nine

stove. Still a mite cold this mornin'," Tobias said as he pointed to a stack of logs near the wood burning stove.

Victor had not yet sat down, so he went to the pile of wood next to the stove. Picking up a split log, opening the stove door, and shoving it in among the hot coals, he said, "I've read the files, and you're right about that Mr. Tobias. Seems like they was a bunch of pilgrims, gettin' lost on day hikes and all."

He was attempting to adopt the vernacular of Tobias in hopes of opening him up. After all, he didn't want to seem like a college boy.

"Call me Smoky! Ever body else does!"

"Okay, Smoky. But you know somethin'? When I looked at the files, only two people was lost who was never found and..."

"Yeah, I know 'bout 'em—kids. Both on day hikes with their families and such. One was lost in up near to Laurel Falls, back in July of eighty-nine. Other 'twas over in the Chimneys back in sixty-seven—May 'twas, if I recall."

"What do you remember 'bout 'em? Lookin' at the files it seemed that they looked pretty hard for 'em," Victor said.

"Hey, it's gettin' long onto thirsty time! Want a bit of a snort?" Tobias said. Not waiting for a response, he deftly wheeled his chair from its place in front of the stove to the kitchen.

Victor was reluctant to refuse as it was only nine-forty five, and still feeling the remnants of last night's hangover, he dreaded the taste of anything that contained ethanol. He was fearful that's what Smoky had in mind but he mustered his courage.

"Sure, whaddya you got, Smoky? I'm always ready to throw a couple down!"

"Special brew, young feller—blackberry wine! Make it myself!" Tobias said, as he wheeled himself into the kitchen.

"Ain't into no moonshine and such. Too tough on an old fart like me!" he said and disappeared into the kitchen.

"Probably too tough on me too, Smoky, some homemade blackberry wine sounds great!"

He heard Tobias rummaging around the kitchen, and in a couple of minutes he came back out and said, "Got 'em sittin' on the counter, young feller, but can't get 'em in here with this chair and all. How 'bout fetchin' 'em for us?"

SmokeFire!

"No problem, Smoky," Victor said, quickly standing up and walking into the kitchen.

Two large water glasses sat on the counter next to an unlabeled bottle of dark looking liquid, which Victor assumed was the home-brewed blackberry wine. Both glasses were full to the top, and Victor's stomach almost rebelled at the sight. Picking them up, he returned and handed a glass to Smoky.

"Thanks, young feller. Hope you like it! Here's to us, and them like us," he said as he tipped the glass to his lips.

"Now where was we?" he asked after resting the glass on the right arm of his wheelchair.

"We were talkin' 'bout them kids who got lost up there who was never found, I think," Victor said, as he raised his glass to his lips.

This is probably going to kill me, he thought, as he cautiously took a sip of the wine.

"Damn, Smoky! This is some pretty good stuff!" Victor said without trying to sound patronizing—and actually, it wasn't all that bad.

"Ain't too bad if I don't say so myself. Been makin' it nigh onto forty year," Tobias said, as he raised his glass once again and took a long swallow. "Git the makin's from a mail order place down Pigeon Forge way."

"Yeah, we was talkin' bout them kids. Only ones who ain't never been found," Tobias said. "Been sixty-three pilgrims who bought it up thare, but them two's the only ones ain't been found—'cept your friends. Heard 'bout 'em last week. Damned shame, that!"

Tobias took another large swig from the glass and almost emptied it.

"What 'bout 'nother one, young feller? Let's freshin' 'em up!" he said, tapping his glass on the wheelchair arm. "You're gettin' behind thare!"

Victor had only taken a couple of swallows from his glass, but did not want to appear as though he was refusing hospitality. "Damn, Smoky, I been so interested in what you're sayin' I almost forgot to take me a swig," he said as he raised the glass to his lips and took a large swallow.

What have I gotten myself into?

Getting up, Victor took the glasses and went back into the kitchen. He refilled both, although his was still half full.

Upon returning he handed Smoky his glass and sat back down. The wood burning stove was raising the ambient temperature in the small

Chapter Nine

room to near flash point, Victor thought. On the other hand, perhaps it was Smoky's blackberry wine.

"Thank ye!" Smoky said, after accepting the glass.

"Yeah, damn strange 'bout your two friends. Heard they's both had themselves some bush 'sperience, but you know somethin,' young feller? Thare's some damn strange goin's on up thare—has been for over a hundret year. Cherokee Indians used to live up thare—many a tale 'bout spirits and all. Now I's can see you're an educated feller, and you probably got no use fer it, but it's true! They had this ole tale 'bout the Little People, lived underground 'neath the Chimney Tops, they did. Snatched Indian chilren."

Taking another hospitality swig, Victor said, "Come on Smoky, you don't really believe that, do you?"

"Ain't got no reason not to, young feller!"

Victor was quickly realizing that this whole thing was going nowhere, just like his last endeavors. Besides, the wine had to be at least a 'hundret proof,' he thought, or perhaps it was just that his hangover had just about dissipated when he got into Smoky's wine and was now being rekindled.

"What about those kids who were never found, Smoky?" Victor asked. "Whaddya think happened?"

"Don't rightly know! Maybe they just run down to them hollers and disappeared, or maybe them Little People got 'em. Worst tragedies in the Park!"

Obviously the wine was getting to Smoky as he was beginning to slur his words, and Victor was fearful that he was going to tap his glass on the wheelchair arm again and demand another. *I've got to make my move now!*

"Let me ask you something, Smoky," Victor said, dropping his 'good ole boy' vernacular. "I think my friends went up to the Panther Creek area, and that was the last anyone ever heard of them. Chief Pike and the Rangers searched for them, but didn't find anything. As I said, they were experienced. In fact, Buddy and I were in Vietnam together, and he was the finest jungle fighter I ever saw. It wasn't like he didn't know what he was doing. What do you think could've happened?"

"Damn! Panther Creek! Nobody done told me that! That's bad country, young feller! No trails. Snakes, bears, and such. But thare be

SmokeFire!

somethin' much worse up thare than them critters. Cherokee's got some bad tales 'bout that place!" Smoky said, then raised the glass to his lips.

"What do you mean, Smoky?" Victor asked, leaning forward from the chair he was sitting in.

Tobias reared back in his wheelchair, finished off his glass, and stared at the wood burning stove as he shook his head back and forth.

"Bad, young feller! Bad country! Don't nobody go up thare! Not now, not evar! Evil spirits! Don't nobody believe it, but it's true!"

Oh please, Victor thought. Tobias's glass was empty. *I've got to get out of here!*

"Come on, Smoky, what are you talking about?" Victor asked.

"Don't remember the Cherokee words fer the evil spirit, 'Ole Red Eye or somethin' like that—don't remember what it meant!"

Tobias was now sitting back in his wheelchair, staring up at the ceiling.

"Smoky, what are you saying?"

"Now I's remembers what it meant. Ain't thought of it in a long time."

He lolled his head back and forth a couple of times. Then right before he passed out, he uttered a single word.

"SmokeFire!"

Chapter Ten

Sunday afternoon, April 25, 1999
Knoxville, Tennessee

Victor had left Smoky passed out in the wheelchair. He thought of moving him to the couch, but felt that Tobias probably had a lot of experience sleeping in that chair.

He had put another log in the stove, closed its door, and made sure the latch engaged so that Tobias wouldn't bump against it causing the door to open and possibly start a fire. He left Smoky a note stating his appreciation for his time and extolled the virtues of his blackberry wine.

It had been a fruitless trip. Smoky did seem to know about the lost people, even recalling the month and year and the places where the children got lost. *He probably has some interesting tales*, Victor thought, *if you can keep him sober long enough to tell them.*

He got back home just after twelve, made a sandwich, and went out onto his patio. It was turning out to be a beautiful spring day—cloudless with a gentle breeze.

Well, what next? he wondered. There were two items on his agenda for tomorrow, not the least of which was to see Vodeski and request some time off to continue his investigation. *That should be interesting.*

He thought of going through the photographs he had taken from the helicopter again but felt that would be useless. He also thought of getting the files back out, and felt that would be equally pointless, as he had gleaned nothing really from his review last night, other than the fact that experienced hikers didn't get lost without ever being found. He did, however, remember the thick file relating to the U.S. Army's survey camp. The more he thought about it, the more it nagged at him.

Jeffers had been an experienced officer, and the other personnel records revealed his soldiers were for the most part highly educated. *How could they have made such a mistake?* he wondered.

For lack of anything else to do, he went back into his office and dug out the file. Taking a bottle of water from the refrigerator, he took both back out onto the patio.

Reading through each of the soldiers' personnel forms—some of which were difficult to decipher due to fading of the ink—he got a better feel for the types of individuals they had been. Most had college degrees in geography or geology and had been in the service only a short time. Their first and only tour, Victor commented to himself.

Examining Jeffers's file again, he saw that he had been in some pretty extensive combat during the Second World War. He had been awarded a Silver Star for valor and a Purple Heart for wounds received in action, but the record didn't provide details of either. He had been the Commandant of the Survey Camp since its establishment, so he had had plenty of experience in running it.

Among the search records was a small paragraph stating the location of the encampment—near Panther Creek.

Now that's strange, Victor thought. *I wonder if there's more to this than is shown here?*

Looking at Jeffers's personnel form, he again saw the Knoxville address.

Was he from here, or did he move here after getting the assignment? he wondered. It was not uncommon for officers—or enlisted personnel, for that matter—to relocate their families to noncombat areas during long assignments.

Chapter Ten

On an impulse Victor went into the kitchen and retrieved the Knoxville telephone directory. Opening it up to the "J" section, he scanned up and down near the "Jef..." names. Lots of Jeffs, Jeffersons, and among them a single listing for "R Jeffers." Oddly enough, the address matched that of the Army personnel form.

A relative? he wondered.

Without really thinking about it, Victor picked up the telephone and dialed the number. While it was ringing, he thought, *What am I going to say?*

"Hello?" a female voice answered.

"Ms. Jeffers?"

"Yes, who's calling?" she asked.

She sounded like she was in her thirties or forties—*a daughter perhaps?*

"Ms. Jeffers, my name is Victor Scofield, and I live here in Knoxville. I'm kind of embarrassed about calling, but I've been doing some research, and I came across a U.S. Army file which listed a Captain George Jeffers..."

"He was my father. He died a long time ago," she said.

Victor detected something in her voice—not sadness really, but almost longing.

"Yes, I've read the account here in the file."

"The file? Mr. Scofield, who did you say you were with?" she asked, her previous tone disappearing behind a wall of formality.

"I'm doing some private research, and..."

"What kind of research?" Now her tone was escalating, not really questioning but more demanding. *She's going to hang up on me*, Victor thought.

"Ms. Jeffers, you don't know me, and I'm sorry for calling, but let me be honest with you. Two weeks ago my best friends—a husband and wife—went camping in the area near where your father's camp was located, and they haven't been heard from since. The Park Service has called off the searches, and I've been looking into it, trying to figure out what might have happened to them. I found the file of Camp Thirteen—your father's—among some other records of lost persons. For some reason it seems strange to me, because..."

Interrupting, she asked, "Strange, how?"

121

"Well, from the records here, it seems that the Army decided that the accident might have been due to some improper handling of seismic explosives. Frankly, given your father's experience, as well as that of others in his detachment, it just seems peculiar how an accident like that could have occurred."

"I didn't know my father, Mr. Scofield. He died when I was very young. My mother died about eight years ago and she never really would talk about it. You see, after the accident she...well, she kind of lost it."

"I don't mean to pry, and in all honesty I'm not sure why I called. I'm pretty shook up over my friends' disappearance, and well, I guess I've been trying to do something, anything, that could help me figure it out. You see, my friends—like your father—were very experienced in hiking in the Smokies. Beyond that there are no commonalities. I really shouldn't have bothered you, and I'm sorry for calling," Victor said apologetically, preparing to hang up.

"No, wait. I think I heard on the news about some hikers becoming lost a week or so ago, but I didn't pay much attention to it. I'm really sorry to hear about your friends, but surely you don't think there's some connection, Mr. Scofield. My father's death happened almost fifty years ago!"

"No, no, of course not," Victor said. "I guess your father's accident intrigued me. Perhaps my subconscious is diverting my own feelings. I'm really sorry for disturbing you. I shouldn't have called."

"Since you're being honest with me, Mr. Scofield, let me be honest with you. I never knew my father, and I haven't heard anyone mention him since my mother died, and she never really talked about him much."

The longing in her voice that Victor had sensed had now taken on a deeper quality, with a weariness bordering on a sigh. Although her father had died almost fifty years ago, Victor wondered if the loss still affected her in some way, but it was not his intent to reopen old wounds.

"His death really destroyed my mother," she continued, "at least emotionally. So whatever happened to him claimed two victims—three if you count my childhood."

She said this in a melancholic tone, and Victor was beginning to feel uncomfortable and to berate himself for his thoughtlessness in calling.

"I'm very sorry, Ms. Jeffers," Victor said apologetically. "I didn't mean to bring up any unpleasantness."

Chapter Ten

"No, it's okay, really. It's just the not knowing what happened to him that's always bothered me. After I grew up, I tried to find out about what happened, but the Army was no help. They said it was an accident."

"I know what you mean," Victor said, lightly, "I was in the army and they told us squat," hoping to relieve the stress of the conversation.

"Mr. Scofield, would you like to meet me for a cup of coffee or something? I'd be interested in hearing about the information contained within the file you have and your thoughts regarding the accident." She paused, "and maybe we could talk about your friends as well."

Victor was somewhat taken aback. He hadn't known what to expect when he called, and in fact had almost hung up the phone before it began ringing. Then, when he had touched a nerve with her about her father, he regretted calling. But there was an honesty and sincerity about her that touched him. It had to be hard on her, he reasoned, especially with the effect it had had on her mother. Maybe there was something he could do to help, even if it was just to listen. Besides, after his meeting with Smoky Tobias he could use the company of someone rational, and she did sound nice.

"I think I would like that, Ms. Jeffers. I live in West Knoxville, and I see from the telephone book that you live on Sutherland Avenue. Do you know a little restaurant off Kingston Pike called Lakes Grill, over in Homberg Place?" Victor asked.

"I don't know where the restaurant is, but I know where Homberg Place is," she replied.

Victor gave her directions to the grill, and they agreed to meet there in an hour.

After replacing the receiver on the phone, Victor thought he must be really losing it. This wasn't going to help anything, but at least it might help take his mind off his problems.

He took a quick shower, got dressed, and headed for the Grill. He wanted to make sure he arrived before her, so that if she showed up early, she wouldn't have to wait alone.

Driving up into the parking lot of the Grill, he noticed that there weren't many cars, probably because it was between the lunch and dinner hours, he thought. It was a small establishment, that served excellent food in a cozy atmosphere, and he visited it often.

SmokeFire!

After passing through the double glassed doors, he stood in the entrance and looked around for a woman sitting alone. Noticing no one, he selected a booth next to the front windows and slid into it.

"Mr. Victor Scofield! What brings you here on this beautiful afternoon?" the waitress asked—the Grill's only waitress, in fact. She was the wife of the owner, and knew him well since he, Buddy, and Donna had been regulars for years.

"Hi, Francis! I'm meeting someone and what better place than here? How are you doin'?" Victor asked.

"Not too bad. Listen, Victor, we're really sorry to hear about Buddy and Donna. We were crazy about 'em," she said as she sat down in the booth across from him and picked up his hand in both of hers.

"Thank you, Francis. It is very tragic indeed."

Francis hadn't bothered to bring a menu, knowing that he was intimately familiar with the courses offered. Buddy and Donna had discovered Lakes Grill many years ago, and had taken Victor there for dinner on his first night in town after moving from California.

"Great food, Vick! Don't be fooled by the size of this place or the Xeroxed menu. Mark and Francis can cook a steak that is par excellence," Buddy had said, in a poor imitation of a French accent. "And he cooks up a breaded filet of sole that is not to die for but to sacrifice one's soul for. Plus," Buddy had added, "they got a wine list that beats anything you've ever seen."

That first night Victor had ordered the sole, and in his mind the meals in the finest four-star restaurants had paled by comparison. Buddy had selected a 1991 Allen Vineyard Chardonnay, with which Victor had been unacquainted, and it had been excellent. So excellent that they had stayed after the restaurant closed sampling other wines with the owners. And they all had to call for taxicabs to take them home. It had been a wonderful evening, and Victor had been coming here ever since.

"So, found a new love of your life? Going to introduce her to the finest restaurant east of the Mississippi? Or meeting some banker puke, in which case we've got some Mad Dog 20-20 for him," Francis said with a coy smile, referring to the wine preferred by street people.

"No to the first, Francis. Yes to the second, and no to the third. How's Mark?" Victor asked, referring to Francis's husband.

Chapter Ten

"Workin' hard back in the kitchen where he belongs. Hey, he said next time you came in to tell you how much he appreciated you helping him get that new computer setup. I swear, Victor, we finish here and go home and he spends hours surfing the Net looking for wines. But I'll have to say, he's found some great new domestics from it," referring to Mark's staunch decision not to serve a French, Italian, or any other foreign wine.

"Glad to hear it. I'll have to try some of his new discoveries," Victor said, licking his lips.

"Victor, it's none of my business, but with what happened to Buddy and Donna, who's going to take care of Jennifer?" Francis asked, suddenly getting serious.

"I've thought about that, Francis, and frankly I don't know. Neither one of them had any brothers or sisters. Donna's mom, Mae, is too old to take care of her permanently. I'm going to talk to their attorney next week and see if they filed a will. Maybe they made provisions for such an event," Victor said with little confidence.

"Let us know if we can do anything to help, Vick," Francis said just as the door opened.

A tall blonde woman was standing in the waiting area next to the 'Please Be Seated' sign, and was looking around.

Francis had swung her head around at the sound of the door opening, and turning back to Victor, she said, in a whispering voice while leaning over the table, "Vick, if that's your friend, you're history. She's gorgeous!"

She wore a bright yellow spring dress with narrow shoulder straps that accentuated her shoulder-length hair, which was a rich blonde color. Her figure, tall and slim, was not full but more like that of an athlete's, as she had wide shoulders. Victor would not have called her beautiful, but he would have labeled her striking.

"Yes, I think this is my time for an exit. Don't blow it, Vick!" Francis said with a wink as she got up from the booth.

Victor stood up and approached her.

"Ms. Jeffers?" Victor asked, while extending a handshake.

"Yes. Mr. Scofield?" Her voice was soft and confident, and she took Victor's outstretched hand and gently shook it.

"It's Victor. Please come and sit down."

SmokeFire!

They walked to the booth, and she gracefully slid into it, with Victor sitting across from her. "I really appreciate your meeting me, Ms. Jeffers. I hope it wasn't an inconvenience."

"If you're Victor, then I'm Ruth, and it's no inconvenience at all. I was just sitting around reading on this gorgeous afternoon, and honestly I was getting bored. Oh my gosh, that sounds horrible!" she said as her left hand covered her mouth to stifle a nervous laugh.

Victor's eyes immediately focused on her hand and he noticed she wore no wedding or engagement ring. He quickly recovered himself.

"It doesn't sound horrible at all, but it does sound honest," he said with a smile.

"I hope I wasn't intruding. The other woman left as soon as I came in," she said, folding her hands on the table.

"Not at all. That's the owner's wife. I've been coming here for years and know them well. We were just talking about some new wines they have. This place serves the best food and their wine is par excellence," Victor said, mimicking a French accent while kissing his fingertips.

Get a grip, Vick! he thought. *You're getting giddy—the woman's going to think you're an idiot!*

"Really? I've never been here, but I do recall reading an article about them in the Sunday paper a while back. Isn't he the one who was a cook in the Army or something?" she asked.

"Yes, he was. In fact, my friends, the ones who got lost, introduced me to them. They used to love to come here."

Just as Victor was trying to think of something else to say, Francis came up to the table and said, "Victor, I must introduce myself to your friend." Turning to Ruth she said, "Hi, I'm Francis Southern," and held out her hand.

Saved by the bell, Victor thought. Francis had been laying back obviously, observing the exchange between Victor and Ruth and not wishing to interrupt. *Probably heard me babbling*, he thought, *and came to rescue me.*

Ruth introduced herself and related Victor's comments regarding the fine food and wine at the Grill.

"I don't know how well you know Victor, Ruth, but Mark and I know him well. He exaggerates everything, always the optimist, and if it wasn't

Chapter Ten

for Mark, my sights would be right on Victor's heart!" she said, laughingly.

Great, Victor thought. *Now Francis is trying to play the matchmaking game. She's the one who's going to blow it! Ruth's going to think I put her up to it!*

"Well, actually I just met him, but he seems very nice so far," Ruth said, turning to Victor and smiling in a way that absolutely embarrassed him.

Outnumbered and outgunned, he thought.

"What can I get you guys?" Francis asked, looking at Ruth. She had invited him for coffee, but it was now nearing four o'clock and coffee seemed a little out of place.

"I think I'd like to try some of this fine wine Victor has told me about. Do you have something by the glass, maybe a Chardonnay?" Ruth asked.

"I think we can find something you'll like. Vick?" Francis said, turning to him with a mischievous smile.

"I think I'll have the same," Victor said, wondering if he would enjoy it more than he'd enjoyed Tobias's blackberry wine earlier in the day. He suspected that he would.

"All righty, I'll see what we can do," Francis said, as she turned from the table and headed for the kitchen.

Ruth looked at Victor, and smiling, said, "She likes you, Victor."

"I like them, too," Victor said, and Ruth responded, "No, I mean she *really* likes you. Oh, that sounds wrong! Not in a sexual sense, but I get the feeling that she genuinely cares for you!"

"It's just pity, because I'm single and she thinks I don't eat well," he said, chuckling. "I like them both, we—I mean my friends and I—have had some good times here over the years, and they're really nice people. Mark's always back in the kitchen. He's a great guy. Those fancy cooking schools certainly could learn something from him. They started this little business many years ago and have refused to open a larger place—a lot of people, businessmen, I mean, have offered to back them, but they're afraid it'll ruin it. They just like what they're doing, and I envy that."

Ruth, reaching into her purse, said, "Victor, I have a confession to make, do you mind?" She took a small cigarette carrying case, outlined with imitation gold metal flake, and placed it on the table. "I know it's a nasty habit, but it's one of my few remaining vices," she said with embarrassment.

She was so open and direct in her look that Victor didn't think he could have refused if he'd been on the President's Council for Physical Fitness.

"Not at all. Used to do it myself, and they don't mind it here especially since both Francis and Mark smoke." Standing up and reaching behind the small bar, he retrieved an ashtray.

As he was sitting back down, Francis approached with two glasses of white wine.

"All righty, here we go," she said, sitting the glasses on the small cocktail napkins. "Mark chose this. It's one of his new selections he's afraid to try on *real* customers, so we thought we'd experiment on Victor and his new friend," she said jovially. "It's on the house. Mark said he'd be out in a few minutes, Vick, to say hello. He's trying to get prepped for dinner tonight."

Getting back to their original conversation, Ruth said, "I'm sorry about them, Victor, your friends I mean. Did you know them very long?" she asked.

"They were originally from Knoxville, and Buddy and I were in the Service together. I moved here about six years ago at their insistence. I'd lived alone in Los Angeles, and, well, to make a long story short, Buddy and Donna loved this area and after a lot of coaxing talked me into moving here."

You're telling her your life history, he thought. *Rambling on like a schoolboy.* She had a way of drawing him out, making him feel at ease, and he felt that she was genuinely interested.

"Well, it's very tragic, and I'm certainly sorry to hear about it. I know it must be very painful. It was for me when my mother died eight years ago."

It's the way she carries herself, Victor thought. She projected sincerity and confidence and seemed comfortable. She looked to be in her late thirties, maybe early forties. Given that her father had died in nineteen fifty-one, and she had said she didn't remember him, she must have been only one or two years old. Some quick math told him she must be closer to his age, which was forty-nine, although she looked a decade younger.

Chapter Ten

"Yes, it is tragic, but life goes on. So what do you do for a living, Ruth?" Victor asked, hoping to get her talking before he said something stupid.

"I'm an RN—Med-Surge, at UT Hospital," she said, referring to the University of Tennessee's teaching hospital, a level one trauma center for the east Tennessee region.

Medical-Surgical nurse, Victor thought. *Firing line medicine. That explains her sense of self-confidence.*

"After my father's death, my mother and I never moved from here. There wasn't anyplace to go. Her only family, a sister, lived in San Antonio. She, Melissa, wanted Mom and me to move there after Dad's death, especially since Mom became psychologically detached when the news was delivered, but we never did. Melissa was a great help, as I understand it, although I can't remember it, during the aftermath of Dad's death. She came to Knoxville and stayed for a couple of months. I don't remember it, of course, but she helped take care of Mom and me. After Mom died, I kept the house. I've never been married, and it seemed pointless to sell it and buy a new one, since I work a lot of shift work. Besides, I suppose the emotional attachments to the old house play a role as well, I mean since Dad and Mom lived there and all."

It just seemed to flood out of her, Victor thought, and he had to resist the temptation to tell her about Vietnam, Cathy, California, and everything else. Perhaps, like himself, she hadn't had someone to talk to in a long time.

"As I got older, she got worse. She wouldn't ever talk about the accident and rarely spoke about him. After her death, I remember her sister telling me that the fire was so severe that his body was never recovered." She said this quietly as she twisted the glass of wine by its stem and stared down into it. "So, I never knew my father or anything about him, or what happened. It left a big void in my life."

They ordered another round of Chardonnay, which Ruth complimented Francis on, and after the wine was served she asked, "You mentioned a file, Victor. I've never seen any documentation about my father's accident. What is this file and where did you get it?"

"I went up to Park Headquarters and met with the archivist," he answered. "I wanted to get information about people who had become lost in the Smokies. There are eighty-five files, and your father's was among them."

"Eighty-Five! That seems like a lot."

"Maybe, but I don't know how it compares with other national parks."

"You know," she said, "when I told you I'd tried to find out what happened, I never thought about checking with the Park Service about Dad's accident. I only contacted the Army and the Department of Veterans Affairs in Washington, but as I said, they were no help."

"I've got the file in the car if you would like to take it with you and make a copy. It doesn't say much, though, just brief service records of the personnel stationed there, including your father's, and their investigation into the accident."

"Yes, I think I would like to have it, if you don't mind," she said and then added, "You mentioned on the phone that the accident sounded strange to you. What did you mean?"

"The report stated that the investigators' conclusion was that the camp was destroyed by improper storage or handling of seismic charges."

"Seismic charges," she asked. "What's that?"

"Seismic charges are relatively low-level explosives. Geologists use them to measure soil and rock density. Anyway, I wondered why your father's camp would have had so much of it on hand that it could cause such devastation," he explained. "Like I said, your father was an experienced soldier, and it just seemed that given his experience, he wouldn't have made such a mistake. I don't know, it just doesn't add up."

Her interest now piqued, Ruth leaned forward and asked, "What do you think happened, Victor?"

"I haven't the faintest idea," he said, shaking his head.

"Do you think we could get the Army to reopen the investigation?" she asked. "Because what you say makes sense, at least to me."

"That's unlikely. It's been such a long time, and there's no real reason I can think of that would compel them to reopen it. Besides, they'd probably say there's nothing to investigate, and that any physical evidence would have long since disappeared."

"There must be other records," she said. "Like requisitions or something."

"They've probably long since been destroyed," Victor said, "and I'm not sure what value they would have anyway."

Chapter Ten

"If I wanted to look into it further, where do you think I should start?" she asked.

"I'm not sure. Maybe with a U.S. Senator or Congressman, you know, get them to plead your cause."

"Oh, I'm sure that'll be effective," she said mockingly, as she smiled and leaned back into the booth. "Those guys don't care about anything that won't get them votes."

Agreeing with her and nodding his head, Victor said, "You're probably right."

"There are some of my father's old maps in the attic. Do you think with your file and the maps that we could find the camp?"

"Sure, but the area is probably overgrown by now, and it might be a little tough getting to."

"I'd like to see it, or at least I think I would. Would you take me there sometime?"

Victor could tell from her questions that she was more than just curious about what happened to her father. It was as if she needed some kind of closure, some finality to fill the void that she had spoken of.

"I'd be happy to, but like I say, there's probably not much to see."

"Anything is more than what I've seen or heard up to now," she said, with some frustration in her voice.

"I don't wish to sound personal," he said, "but I think you should give this some serious thought. It might be traumatic, I mean, it might do more harm than good."

"I'm sure it would be painful, but, I don't know..."

Victor had visions of them hacking their way through the underbrush and coming upon the overgrown site. He could see himself trying to console her as she cried, standing among the reminders of what had robbed her of a happy childhood. It was a vision he did not relish.

"Give it some thought, and if you decide that's what you want to do, then I'll help."

Reaching across the table, she took his hand into both of hers and looked him straight in the eye. With a sad smile she said, "Thank you, Victor."

"You're welcome."

She gave his hand a slight squeeze and released it.

They talked on until it was nearly six o'clock and Mark and Francis coerced them into staying for dinner.

The conversation shifted to the lighter subjects of work, favorite recreational activities, and the other trivialities explored by two people who have just met. Francis brought their dinner, a new rainbow trout dish that Mark had been experimenting with and wanted to try on them.

At one point, Ruth asked him about Buddy and Donna, but sensing his mood, she quickly moved onto other subjects.

After finishing dinner, they agreed that neither of them had room for dessert and indulged themselves instead in an aperitif. Ruth chose a fine Port wine that Mark recommended, and Victor had an Irish coffee.

Although Victor had wanted to be home by eight so he could talk with Russell, he had been having such a nice time and it seemed that Ruth was also glad that they had decided to stay.

Mark came out as they were finishing up and spent some time chatting with them. He and Ruth hit it off immediately, with talk of cooking, wines, and Knoxville. Mark told her a joke about a hospital and she laughed, saying it might be closer to the truth than he knew.

She fought back with a joke about a cook that was funnier than his joke, Victor thought, to which Mark howled. Then, wiping his tears away, he fired back with, "Whaddya think you just ate, a fish?" which caused all three of them to explode with laughter. Their humor seemed to be more jovial because of the heaviness of their earlier conversation and their mutual losses.

The evening ended about nine-thirty. They had talked for almost six hours. They bid Francis and Mark goodnight with hugs and Victor walked Ruth to her car, a black Nissan Pathfinder. "In case it snows," Ruth explained, "I can still get to the hospital." Then she asked, "What is that you're driving, Victor? It sure is pretty."

"Thank you. It's a 1977 Datsun 280-Z," he answered. "I bought it new, and I've become kind of emotionally attached to it."

He retrieved the file from his car, and opening Ruth's door, said, "Here's the file." Before she could respond, he continued with, "I positively enjoyed this evening, Ruth, not because of what has happened, but because it was really nice. Thanks!"

Chapter Ten

Accepting the file and laying it onto the passenger seat, she turned back and said, "I enjoyed it too, Victor, or should I say Vick?" as Mark and Francis had referred to him this evening.

"You can call me Vick on one condition, that we can do this again," he said, before he really had a chance to think about it.

"Okay, Vick," she answered with a smile. "I think you have my number, and thank you for a very pleasant evening."

With that Victor closed the Pathfinder's door. While he walked back to his car he noticed a feeling. He didn't know why, but for the first time since Buddy and Donna left, he felt good.

He drove home, anxious to see if Russell had left a message on his telephone recorder.

* * *

While Victor was saying goodnight to Ruth, flight 5701 from Chicago O'Hare landed at McGhee Tyson Airport in Knoxville, on time at nine-thirty-five. It was a Sunday night flight, occupied mostly by businessmen flying in for early meetings the next day, with the exception of the well-dressed first-class passenger in seat 3A.

Franklin DeVarra, also known as Franklin 'The Nailer' in Chicago circles, removed his briefcase from underneath the seat. He stood five feet eleven inches, lean, with black bushy hair barely streaked with gray. At thirty-five years old, he had the appearance of a successful businessman with his two-thousand dollar Italian tailored suit and three-hundred dollar Italian loafers. Even the first-class flight attendant had noticed him. Upon leaving she said, "Enjoy your stay in Knoxville, Mr. Valletti," in a provocative tone, to which he responded without expression, "I shall," and exited the aircraft onto the jetway without giving her a second glance.

He felt certain that he could have had her; she had hovered over him during the flight to the point of vexation, as he couldn't review his files without drawing attention. He would have to remember that in the future—dress more slovenly, appear less successful, and give an air of apathy.

DeVarra walked to the baggage claim area and retrieved two suitcases. Besides his clothes, these cases contained the tools of his trade: disguises, binoculars, night-scope, and false identifications.

Due to airline security, the most essential tools of his profession had been shipped to his contact in Knoxville the previous day and were to be delivered to his hotel.

This included a myriad of weapons, not the least of which was a Sig Sauer nine-millimeter, complete with silencer and the new holographic sight system, the handgun of choice for professionals, from the FBI Hostage Rescue Team to persons like DeVarra.

Franklin DeVarra, never 'Frankie,'—he had once severely beaten a man for calling him that—was educated, having a degree in Criminal Justice from Chicago City University, with honors.

Before his graduation he had gotten into an altercation in a nightclub with someone who had insulted his extremely attractive date, asking her what she was doing with a wop.

Having grown up in the streets of Chicago, DeVarra was no stranger to violence.

DeVarra had stood up from the table and broken the man's jaw with one stroke. The man had quickly pulled a knife and come at DeVarra.

Franklin had allowed the man to approach him, let him get close, and then had taken the knife from him and cut his throat.

He was arrested and charged with manslaughter, which had delayed his graduation by one semester and severely threatened his career and freedom. He had had visions of becoming a law enforcement officer, perhaps even pursuing a law degree, when the unfortunate incident had occurred.

Having no money, he was assigned a Public Defender, quite a good one, in fact, and was later exonerated on the basis of self-defense. As it turned out, the PD selection had been arranged by the famous, or, rather, notorious, Cavennetti mob, an elusive organization of the new 'Wise Guys,' whose attention was drawn to this very bright and dangerous individual based upon his academic record and the ruthless manner in which he had killed his assailant.

During the time consuming and emotionally debilitating legal process, young DeVarra's ideals about the legal system were tarnished and his career goals shifted. He felt that the legal system had let him down, as, after all, he had been attacked while defending his honor. The Cavennetti organization fueled and nurtured this disillusionment, knowing that such a man could be useful to them if molded in the correct way.

Chapter Ten

They had secretly paid for all of his legal fees, and upon his acquittal aided in his reinstatement into the College of Criminal Justice so that he could graduate. They had also paid his college tuition and provided him with a generous stipend. Throughout this legal process, Franklin DeVarra and the legal counsels of the Cavennetti held many discussions. Through subtle, effective indoctrination, they sought to convince him to join their ranks. And, of course, there was the money.

Having come from a poor Italian immigrant family, DeVarra was unacquainted with the lifestyle to which the organization now introduced him: cars, clothes, women, fancy restaurants, influence, and cash.

Franklin 'The Nailer' DeVarra had over the years been slowly brainwashed, manipulated, and cultivated by the Cavennetti organization, and with their extensive psychological and legal resources, their investment, although costly, had rendered a generous return. Franklin 'The Nailer' was a killer of the worst order: intelligent, resourceful, and, most importantly, an assassin who followed orders and acted without hesitation or remorse.

At eleven-thirty Franklin DeVarra checked into the Knoxville Hilton under the name of Vincent Picatto. He unpacked his suitcases in the Presidential Suite, and while Victor slept a dreamless sleep, DeVarra opened his briefcase, removed his files, and went over them once more.

As was the norm, he was never informed as to the reasons why 'The Organization' wished to eliminate someone, and he never speculated or asked questions.

Early yesterday his superiors had contacted him and supplied an intelligence file that provided detailed information about his targets including descriptions of history, background, patterns of behavior, and most importantly, photographs.

Rereading the file he reasoned that this job should prove to be a simple one. Looking again at the photographs of the primary target, which had obviously been taken using a telephoto lens, he studied a close-up shot of a middle-aged man getting into his car. After committing the features to memory, he gathered up the file. Placing the photograph of Victor Scofield on top, he closed it.

Chapter Eleven

Monday morning, April 26, 1999
Knoxville, Tennessee

When Vodeski walked into the reception area outside his office, Victor was standing at the mahogany counter that stood in front of Brenda's desk and work area, with a cup of coffee in his hand.

"Scofield! Where the hell were you Thursday and Friday?" he shouted.

"I'd like a chance to explain that, Mr. Vodeski, if you've got a minute," Victor said, setting his coffee cup down on the coaster.

"A minute's all I got, Scofield. I've got an important meeting at eight-thirty, so if you've got something to say, get in here and say it," he said without waiting for a response. Then he walked through the double hung doors into his office.

"Brenda, get me a cup of coffee!" he barked as he set his attaché case down on his desk, in his large, richly appointed office.

SmokeFire!

Turning towards Victor, he pointed his finger and with contempt, said, "Before you start, Scofield, I want you to fire that idiot Systems Manager you got. Today! Now!"

"Mr. Vodeski, why do you want me to terminate Frank? He's a very talented and dedicated employee," Victor said, rushing to Frank's defense.

"Because his attitude sucks, that's why, and because I told you to! Understand! When you leave here, do it first thing!"

"Mr. Vodeski, with all due respect, all terminations have to be reviewed by the Human Resource Department prior to any action. It's SNB policy—a policy I agree with, as terminations should not be made lightly, and it's for our own legal protection as well. As an attorney, I would think you would be aware of that," Victor said as he stood before the massive desk.

"I'm an expert on legalities, and I've got news for you, Scofield, HR doesn't run this bank, I do. You go fire him and I'll deal with HR!" he growled as he removed some files from his attaché case and laid them on the desk, without ever looking up.

"I'll require that in writing, Mr. Vodeski, as I cannot and will not violate bank policy. But could we discuss something else for a minute?" Victor asked, and without waiting for a response, went on.

"As you may or may not know, my friends, the Tippinses, disappeared on the camping trip that I was supposed to go on. To say that I'm very distressed would be an understatement. The Park Service has called off the searches, and, well, to be honest, I'm kind of looking into it myself," Victor said, continuing to stand in front of Vodeski's desk.

At that moment Brenda walked in and handed Vodeski a cup of coffee. Turning her back, she looked at Victor and, without smiling, briefly winked and left.

"Scofield, I heard about your friends. It's regrettable and you have my condolences," he said, raising the cup to his lips. After taking a sip he laid the cup on his desk, sat down and leaned back in his massive leather chair. "But there's nothing you can do, other than be grateful you didn't go with them, or you'd be dead too."

Chapter Eleven

"I don't know that they are dead," Victor said quietly, "and since they've called off the search, I feel a responsibility to look into it further. All that I'm asking is..."

Leaning forward, Vodeski looked directly at him and interrupted forcefully, but with a certain degree of self-control, "I know what you're asking, and the answer is an emphatic 'No'. The bank's got enough computer problems without you going off on some wild goose chase."

Victor felt himself rising to anger, and he could see that Vodeski's temper was reaching a climax. His face was becoming a very deep red color.

"Please, hear me out. I need..."

With his voice at a fever pitch, Vodeski slammed his palm on the desk and raged, "No! I've told you before, and I'm telling you for the last time, no time off! Not for anyone in your department, and that includes you, dammit! That's final!"

As Victor clenched his teeth, he could feel the heat of anger blaze from his neck into his face.

Calmly closing his attaché case, Vodeski pointed his finger again at Victor and said, beginning almost under his breath, but raising his voice in a crescendo, "Now go down...and...ax...that INSUBORDINATE ASS OF A SYSTEMS MANAGER!"

It is said that every man has his breaking point. Vodeski's insensitivity and bullying had reached an all-time high, and Victor's patience had, at that moment, reached an all-time low.

He stepped forward, placed both hands on Vodeski's desk, and leaning over to within a foot of his face, solemnly said, "Okay, Vodeski, that's it! Now I'm going to impart some of my wisdom to you. I'm only going to put it down one time, and I don't give a damn whether you pick it up or not. Here it is! First, I have suffered your bullying, vulgarity, and total lack of professionalism for far too long, but no more." In a calm but forceful manner he continued with, "Second, I don't know what your problem is, but I do know this—you have an extremely serious psychological disorder, coupled with an over inflated ego and feeling of self-worth."

"Listen, Scofield, you better..." Vodeski interrupted, as he anxiously retreated into the large executive leather chair.

SmokeFire!

Leaning farther over the front of Vodeski's desk, Victor said, "I'm not finished, Vodeski, and you shut the hell up before I come over this desk and rip out what you call a heart!"

"Now, here's the important part! First, I quit, effective right now, this second! Second, if I hear of you being abusive to anyone in this bank—and I can assure you I will hear of it—you'll be dealing personally with me, mano-a-mano! Third, and here's the punchline," Victor said as he reached across the desk, grabbed Vodeski's silk tie, and pulled him forward. Bending down, he put his mouth to within an inch of Vodeski's ear and whispered, "If I even think you and I are ever going to cross paths again, under any circumstances—your fault, my fault, nobody's fault—I'm going to put my fist so far up your ass you'll chip a tooth on it. Now, do *you* understand?"

Victor jerked hard on the tie, then released it and stood up. Vodeski glared at Victor with barely-controlled rage, and was about to speak when Victor held up his hand.

"Don't do it! Don't say a word!" Victor said, then turned and walked out of the office.

Brenda, who had obviously overheard the exchange through the open doors, could only look up at Victor with her mouth gaping.

Walking in front of the counter Victor placed his index finger to his lips and whispered, "Shhh, don't say a word!" and giving her a wink said, "I'll call you," before he proceeded down the hall to the elevators.

She stood and watched him as he walked confidently down the hall, and hoped that if she ever got married, it would be to someone like that. *Boy, I like that guy!* she thought as she smiled and sat back down. Putting her face into her hands, she began to silently giggle, her shoulders shaking with the effort to keep silent.

Earlier that morning Victor had removed his personal belongings from his office and put them into his car, expecting something like this to happen. "But not quite like that," he said to himself. After all, wasn't it Buddy who had said, "Why don't you tell him to kiss off?" Well, he had, but as the adrenaline left him on the ride down the elevator, he began to regret losing his temper.

Screw it! he said to himself. *Damn bully had it coming. Besides, in whatever afterlife Buddy was in now*, Victor thought, *Buddy would have just loved that!*

Chapter Eleven

He didn't proceed directly to his car in the SNB lot, but walked out the front doors of the bank and proceeded down Gay Street, turning left on Clinch Avenue. He had one more stop to make, and it was within walking distance.

* * *

The John Duncan Federal Building was located at the corner of Locust Street and Clinch Avenue. Victor had only visited the building once to pick up some IRS forms. Walking into the lobby, he went to the building's directory that was posted on a side wall and looked up the floor for the Knoxville Field Office of Federal Bureau of Investigation.

It was listed as Suite 600. He asked the building's guard for directions to the elevator, stepped on and pressed the button for the sixth floor. He hadn't really formulated what he was going to say, other than that he would ask what the procedures were for investigating missing persons who had disappeared on federal property.

The elevator doors opened, and he stepped into the foyer of the Field Office. It was traditionally furnished, like any other office waiting area. It had a couch, two end tables, a coffee table, and two matching chairs. But his eyes were drawn to the large circular blue and gold shield that read "Department of Justice" along the top and "Federal Bureau of Investigation" along the bottom, the seal of the FBI.

He approached the receptionist's desk and was greeted by a middle-aged woman who, setting down her letter opener among a large stack of unopened mail, smiled and said, "Can I help you, sir?"

"I hope so. My name is Victor Scofield, and I'd like to speak to an agent, please." He was beginning to feel slightly uncomfortable. *Probably a normal reaction that anyone would experience in an FBI office*, he thought.

"Do you have an appointment, Mr. Scofield?" she asked, while still maintaining her pleasantness.

"No, I'm afraid I don't, but I'll only take a few minutes of their time if that's possible. I'd really appreciate it."

"May I inquire as to the reason of your visit, Mr. Scofield, and I'll see who's available?"

"Well, it's kind of a long story, but it's in regard to some missing persons who disappeared on federal property. I really don't need but a few minutes, and I'd just like to ask a few questions about missing person investigations."

"Please be seated, Mr. Scofield, and I'll see if anyone's available. Can I get you a cup of coffee or anything?" she asked as she picked up the telephone.

"No, thank you, I'm fine," he said sitting down in one of the chairs.

She picked up the phone, punched a button that Victor assumed was an interoffice speed dial and spoke softly. In a moment she replaced the receiver and said, "Someone will be with you in just a few minutes, Mr. Scofield," and returned to opening the mail.

Within several minutes a young woman walked out of the hallway and into the foyer. She was approximately thirty years old, Victor guessed, attractive, with short dark hair; she was dressed in a conservative navy blue suit and white blouse which had a small cream-colored scarf attached at the neckline. As she approached him, he wondered if female agents used shoulder holsters or carried their weapons in some special purse.

"Mr. Scofield, I'm Special Agent Virginia Clevenger," she said as she extended her hand.

"Hi, I'm Victor Scofield. Thanks for taking the time to see me," he said as he stood and shook her hand.

"No problem, sir. Would you like to come back to my office where we can talk?" she asked with a smile.

"Yes, I would appreciate that."

He walked down the hallway beside her. As he walked, he noticed there were private offices, some with their doors opened, and some closed. They passed a large conference room, and she turned into the office next to it and went behind her desk but didn't sit down.

"Please, make yourself comfortable," Clevenger said, indicating one of the vinyl office chairs.

"Can I get you anything? A cup of coffee or a soda?" she asked.

"No, thank you, I believe I've reached my caffeine level for the day," he said and sat down in the chair. She turned and sat down behind her desk, which was of a standard variety that one would see in any office. In fact, the entire facility, what little he had seen of it, could pass

Chapter Eleven

for just about any type of business. He didn't know what he had expected, but somehow he felt that the offices of the federal police force would not look like that of a traditional business.

"Now, Mr. Scofield, how can I help you?" she asked. Opening her top desk drawer, she removed a yellow legal pad, placed it in front of her, and then moved her chair up to the desk and folded her hands upon it.

"Well, I'll try to be brief. I have two close friends who disappeared while on a camping trip in the Great Smoky Mountains National Park. They were due back on April seventeenth, and haven't been heard from."

He went on to describe the events to date, his efforts, excluding the helicopter trip. He related his conversations with Steve Russell and Marsha Benton and his review of the files. He further explained that since their disappearance had occurred on federal property, he wondered if there was anything the FBI could do.

"Mr. Scofield, I'm terribly sorry about your friends, but the FBI does not investigate missing persons, as that is not classified as an offense—a crime, if you will."

"I can appreciate that, Agent Clevenger, but frankly I'm convinced that this incident is not a missing person, but rather an abduction or perhaps murder," Victor said. He went on to describe his friends' backcountry experience and his review of the files citing the fact that no two experienced hikers had ever vanished without a trace in the Great Smoky Mountains National Park.

"What evidence do you have, Mr. Scofield, that leads you to believe that a crime has been committed?" she asked, while making notes on the pad.

"I don't have any evidence per se, but given their backcountry experience, especially Mr. Tippins', I can come to no other conclusion. The park ranger I spoke with, Steve Russell, also considered that fact a possibility, and there have been some past incidences of murder within the Park," Victor explained.

She had continued making some notes as Victor spoke, but he could not see exactly what it was she was writing down. He leaned forward slightly and glanced down at the paper and saw that she had written today's date, his name, and that of Steve Russell's. There were some

SmokeFire!

other notes; however, he didn't want to seem obvious by staring down at the pad.

"Well, I'm not much of an outdoors person, so I don't know a lot about the Park. Tell you what, though, why don't you give me some additional information on your friends and I'll look into it. That's really about all I can do without any evidence," she said as she turned the pad to a new page.

Victor gave her all the information about Buddy and Donna that he thought was pertinent, including their birthdays, address, and occupations. He also added that he had considered the fact that their disappearance might have been intentional, except for the fact of Jennifer and went on to elaborate how they would not have, under any conditions, left her behind.

Clevenger made copious notes while Victor spoke and then set down her pen.

"All right, Mr. Scofield, I'll make a few calls and get some more information. Is there a number where I can reach you?" she asked politely.

Victor gave her his home and cell numbers. He almost gave her his office number but caught himself. She asked for his home address, jotted that down as well, then stood up and walked around the desk.

"I'll let you know, Mr. Scofield. Give me a couple of days, though. Here, I'll walk you out."

Walking down the hall, she asked, "What do you do for a living, Mr. Scofield?"

"Well, I used to work for Second National Bank up until about an hour ago. I was Vice President in charge of Data Processing. But, well, honestly, I had a serious disagreement with my boss and I resigned."

"Well, sometimes we all have to make important choices, Mr. Scofield, and I wish you luck," she said, as they reached the foyer. Victor offered her his hand, thanked her for her time, and left.

Riding down on the elevator, he thought that the first thing that Clevenger would do would be to research the disappearance of Buddy and Donna rather than performing a background check on them. Undoubtedly she would be in touch with Pike, which Victor felt should be interesting. *That'll throw the fat in the fire. Pike will go ballistic*, he

Chapter Eleven

thought, as he stepped onto the street. *Hopefully she'll talk to Russell as well.*

Walking back toward the bank, he looked up at the massive structure and felt a sense of relief that he didn't have to go back, while at the same time wondering what he would do for the rest of the day, as it was now only ten o'clock. In fact, he thought, *What am I going to do with the rest of my life?* He felt that same old loneliness to which he had become so accustomed, especially since Buddy and Donna were gone, but even when they had been here, it still crept into his life far too frequently.

Getting into his car he noticed that Vodeski's car was missing from his personal parking space. *Probably going down to the courthouse to swear out a warrant for my arrest on assault charges,* Victor thought. But there had been no witnesses, and it would be his word against Victor's, as Brenda had not actually seen him jerk Vodeski's tie.

Pulling out of the SNB parking lot, he decided he would call Russell at the Ranger Station when he got home to see if he had turned up any new information. He also thought about Ruth. He had really enjoyed talking with her last night at the Grill, and she seemed to enjoy it as well. When she had spoken of her father, Victor had been charmed by her openness and vulnerability.

Thinking back, he realized that it must be difficult for her, never knowing exactly what happened to her father.

He wondered if he were being too obvious in his interest of her if he called her tonight. *Would that be too forward?* he asked himself. She seemed like an honest and straightforward woman, and perhaps she would respect a call from him. He would think about it, as she had said that her next shift wasn't until Wednesday, and after all, she *had* said for him to call her. Maybe he would call in the morning and see if she would have dinner, perhaps on the pretense of picking up his file on Camp Thirteen.

When he arrived home, he pulled into the garage. Opening the door into the kitchen from the attached garage, he set the car keys on the kitchen countertop and thought about getting a beer, but looking at his watch saw that it was only ten-thirty, so he pulled out a soft drink instead.

SmokeFire!

He took a long pull from the can, went into his office, and turned on his computer. He'd have to update his resumé, he thought. However, with his investments, there was no real hurry to find something new as he could continue his relatively frugal existence for years. But he would miss the hundred-thousand dollar per year salary. He also remembered that there was over a hundred thousand in his SNB Money Market account. Legally, he didn't think Vodeski could do anything to block that, but knowing Vodeski, there was no end to what the man might do. He would have to transfer that out, he thought, but tomorrow. He had his Money Market checkbook, and it would be a simple matter of writing a check and having SNB issue a certified check, which he could use to open an account at another institution.

While sitting at his desk, he pulled out the paper that Russell had given him and dialed the Abrams Creek Ranger Station. There was no answer after about fifteen rings, and he replaced the phone in the cradle. He wasn't really surprised, as he was sure that park rangers were rarely relegated to sitting behind the desk all day, and he decided that he would call back after lunch.

Looking over at the table that sat in front of his desk he saw the stack of photographs from the helicopter trip, his map, and underneath the table the file box of incident reports. *What to do next?* he wondered as he tapped his pencil absent-mindedly on the desk.

He looked down at his old oak desk and thought again of Cathy. Her hands had touched, sanded, and skillfully refinished its surface. He remembered coming home, when they had lived in L.A., just after she had completed staining it. The small house in which they lived had smelled like a paint shop when Victor had walked through the front door. She had come out of the little office dressed in one of his T-shirts and an old pair of shorts, both of which had stain all over the front.

"I've been refinishing your desk, Master," she had said coyly, "Come see it. I think it turned out pretty good!" And taking his right hand in her stain-covered left hand, she had led him into the little office.

Indeed, it had turned out well, and Victor had been impressed. There was sawdust coating every surface in the room, and the newspapers she had placed underneath the desk were splattered with stain.

Chapter Eleven

"It's still wet, or at least I think it is. So what do you think?" she asked, proudly looking up at him. He could still remember the big blotch of stain on her left cheek.

"Well, it does seem that you managed to get a little stain on the desk besides just on your shirt, your shorts, the newspapers, and your face," he chuckled. She had swatted at him with the stain covered rag, then exclaimed, "My face? I've got stain on my face?"

He had grabbed her around the waist as she was turning to run into the bathroom. Turning her to him and pulling her close, he had said, "I don't know what looks more beautiful, you or the desk. You did an amazing job, honey," and with that put his arms around her neck and affectionately kissed her, stain and all. At that moment, she had looked so beautiful.

He rubbed his hand gently across the desk surface, and a silent tear ran down his cheek. *I miss you hon!* He wondered how his life would be different now if she were still here with him.

Wiping his eye with his hand, he got up and went into the kitchen with the intention of fixing a sandwich, but upon opening the refrigerator door decided he wasn't hungry. He was very tired, probably from the stress, he thought, and went to the bedroom to take a nap. He lay down and drifted off to sleep immediately.

He was awakened at about three o'clock by an insistent knocking at his front door. He swung his feet off the bed and ran his hand through his hair, then wiped the sleep from his eyes. Standing up, he walked into the living room and said loudly, "Just a minute, be right there!"

He walked across the living room to the front door and opened it only to realize the chain lock was still attached. He rarely used the front door, preferring to come in by the garage using his remote opener, and then through the kitchen.

As the door banged against the chain lock, he noticed a rather large man, dressed in a gray suit, whom he did not recognize. He also noticed that there were two marked police cars parked on the street in front of his house. Four uniformed police officers stood behind the big man. Next to the man in the gray suit stood Virginia Clevenger.

He looked from the man to Clevenger, just in time to see her give a slight nod of her head to him, and then he looked back.

SmokeFire!

"Victor Scofield? FBI. We have a warrant for your arrest—for homicide," the man said, offering no identification, but he raised a large pistol and pointed it through the crack in the door directly at Victor's chest.

Victor felt the adrenaline rush into his system, a rush he had not felt since his time in Vietnam, and like he did in Vietnam he reacted. He didn't think.

"You got no time to think," Buddy had said more than once. "You think—you die!"

In one quick move, Victor slammed shut the heavy oak door and threw the dead bolt lock. He turned and ran into the kitchen, grabbing his car keys from off of the countertop. He ignored shouts of "Open the door!" and the heavy thudding behind him and ran into the garage.

Oh no, he thought. *They'll have the driveway blocked!* He jumped into the 'Z' and started the engine.

Victor's garage, on the inside, was unfinished two-by-fours. Since the house was an English Tudor it had been constructed of stucco over wood on the exterior, so the walls in the garage were relatively thin. He revved the engine, put the car in first gear, and popped the clutch.

The 'Z' shot forward, the tires screeching on the concrete floor. Then they picked up traction. The car hit the backside of the garage with an astounding collision, but never really slowed down.

He crashed through the exterior with shards of wood flying everywhere as he fishtailed across his backyard. A startled uniformed police officer was at his back door, and all he could do was stare in amazement, his handgun hanging at his side.

Victor shifted into second gear and drove through some bushes at the edge of his backyard and into his neighbor's yard. He emerged onto the back street with leaves and shards of wood attached to the 'Z'. The car jumped over the curb, and Victor spun the wheel, shifted into third gear, and floored it.

He sped down the back street, took a right, then a left, and after about a half mile emerged onto Kingston Pike, the main West Knoxville thoroughfare. He turned right onto the divided highway with his heart pounding and slowed down, as it was a crowded highway.

Dammit! he thought. *Murder? Who?* He was in too deep now. He had crossed the line. *Okay*, he thought, *calm down. Think it through!*

Chapter Eleven

He had to run. He had no choice now. He drove down Kingston Pike and saw West Town on the left, Knoxville's largest shopping mall. Turning into the main entrance, he drove to the center of the huge parking lot and swung the 'Z' into an open slot. He turned the ignition off and slumped forward. Resting his forehead on the steering wheel, his breath came in gasps. After about a minute he got out of the car, leaving it unlocked, with the keys in the ignition. *Maybe somebody will steal it before they find it,* he thought.

Without thinking he walked across the parking lot and entered the busy mall. He immediately found a restroom, went into the stall and retched.

When he emerged, he went to the sinks and looked into the mirror. The face that stared back at him was a wreck. He washed his face and combed his hair, and leaning forward on the counter thought, *what next?*

Evasion was the only word that came to him, words from Vietnam a time long ago in the event he was facing capture—*escape and evade.* Okay, he thought. *I'm going to need some resources.* He exited the restroom and went to the mall's directory, which was located in the center of a large intersection. Scanning down, he found the location of the SNB branch located within the mall. He got his bearings and proceeded towards the bank's branch.

They haven't had time to lock the account, he thought—he hoped. *I was just at the FBI this morning.* He walked into the little branch office and approached the teller's booth.

"I'd like to withdraw some money from my Money Market account, please," he stated to the young teller, as he withdrew his wallet. At least he'd been so tired that he had not removed it from his hip pocket when he lay down. He always carried a single Money Market check folded behind his driver's license for emergency purposes.

He unfolded the check, wrote out the amount, and passed it to the teller. She looked down and raised her eyebrows.

"Do you have any identification, Mr. Scofield?" she asked.

"Certainly," he said, handing her his driver's license.

"Just a minute sir, I'll be right back," she said as she turned and walked down the teller counter toward an older woman who sat at a desk in the corner.

He tried to appear nonchalant, tried to convince himself that the FBI wouldn't have frozen the account. *But who knows, maybe that's one of the first things they do.*

The young teller handed the older woman, the cashier, the check, which she scrutinized before looking up towards Victor. Then she came over to the counter with the girl.

"Mr. Scofield, could you please come to my desk?" the older woman asked while holding his check and driver's license.

"Certainly, but I'm in a bit of a rush if you don't mind," Victor replied.

"I understand, sir, just a few formalities. If you'll please follow me," she said as she turned and walked toward her desk.

"Please sit down, Mr. Scofield," indicating a chair in front of her desk, as she primly sat in her chair and put on her reading glasses. While holding his check, she continued. "Mr. Scofield, I'm sure you understand that on withdrawals of this magnitude, we have certain procedures, and..."

"Ms. Tennison," Victor interrupted, noticing the nameplate on the desk, "I fully understand the procedures. I'm a Vice President of SNB, Data Processing, and I am totally familiar with all banking procedures including that of possible customer extortion. I can assure you that I am not being extorted in any way," he said firmly. "It's just that I have an investment opportunity that I simply cannot pass up, but I must move quickly to take advantage of it."

"Now, you have my identification, my check, and my signature's on file, so if you'll please cash the check, I'd appreciate it, or you can hand me the telephone so I can call Brad Heron, the President of SNB. I was with him only an hour ago, and, well, confidentially, this is an opportunity that we're both seizing," he said in his most authoritative voice.

"That won't be necessary, Mr. Scofield." She pecked the information from his check into her computer terminal. Looking at the screen, then back at the check, she turned to Victor and asked, "In what denominations would you like that, Mr. Scofield?"

"I'd like two thousand in twenties, and the rest in hundreds, if you don't mind," he replied, leaning back into the chair.

Chapter Eleven

"It'll be just a moment, Mr. Scofield," and with that she left and went into the vault area.

If his instincts were right, the FBI and police would be entering the bank just about now if they'd put a lock on his account. *If they are*, he thought, *there's nothing to be done.*

A long five minutes later the cashier came back with a large envelope and handed it to Victor saying, "I suggest you count it, Mr. Scofield, and would you like someone to walk you to your car?"

"Neither will be necessary, Ms. Tennison," Victor answered as he stood up. "I'm acutely aware of the accuracy of cashiers, and I have some associates waiting outside in the limousine for me, so there are no security concerns. I appreciate your expedient and courteous service, and I'll be sure to mention your name to Brad," he said as he stood and offered her his hand.

Placing the large envelope underneath his shirt and tucking it into his pants, he walked from the bank and out into the mall area. He turned left and went towards the main entrance.

He was now a fugitive, he thought, but a fugitive with a hundred thousand dollars in cash, and that could take him very far.

Chapter Twelve

Monday afternoon, April 26, 1999
Knoxville, Tennessee

Victor walked toward the main entrance of the mall while he tried to decide his next move. He knew from his training in the military the tactic in an enemy search was for them to set up a perimeter, then to slowly close it until you were trapped. The tactical advantage, he had been taught, was to be outside the perimeter before they started to close it, and that meant that you had to move fast and remain undetected.

As he approached the entrance, his mind turned to exactly that: how to move fast and not be detected. He could perhaps steal a car, but since he knew nothing about "hot-wiring" a vehicle, he would have to find one with the keys in it. Second, a stolen car would in all likelihood be quickly reported to the police, and that would draw attention to him that could lead to his capture.

He could take a taxi, he thought. However the FBI could—and probably would—check all records of taxi cab companies for their pickup and drop off points, again opening himself to exposure. Rental cars were also out for the same reasons.

He supposed he could call his friends Francis and Mark, but the FBI would probably eventually get around to talking with them, as he had know them for a long time, and he preferred to keep them out of it, at least for now.

As he stood inside the multiple glass doors that marked the main entrance to the mall and contemplated his next move, an option immediately presented itself.

Pulling up next to the curb out in front of the mall was a KAT bus, short for Knoxville Area Transit. Without delay he walked through the double glass doors and stepped onto the bus along with several other shoppers. He had never ridden a bus in Knoxville—he never had had any reason to, and he didn't know how much the fare would be. In order to draw less suspicion to himself, as the FBI might contact the transit authority, he handed the driver a one-dollar bill hoping that would cover it. The driver took the bill, and reaching up to the center of the dashboard, ejected a single quarter from the change dispenser and handed it to him.

Victor then turned and walked to the back of the bus and chose a seat near the rear door. As the driver closed the door and slowly drove off, Victor wondered where the bus was going, and what its route was.

Sitting across the aisle from him was an elderly lady, and he leaned across and asked, "Pardon me, could you tell me where this route stops—where it ends, I mean?" She turned and said, "Why yes, it ends in East Knoxville over on Magnolia, then turns around and makes the trip back. It takes about thirty minutes, with the other stops and all."

He thanked her and leaned back into his seat thinking, *Magnolia, that's on the other side of town in east Knoxville. That should do it.*

The bus pulled out onto Kingston Pike, and he looked out the window, wondering what the FBI was doing now, probably putting out an all points bulletin and contacting the bank. If they talked to Vodeski, Victor thought, that ought to be a real treat for him. It would presumably please Vodeski to no end that the FBI had a warrant out for

Chapter Twelve

his arrest, while at the same time scaring the hell out of him since Victor had threatened him. The thought pleased him.

* * *

To say that the Special Agent In Charge (SAIC) of the Knoxville FBI office, Bill Richter, was livid was an understatement.

"Damn it, Clevenger!" he yelled as he stood at the head of the large conference room table in the office. All the other agents in the field office were sitting in chairs that surrounded the table. "You told me that Scofield wouldn't be any trouble!" he shouted. "Oh, he won't resist, Bill, he's a banker," he said, in a falsetto voice, mimicking her while holding up his hands. "Damn it! He slammed the door in our faces! And that idiot cop at the back door just stood there! Okay, here's what we're gonna do. Clevenger, you get your butt over to Second National before they close. Don't call for an appointment. Just show up and talk to one of the senior VP's. Find out everything about Scofield you can."

Calming down, he then pointed to two of the junior agents and said, "Cox, you and Winslow contact the cab companies, find all fares taken by one man—I don't care in what part of the city. Start with fares from three o'clock on, and then check the rental car companies. Hayes, get over to the phone company and get Scofield's phone records from the past month, then check out all the numbers. I want to know who he's called, especially within the last week. Also, get a listing from the phone company of all pay phones in the city, and then cross index it with his phone bill. Let's see what turns up."

Richter went on assigning other tasks to the remaining agents, and dismissed the group with instructions to meet back in the conference room by six-thirty.

"Clevenger, I want you to stay," he said. As the others left, he slumped down in the chair next to her. "Virginia, I apologize about blowing up at you like that. It wasn't justified. I'm sorry," he said, "it was my responsibility."

"It's okay, Bill, don't worry about it," she said, folding up her notepad. "I better get over to the bank before they close and see what I can dig up." Standing up she walked to the door and paused. "You know, Bill, there's something that bothers me. Why would Scofield

SmokeFire!

come here this morning and then drive up to Abrams Creek and commit homicide? He was distressed, but he just doesn't fit the profile. Why would he drive back home? He's smarter than that, or at least he gave me the impression he was."

"Virginia, when you've been in the business as long as I have, you'll see people do some pretty crazy things. We go on standard investigative protocol—evidence is evidence. Coupled with what the Chief Ranger told us at the scene, that Scofield blames the Park Service for his friends' disappearance, it's a pretty strong case, and the U.S. Attorney thinks so too. He did it, Virginia. Of that I have no doubt. The man's over the edge," he said, rubbing his eyes with both hands. "Also, while you're at the bank, lock his accounts and see what credit cards are issued to him. Don't lock those. We'll put 'em into the system so if he uses 'em we'll know about it."

Virginia left Richter sitting in the chair, twirling his Cross pen while he stared down at his notes.

* * *

The KAT bus stopped at the corner of Magnolia and Jessamine Avenue, and Victor got off with several other people. There was a small diner across the street, and he crossed over, went in, and ordered a cup of coffee. He had been toying with an idea of who to contact, as he needed some help. Getting his wallet out of his hip pocket, he opened it and pulled out the little slip of paper with Ruth's number. He didn't want to get her involved, but he also recognized that there wasn't anyone else he could call. Besides, he said to himself, nobody knows that we know each other, which should make it difficult, if not impossible, for the FBI to trace him through her.

Walking to the pay phone in the corner, he dialed her number, and after the third ring, she picked up.

"Ruth, it's Victor," he said after she had answered.

"Hi, Vick, how are you doing?" she asked cheerfully.

"Not too good. Listen, I know it's short notice, but there have been some new developments. Could you meet me?" he asked, speaking softly, although there were only two other people in the diner.

"Sure, Vick, when?" she asked, more seriously.

Chapter Twelve

"As soon as possible—now, if you can."

"Okay, it'll take me a few minutes to get ready. What new developments, Vick?" she asked, "What's happened?"

"A lot, but I'd rather not go into it over the phone. There's a Home Depot over off Magnolia, you know where it is?" he asked. She said she did, and he told her to meet him in the electrical department. That he'd be there in about ten minutes.

"Victor, are you okay?" Ruth asked in a concerned voice.

"Yeah, I'm okay. I'll see you there," and he hung up before she could say anything else. He laid two dollars on the counter for his coffee and walked out of the diner. He didn't want to meet her there, as police officers were notorious for stopping into diners and such places, and he didn't want to take the chance that he might be recognized. He doubted that the FBI had gotten any photographs out on him yet, but he didn't know the extent of their resources.

"Never underestimate your enemy's intelligence," they had said back in Vietnam. "Always overestimate it. That way you won't get surprised."

Walking out of the diner toward the Home Depot, he wished Buddy were here now, as he could certainly use some of that wisdom.

Victor was standing in the electrical department pretending to look at some light switches when he saw Ruth walk down the aisle. Placing the light switch back in the bin, he turned and gently took her by the arm and proceeded towards the front of the store.

"Victor, what's going on? Why did you want to meet here?"

"It's a long story, and I'll tell you when we get to somewhere more private," he replied while still walking.

They walked out and got into Ruth's car. Turning the ignition key, Ruth asked, "Where to, Victor? You've got to tell me what's going on," with a degree of anxiety in her voice.

He had already decided that he didn't want to tell Ruth that the FBI was looking for him while she was driving, as she would probably be shocked. Rather, he wanted to go someplace private where there was little risk of being noticed and take her through the sequence of events of the day, culminating with his evasion of arrest. He was worried that she would be angry, maybe even scared since she really didn't know him, and that she would simply ask him to get out of the car, then go

157

call the police. And he wouldn't blame her. It was a chance he was willing to take, however, as he had few other alternatives.

"There's a Sonic drive-in restaurant about three blocks from here. Drive over there and we'll get a soft drink and I'll tell you all about it. I appreciate you coming, Ruth. I didn't have anyone else to call and I need some help."

She seemed to accept his response, and drove down Magnolia to the Sonic and turned into an empty stall. Turning off the ignition, she said, "Okay, we're here. Now, what's going on, Victor, and why all this cloak-and-dagger behavior?"

"Order us a couple of Cokes and then I'll tell you, okay?"

She pressed the intercom button and ordered two Cokes, then turned back around, a deep look of concern on her face, and he knew it would only get worse as he related the events.

He started with the meeting this morning with Vodeski, told her of his resignation, and how he had handled it, word for word. If he was going to ask her for help, he decided, then he would have to be totally honest and let her make the decision to help him or not.

He briefly told her why he had treated Vodeski in the manner he had, and she responded with, "Sounds like he had it coming, but you probably shouldn't have grabbed his tie."

He admitted that she was right and made no excuses. He then related his trip to the FBI office and his discussion with Virginia Clevenger.

"Why did you go to the FBI?" she asked, "I thought they only investigated federal crimes."

The Cokes arrived, and Victor pulled out five dollars and gave it to Ruth who, in turn, handed it to the waitress. As the waitress was counting out change, Victor leaned across and told her to keep it.

Sliding the straw into the cup, he said, "They do, but Buddy and Donna disappeared on federal property. I thought that might justify their involvement."

He went on to say that Clevenger said she would look into it and get back to him, and that he then went home and took a nap.

She listened attentively and without interrupting, and he paused and set his Coke down on the dashboard.

"You're not going to like the next part, but please hear me out."

Chapter Twelve

He then related the entire events from when the FBI attempted to arrest him until he called her. As he told the story, her look went from amazement, to deep concern, and then, almost to terror.

"I didn't kill anyone, Ruth, you have to believe that! I mean, I went to the FBI office this morning and..."

She paused for only a moment while looking down, then raised her head and looked him squarely in the eye.

"Victor, I know you didn't kill anyone. Admittedly, I don't know much about you, but I'm a pretty good judge of character. What the hell is going on? Who was killed?" she asked.

"I don't know, but since the FBI's involved, I can only assume it's a federal crime and that suggests that it was a Park Service employee. I'm afraid it was Steve Russell. He said he would call me last night after going back up Panther Creek but he didn't. I've tried to call him since last night and earlier today, but never got through to him."

"If you didn't kill him, who did? How? When?"

"I don't even know if it was him. In fact, I don't know anything, but I've got to find out."

She then asked him why he had evaded arrest, and he explained that he had just reacted without thinking. They discussed getting an attorney and Victor turning himself in, but he argued, "I think it's deeper than that. If I'm out of commission, then we may never find out what this is all about. Besides, in all likelihood they would not allow bail with it being a capital offense, not to mention the fact that I ran."

"What's deeper than that, Victor? What are you talking about?"

"I don't know, I haven't had a lot of time to formulate any ideas really, but I do know this. Either it's a case of the FBI drawing a false conclusion—which they've obviously done—or it's something else. I don't know much about the FBI, but I doubt that they could obtain a warrant without some kind of evidence."

"What do you mean something else? You said you were there this morning, and they didn't say anything? Maybe they got your fingerprints from his house or something," she said.

"I doubt they could get a warrant just from my fingerprints being there. It has to be something else. Let's break it down. First, you're right, I was at the FBI this morning and they seemed totally unaware of why I was there, and Clevenger even offered to look into it. Therefore, whatever happened, happened after that. Second," he said, holding two fingers up, "something occurred—some event came to light. That something must have been the homicide on federal property, i.e. the Park. Third, they found something, something so compelling, so absolute, that they were able to get a warrant issued on quick notice, by a Federal Magistrate, I presume. Now, we are left with two questions. First, who was killed? Second, why do they think I did it? Those are the two questions which I must get answers to."

"Oh, Victor, this is horrible. They're the FBI! You can't hide from them. They'll find you. It's only a matter of time, and when they do, whatever they've got is going to seem much worse because you're running from them. You've got to trust them. You've got to turn yourself in! I'll be with you, I promise, every step of the way," she said pleadingly.

"No, I'm in too deep now, and I've got to see this through. Let me ask you something. What if, and I mean *what if*, really, it is something deeper? What if we're being manipulated? It would explain certain things," he said pessimistically.

"Somebody manipulating the FBI? You've got to be kidding. Nobody could do that!"

"I agree, I don't mean somebody manipulating the FBI, but what if they could make the FBI think I did it?"

"That doesn't make any sense, Vick. What could someone possibly do?"

"I don't know!" he said, shaking his head, "but I've got to find out the answers to my two basic questions: who was killed, and why do they think I did it? There's only one way to find that out."

Picking up Ruth's cell phone, which was lying on the console, he dialed information.

"Knoxville," she heard him say, then, "Federal Bureau of Investigation." After a few moments he pressed the 'end' key on the phone and set it down.

"You're going to call them?" she asked incredulously. "And say what?"

He could see she was becoming emotional, and he couldn't blame her.

Chapter Twelve

"Yes, I'm going to call Virginia Clevenger. Don't worry, there's no way they can trace a cell call, at least I don't think so. They might have the technology, but I doubt it. Anyway, let's not stay stationary. Pull out and head back into the city, there's a lot of cell towers there, and in case they can trace it, that ought to make it more difficult."

Exasperated, she backed out of the stall and headed down Magnolia back into the downtown area. As they pulled onto the interstate on-ramp, Victor dialed the number of the FBI. It was now six o'clock, and he didn't know what hours they kept, but he doubted that after the events of the day they would have left.

"Federal Bureau of Investigation, can I help you?" the operator said, and Victor wondered if it was the same woman who was in the reception area earlier.

"Yes, I'd like to speak to Special Agent Virginia Clevenger, please," he said.

"May I say who's calling?" the operator asked.

"Yes, tell her it's Victor Scofield, and that I've only got a minute."

"Just a moment, please," she said, and he was put on hold.

* * *

Clevenger, Richter, and the rest of the investigative team were in the conference room giving reports of their efforts and exchanging ideas of how to apprehend Scofield when there was a knock on the door. Without waiting to be asked, the receptionist opened the door halfway and said, addressing Richter, "Sir, Victor Scofield's on the line. He wants to talk to Virginia," nodding towards Clevenger.

"Get Cooper to record and trace—now! Tell him to buzz this phone when he's set up," Richter said, referring to their technical agent who performed such tasks. Dropping his pen onto the table, he said, "Tell Scofield she's in the restroom—no wait, he won't buy that! Tell him it will be just a moment, that you're trying to locate her. Remember, Terese, act normal, Cooper first, then Scofield, and do it now!"

The receptionist gently closed the door, and Richter said, "Damn it, will someone please tell me that asshole's not calling from a cell phone!"

SmokeFire!

"He's too smart not to, Bill," Clevenger said, "I wonder what he wants."

Within thirty seconds Cooper, the FBI's resident technical agent, buzzed the conference room and told Richter that Scofield was in fact calling from a cell phone, but he had the recorder set up.

"Okay, Cooper, we're ready. Go tell Terese to put him through. Virginia, since he wants to talk to you, pick up on this phone," he said, pointing to the phone sitting near her, "I'll pick up on this one."

"Mr. Scofield, this is Special Agent Clevenger," she said after picking up the receiver.

"Agent Clevenger, what is going on here? Who was killed and why am I being accused of murder?" Victor asked.

"Mr. Scofield, where are you?" Clevenger asked, while Richter listened on the other line.

"Let's skip that for now. Please answer my questions," Scofield replied firmly.

Clevenger looked over at Richter who nodded his head, and said, "Park Ranger Steven Russell was found dead in his home early this morning by Chief Ranger Pike. His throat had been cut. The murder weapon, a butcher knife that was found at the scene, had your fingerprints on it."

Victor exhaled a deep breath. He'd been afraid it had been Russell.

"My fingerprints, how? I was at Russell's Saturday morning, but the only thing I touched was a coffee cup. Then a thought struck him. "What kind of knife? Describe it."

Again Richter nodded, and Clevenger said, "It's a Gerber Balance Plus eight-inch cooking knife. Stainless steel with a triple studded black handle."

"I don't know about Russell, but I have an entire set of Gerber knives," he said, which they probably already knew, as he was sure they had searched his house.

"We know, and of your set one large knife is missing, obviously the one which was used during the crime. Mr. Scofield, why don't you turn yourself in and make it easier on everyone?" Clevenger asked.

"Agent Clevenger, I told you this morning that I had been at Russell's Saturday and why. Why would I have even come to you if I were about to commit a murder? Further, if I was going to kill him—

Chapter Twelve

which I did not—I wouldn't use a knife from my kitchen, for God's sake."

"Just tell us where you are and we'll come to get you. I'll be there and nothing will happen. Then we can come back and discuss this before anyone gets hurt," Clevenger said.

"Listen to me! I didn't kill Russell, but somebody did, and that somebody is still out there. If you're so concerned about anyone getting hurt, maybe you should spend your time finding the real killer instead of chasing me. Now, I don't know what's going on here, but I'm going to find out. Somehow I believe this is all interrelated, and..."

"Mr. Scofield, this is Bill Richter, Special Agent In Charge of the Knoxville office," Richter interrupted, holding his hand up to Clevenger. "Virginia's right. If you're innocent, then let us come get you and we'll get this straightened out. If you are innocent, and maybe you are, then we'll get this cleared up. So, where are you?"

"Agent Richter, all I've tried to do is find out what happened to my friends. So far I haven't talked to anyone—other than Russell—who has been of help, including your office, and there's absolutely no reason for me to believe you won't just lock me up and let it go before a jury. Steve Russell was helping me—the only person who ever offered to do so, I might add. So no, I'm not telling you where I am, but I will tell you this. I liked Russell, and maybe he got close to something. I'm not coming in until I get some answers. Then we'll talk. Now, I'm not going to leave town because I didn't do it. When I find out what's going on, and I will, I promise you, then I'll gladly meet you. I'll make a deal with you. I talked to the park archivist, Marsha Benton, and she provided me with the incident files, which I'm sure you have. If the FBI is as good as you're supposed to be, then you'll get up there and protect her. She could be the next victim. If I don't find out anything by Friday morning, then I'll meet you and turn myself in. Do we have a deal?" Victor asked resolutely.

"The FBI doesn't make deals, Mr. Scofield, and..."

Victor interrupted Richter. "Well, it's the only one you're going to get, so you better take it. Now, get somebody up there to protect Benton, and I don't mean that ass, Pike. I mean your people. I'll get back with you when I have more," Victor said, and then ended the call.

Clevenger placed the phone back on the desktop unit and sat down. Richter pressed the intercom button and said, "Cooper, bring the tape of that conversation in here," and without waiting for an answer went on to say, "and contact the cell phone companies. See if they can tell us who's cell phone that call came from." Sitting down at the head of the table, he ran his hand over his short cut hair and said, "Damn Scofield, he's not going to make this easy."

Clevenger spoke up. "Bill, there's something about this that doesn't feel right. Scofield's right. Why would he have come in here this morning if he was going to immediately go up and murder Russell? The Coroner said Russell had been dead only a couple of hours, and that was just a guess at that point. Scofield would've had to drive directly up there and kill Russell. Then why would he go back to his house?"

"I don't know, maybe the son of a bitch is crazy. Hayes, you coordinate with the locals," referring to the area police and sheriff's departments, "and the Park Service as well."

Cooper then came into the conference room with the tape and a cassette recorder and laid both on the table.

"Cooper," Richter said, "find out about that cell call. Scofield's was in his car, which KPD discovered," referring to the Knoxville Police Department. "If he didn't have two, I want to know who the other one belongs to."

"It's going to take a while, boss," Cooper said. "The cell companies aren't as quick to respond as the local land line service. I'll have to go through their central billing offices, and they might be closed. It'll take some time."

"Just get it as quickly as possible, okay? Now, let's replay that tape, Virginia, and see if we can get anything from it."

As the FBI was replaying the tape, Victor and Ruth were on the interstate in downtown Knoxville about two miles from the FBI office. He related to her the conversation, and she said, "Victor, this is bad, real bad. Are you sure you won't reconsider meeting them? I mean, if you're right—and I believe you might be—then you might be safer with them."

"No. I meant what I said. The only one I've really trusted in this has been murdered. There's absolutely no reason for me to trust them."

Chapter Twelve

"So what are you going to do?" she asked.

"I need some things. Will you help me?"

"Victor, I believe you. I know you didn't kill Russell, but I can't help you run from the FBI," she said, adamantly, and then continued with, "They *will* eventually catch you, and if they found out that I helped you, which they *will*, they'll put me in jail too! I'm sorry. I just can't do it!"

As she stared through the windshield, Victor turned and said, "Listen, Ruth, I know you're scared. I'm scared too, but something's going on here. Russell's death is somehow connected to all of this, I need some help, and..."

"No, Victor! Absolutely not," she said unyieldingly, "If the FBI arrests me, I'll not only lose my job, but my nursing license too, not to mention going to jail. I simply can't do it!"

"Just hear me out, okay?" he asked.

"Crap!" she said impatiently, "Okay, but make it quick. I don't want to get stopped with a fugitive in my car!"

"Me either, but listen to this," he explained, "I can't believe it's a coincidence that Russell was murdered. Either he found something or it was because they found out he talked to me, and..."

"They?" she said excitedly. "They, who?"

"Just calm down, okay?"

"I can't calm down, Victor!"

"Look, take this exit and pull into that parking lot," he said calmly while pointing towards a large church. "This is getting out of hand."

Pulling into the parking lot, she switched off the engine and turned to him, saying, "Okay, last stop. Make it quick!"

Speaking softly, he said, "Like I was saying, this is not some coincidence. Whoever killed Russell did so for a reason. Also, they broke into my house, got one of my kitchen knives, and..."

"One of your kitchen knives?" she asked with disbelief and astonishment.

"Yeah, the FBI confirmed that. That's how they got the warrant. That's not important," he said. "What is important is the number of connections. It's all about connections!"

"Connections," she asked, starting to calm down. "What connections? What do you mean?"

SmokeFire!

"I mean, step back and take a look at it," he reasoned. "Buddy and Donna's disappearance, my nosing around, Russell's murder with my kitchen knife. Somebody's getting nervous. Why?"

They were both getting frustrated, and while Victor was thinking she asked, "Victor, let me ask you a far-out question."

"Ask away."

"Okay," she said, "but this is going to sound pretty stupid. Do you think my father's death could somehow be, to use your words, connected?"

Contemplating her question for a moment, he said, "I don't see how. Ruth, that was almost fifty years ago!"

"You said it yourself. Step back and take a look at it. Can you say it's *not* connected, related in some obscure way, maybe even directly?" she questioned.

"No, I can't, but I don't see how it could. Do you?"

"No, I don't know," she said. "I guess I'm just thinking out loud. I read Dad's file you gave me—several times—and what you said in the restaurant yesterday, about the facts just not adding up, well, I guess it just got me to thinking. Maybe my imagination is just running away."

He was beginning to think that calling her yesterday had been a bad idea. Now he was sure. He had opened some old wounds, giving her the file and calling her today. *What am I doing to this woman?*

"I'm sorry," he said apologetically, "I shouldn't have called you. This doesn't have anything to do with your father, Ruth. It's my problem, and I'm sorry I brought you into it."

"Don't apologize, Vick, I got myself into it. I stayed awake late last night thinking about your friends, my father, and what's happened. Now with all the crap that's gone down today..." she continued. "It makes me wonder. Maybe you're right."

"Right how?" he asked. "It makes you wonder about what?"

"I don't know. This is all so bizarre I can't think straight..."

"Well, there's definitely something here I'm not seeing, and I do think Russell's murder is connected, but I don't see how it could possibly be connected with your father's accident," Victor said. "If there is something here, it's more about Buddy and Donna and what happened to them. Not about your father and the camp."

Chapter Twelve

She leaned back into the car seat and closed her eyes. He said nothing, and just as he was about to tell her he was going to go it alone and get out of the car, she opened her eyes and turned towards him.

"Okay, I'll do it. I'll help you," she said with finality. "So what do we do next? If you're right then someone out there wants you out of the way. That's pretty scary!"

"Yes, it is," he agreed. "So we keep out of their way—low profile I mean. Ruth, I want to be honest with you. There's risk here—serious risk. Are you sure?"

"If it helps me to find out about Dad, then it'll be worth it," she said with that hint of yearning in her voice again.

"Thank you! We are going to need some stuff. Pull onto the Interstate and head west," he instructed. "First thing I'm going to need is a new cell phone. Let's drive down Kingston Pike. There's an Office Depot and we can get one there," he said as she started the car. "I'm going to need you to purchase it because if they run a credit check, the FBI probably has markers on my social security number by now."

Looking over at him, she smiled and said, "You run from the FBI often, Scofield? You sound like an expert."

The tension of the last half-hour gone, he replied with a wry smile. "I try to keep it to a minimum."

Pulling into the Office Depot, he said, "I'll give you the cash to pay for a year in advance. Get one of the small ones with the widest possible range, and get some extra battery packs—lithium ion type—and an AC quick charger, plus one of those cigarette lighter chargers," he said, scribbling it down on a piece of paper. "Next, I'm going to need some transportation. We're not going to rent a car because that's too traceable, even if you rent it. There's a bunch of used car lots up and down Kingston Pike. We'll stop in and I'll pick one up. Then you can go home, and I'll take it from there, okay?"

"Where are you going to go? They require identification at motels, and I'm sure the FBI has put out some kind of alert."

"I'm sure they have too, but there's about a zillion motels up near the Gatlinburg area, and I'll get me a room at a cheap one. It'll take them forever to put out alerts at the mom-and-pop places. Then I'll decide what to do next."

SmokeFire!

They pulled into the parking lot at the Office Depot, and in about twenty minutes Ruth came back with a new Nokia cell phone, spare battery packs and chargers.

"I signed you up for the Platinum Plan. You get six-hundred free minutes a month," she said and handed him the bag.

Victor unpacked the box and put it in the back seat with the other accessories, then plugged the charger into the cigarette lighter and connected it to the phone.

"There is one more thing I'm going to need, and you're probably not going to like it. I want to go to Sears and pick up a shotgun."

"A shotgun! Victor, this is getting out of hand."

"It's only for self-defense purposes, and I don't mean against the FBI. I don't know what I'm dealing with here and until I do I want some protection. Will you do it?" he asked.

"I'll do it, but I don't like it. I don't know what to ask for, though. I don't know anything about guns."

She gave him a piece of paper from her purse, and he wrote down the instructions.

"Tell them it's a gift for your brother. If they ask you any questions, just say that this is what your sister-in-law told you to get, that you don't know anything about guns. You'll have to fill out some paperwork, but there's no waiting period on shotguns like there is for handguns," he said as he tore the paper from the pad and placed it in her purse.

"It's a Winchester twelve gauge pump. If they don't have Winchester, get a Mossberg or whatever they have. Just make sure it's a twelve gauge pump. I also wrote down the type of ammunition. Get the clerk to pick it out for you. Ruth, I hate dragging you into this and it's not too late to change your mind."

As she drove onto the mall road exit she said, "You didn't drag me into this. I volunteered, remember?"

"Well, you didn't exactly volunteer, but..."

Stopping at the traffic light, she turned towards him and interjected, "I agreed to help you because if somehow it is connected with my father's accident, then I want to know. I've already helped you, and now I'm involved in it too. Besides, there may be something I can do that you can't."

Chapter Twelve

The light changed and she pulled into the intersection. Victor was having second thoughts about getting her involved.

"Ruth, any connection with your father is tenuous at best. I think it would be better if you just got me the shotgun and dropped me off at a car lot."

"I'm a big girl, and my mind is made up, so don't try to talk me out of it."

"Okay, okay," he said, as the tone of her voice made it clear that she wasn't going to change her mind.

They swung into the parking lot of the Sears store, which, ironically enough, was located in the mall where Victor had left his car. Gathering up her purse and opening the car door, Ruth turned and said, "I'll go get the shotgun, then drop you off at the car lot. You get a car while I go home and quickly pack some things. Then I'll call you on your new cell phone. Don't forget to give me the number."

Before he could argue any further, she stepped out and shut the car door.

* * *

The FBI has many resources, but Franklin DeVarra had something much better—luck. He, too, had contacted the telephone company, via a personal visit, and after a rather large bribe to a clerk had obtained Victor's home telephone records and the records of pay phones in Knoxville as well. Unknown to many people, the telephone company maintains records of all calls, local and long distance. The FBI had gotten the same information, but they had acquired it prior to Victor's call from the diner. DeVarra, on the other hand, had not. Sitting in the public parking lot near the phone company, it had taken him about an hour of scanning through the records before he found a match on Victor's home phone with that of one of the pay phones. He then picked up the cell phone and called the contact whom he had earlier bribed and asked for the name and address of the person.

DeVarra was now in possession of Ruth's name and address. He looked on the city map, started the car, and drove towards her home.

Chapter Thirteen

7:00 p.m. Monday, April 26, 1999
Knoxville, Tennessee

Ruth and Victor had gone to the AutoMart where he purchased a 1993 Jeep Wrangler, after a little haggling so as not to arouse any suspicions. They'd decided that Ruth should wait until he completed the purchase so that he could transfer the shotgun to his Jeep. "After all," Ruth had said, "you just can't stand there with a shotgun in your hand and haggle with the salesman," and she did have a point.

Afterward, he had stopped off at the Ace Hardware store where he purchased a hacksaw, locking pliers, and other assorted tools.

He was now driving east on Interstate 40 just outside of Knoxville. He would find a room on the south side of the Park, which was less populated than Gatlinburg or the surrounding area, and where he hoped the small motels would be more prolific. He chose the long route around the Park rather than taking Highway 441 over Newfound Gap on the off chance that the two-lane highway might be being watched by the authorities. During the drive he contemplated Ruth's continuing

SmokeFire!

involvement and the events to date. He didn't want to put her in harm's way and had probably gotten her too involved already, but since she had seemed to want to help him, he could hardly deny her. Besides, he too wondered if, although it was almost fifty years ago, the destruction of Camp Thirteen was somehow related, even remotely. He also thought about Steve. *Damn*, he thought, *I really liked the guy!* He felt somewhat guilty in that if he hadn't approached Steve, the ranger might still be alive. Then his thoughts turned to who might have killed him, especially in such a gruesome way. *Who? Pike?* he thought. *But why would he do that?* There was something about Pike that Victor didn't like, but he didn't think he was a murderer.

Russell had told him that he had been at the Park for two years; then, two days after meeting Victor, he was murdered. *There's got to be a connection*, he thought. *Okay, why would someone kill Russell?* he asked himself. *Narrow it down. It must have been something he knew or was about to find out. Something he'd seen, heard? Was it connected to Buddy and Donna?*

Okay, he thought, *if it's connected, then it's either connected to someone I've already talked to or someone they talked to.*

He went over the people he had discussed this with, leaving absolutely no one out. Pike, Mae, Russell, the two rangers at the main headquarters desk, Marsha Benton, Smoky Tobias, Virginia Clevenger, Ruth, and lastly, but only briefly, Vodeski.

Ruth? She did want to be involved. *What better way to keep an eye on him than to stay with him? That's crap,* he thought, *why would she be involved?* He had approached her by calling, not the reverse. She had a great career and seemed like a delightful person, and besides, he was attracted to her.

No one on his list was even a remote suspect for murder, so he decided that it must be someone else. *But who? If it was someone else, then they had to be connected to someone on the list.* There just had to be a connection.

Maybe the connection wasn't a person, he thought. *Maybe it's a thing, a place. Panther Creek? That's possible.*

He decided that, in any event, the priority now was to find a secure place to hide until he figured out his next step, and he had an idea about that.

Chapter Thirteen

He exited the Interstate at Highway 276, choosing the long way around the Park in the event the FBI or Park Service was monitoring the park roads. His destination was the Cherokee Indian Reservation, which was situated on the south side of the Park. Although he'd never been there, he supposed that there must be a lot of small, independently-operated motels where he could hide for the next four days. If he couldn't get some answers by Friday, he'd stand by what he had told Richter, turn himself into the FBI, and go from there.

He was passing the small tourist community of Maggie Valley on the south side of the Park when his cell phone rang. Although he had great trepidation about Ruth's involvement, he felt his pulse slightly quicken when the phone rang. *Are you glad she's calling?* he asked himself. *Were you afraid she wouldn't?*

He picked up the new cell phone and realized he should have tested it because he had a little difficulty opening the small door that covered the keypad. He finally pulled it down and placed the phone to his ear.

"Hi, Ruth!"

"Hi, Vick. Okay, I've got some stuff packed and I've called my supervisor and arranged for some time off the rest of the week, and before you start. It's no problem, okay?"

Smiling to himself, he said, "I'm not going to start...so you're leaving now?"

"Yeah, where are you?"

"I'm not entirely certain, but I'm going to find us a place within the next fifteen minutes or so. Why don't you go ahead and get started and call me on your cell phone."

"Okay, I'll call you in about, say, thirty minutes?"

"Perfect. I'll be waiting on it. By the way, there haven't been any problems, have there?" he asked.

"No, why do you ask? Are you expecting some?"

Not yet, he thought, *but they're coming.* "No, just being paranoid, I guess. I'll wait for your call. And Ruth?"

"Yes?"

"Thanks. I've thought about it and I really do need you, I mean..."

"Vick, we can talk about it when I get there, okay?"

SmokeFire!

"All right, talk to you in a few minutes. Bye, bye," he said and flipped the cover closed on the little phone, setting it back down behind the gearshift.

He entered the Cherokee Indian Reservation but didn't stop at the first place he saw. Driving on, he came to a little motel named "Tomahawk Inn" that had a neon sign depicting an Indian in blue and red headdress swinging a red tomahawk. He pulled into the parking lot, detached the cell phone from the cigarette lighter charger, put it in his pocket, and went in.

An old Indian with long straight gray hair sat behind the counter reading, of all things, a paperback Louis L'Amour western.

"Howdy, you needing a room or directions, sir?" he asked in a friendly voice as Victor walked up to the little counter.

"A room if you've got one, sir."

"Got plenty, little early in the season for tourists, and 'sides, they don't stop here a lot anyway. Where you from?"

"I just drove in from Raleigh, gonna meet my wife here. She's driving up from Atlanta, we've been traveling—separately, I'm afraid—but business is done and we thought we'd meet up here, stay a few days, then go on home. We live in Nashville."

"Ah, double income—no kids!" he said, smiling in a friendly way. "Got just the room for you. Private and out of the way," he said, winking.

"You've read my mind, sir. By the way, my name's Thomas Halloran, what's yours?" Victor asked in an equally sociable tone.

"Dan Red Feather. Pleased to meet you," he said as he extended a weathered and bony hand across the counter.

As Victor signed the guest book, he said, "Mr. Red Feather, all I got is my company credit card and since this is personal business," with a wink and smile, "I can't put it on that. Don't think my boss would like it, if you know what I mean. Wife's got our cards, and they're probably up to their limit after her being in Atlanta. You know women. Is cash okay?"

"Ain't nobody knows women, Mr. Halloran. Not even them who claim to. Cash'll be fine."

Chapter Thirteen

Victor handed him three hundred dollars, stating that they would only need the room for three or four nights, and Dan handed him back change of forty-five dollars.

"It's around back, down on the end. You can't miss it, Mr. Halloran. Let me know if you need anything," he said as he handed Victor two sets of keys.

"Thanks. Where's a good place to eat? My wife ought to be getting here in a couple of hours, and knowing her, she'll be hungry."

"Go on down 'bout a mile to Squaw Restaurant. Dumb name, but great food. Tell Annie that Dan sent you. She's a dish that one is," he said with a wide grin. "Tell her I still want to marry her."

"Thanks, Mr. Red Feather. Appreciate the hospitality," he said as he turned to leave.

As he was opening the door, Dan remarked, "One more thing, Mr. Halloran. I am discreet, if you know what I mean," he said in a serious tone.

"That sir, I am sure of. Thank you," Victor responded with a polite nod.

As he opened his car door to get in, the cell phone rang. He flipped open the little cover, stepped into the Jeep, and said "Hi, Ruth."

"Hi, Vick. I'm just getting onto I-40. Should I go east or west?" she said.

"Go east, exit at 407, go through Sevierville, then take 441 across the mountain. That should put you here in about an hour and a half. When you come off the mountain, you'll be in Cherokee. Turn left and give me a call. I've booked us a room at a place called the Tomahawk Inn. It'll be on your left. You can't miss it. We're in room 101."

"Hmm, sounds cozy. Got a Jacuzzi?" she asked whimsically.

"I doubt it, but it seems perfect for our needs."

"Okay, see you then," she said, and hung up.

How long has it been since you've been in a hotel with a woman, Vick? he thought. *Oh no, maybe she thinks I got two rooms!* Well, it couldn't be helped now, he thought as he drove around the back.

He unlocked the door to the room and walked in. To his surprise it was very clean and tastefully decorated, nothing extravagant but with quality contemporary furniture. There was a double bed and no sofa. *Damn floor's going to break my back*, he thought.

SmokeFire!

He went back out to the Jeep and unloaded the shotgun, ammunition, and tools. *Going to have to get me some clothes and toiletries tomorrow*, he thought. But first things first. He laid his purchases on the bed and went to work.

As Ruth turned off I-40 onto Exit 407, Franklin DeVarra followed her, two cars behind.

* * *

Victor, after cleaning up the metal shavings and sawdust from his work on the shotgun, examined it. It was a Winchester pump action model 1300, not designed for hunting game but rather, as a defensive weapon, and it had originally had an eighteen-inch barrel. Using the hacksaw, he had cut the barrel down to within one inch of the four shot magazine, and had shortened the hardwood stock to the grip. The overall length of the weapon was now about twenty-four inches long, which would make it easier to carry and conceal. Sitting down on the bed, he inspected the chamber, worked the pump action several times, and tested the trigger pull. Opening up a box of shotgun shells, he placed five rounds on the bed and set the box aside. They were magnum double-O—'double ought'—buckshot, favored by military and law enforcement personnel. The magnum was an extremely powerful load, comprised of nine thirty-two caliber "pellets," and would totally decimate anything within a thirty-foot range. He inserted four rounds into the magazine, worked the pump action to chamber a round, and then inserted the fifth shell into the magazine. Generally, it was deemed unsafe to keep a round chambered, but as Buddy had once said, "A weapon's no good unless you can get it into action fast—when you need it, you're gonna need it quick!"

He leaned the shotgun out of sight against the wall between the bed and nightstand, gathered up the stock and barrel that he'd cut off and placed them in the Jeep with the remaining shells and tools.

At nine o'clock there was a knock on the door, and without opening it he said, "Yes?"

"It's me, Vick," replied Ruth. He opened the door and let her in.

* * *

Chapter Thirteen

Franklin DeVarra was a hundred yards behind and had seen Ruth turn into the single level Tomahawk Motel. Not wanting her to notice him, he proceeded past the motel, turned around, and drove into the back parking lot from the opposite side. He backed into an empty slot in the dark back corner of the parking lot with his headlights off and waited. He didn't know exactly which room she had gone into, but he suspected she had parked directly in front of the room since the hotel was practically empty. There had only been two cars parked out front, and none was parked in the back lot, except hers and a Jeep that sat in front of the only room that had a light on. Obviously she was meeting someone, as she had driven directly to the room without checking in and getting a key. *A lover? Scofield? Or someone else?*

When he had been reviewing Scofield's home telephone records, there had only been a single call to Ruth, and that on the previous afternoon, so he doubted if they were lovers. Maybe following her had not been such a good idea after all, as it could lead to nothing. He reached into the back seat and extracted a set of high-powered binoculars. He had night vision goggles, but the ambient light from the room, even though the curtains were drawn, would flood the vision, as the NVG's were highly light-sensitive. He decided to sit back, keep the room under surveillance, and see what happened.

* * *

"I stopped off and got us some deli sandwiches for supper," Ruth said as she set the bags down on the little table. "I figured you wouldn't want to go out."

"Great, I am hungry. The desk clerk mentioned a restaurant near here, but I think I'm just too tired to get back out."

"Me, too. Why don't you see if you can find a soft drink machine and I'll unpack this luxurious meal."

"All righty," he said as he extracted some singles from his wallet, which he had earlier placed on the nightstand. "Be right back."

Victor left the room, and Ruth carried her case into the bathroom and began unpacking her toiletries. She had also packed a carry-on

SmokeFire!

fabric bag that contained some jeans and other casual wear that she would unpack later.

* * *

Scofield! DeVarra thought, as he watched him exit the room and close the door. *Son of a bitch! This is my lucky day!*

As he watched him walk down the sidewalk that ran along the front of the rooms, DeVarra lay the binoculars down in his lap and slouched down in the seat so that his eye level was at the edge of the dashboard. Scofield approached the soft drink machine, fed some bills into the slot, and carried several cans back to the room.

Franklin DeVarra prided himself on his professionalism. He never took unnecessary risks, never left any clues—unless they were intended—and, as a result, had never been arrested in any of his assassinations, of which there had been over thirty since he entered his profession.

This is perfect! I've got them both together in an isolated place!

As Scofield went back into the room, DeVarra sat up. He pulled the Sig Sauer out of his briefcase, attached the silencer, then took the briefcase and walked toward Scofield's room, keeping in the shadows.

* * *

"So, what have you been doing since I left you?" Ruth asked, taking a bite out of her sandwich.

"Not a lot, worked on the shotgun," Victor said as he nodded to where the gun leaned against the wall "Cut it down so it'll be easier to carry. It's loaded, so be careful."

"Don't worry, I wouldn't touch it for the world. So, what is our plan, Victor?"

"Our plan? I've been doing some thinking, and I think the next step is to..."

Before he could continue, there were three sharp knocks on the door. Victor looked up directly at Ruth while he dropped his sandwich and raised his eyebrows. She shook her head, which Victor took to mean she didn't know who it could be.

Chapter Thirteen

Standing up, he approached the door and asked, "Who is it?"

"Front desk, sir. You dropped some papers out of your wallet when you checked in. Just found 'em lying on the floor at the counter."

Papers? He had taken out his wallet when he paid for the room. Maybe something had fallen out and Red Feather had found it.

He left the chain lock attached and slowly opened the door. Before he had a chance to look outside, the door came crashing into his face knocking him backwards, the chain lock ripping off the door frame. He fell against the dresser and caught his fall by grabbing the corner of the bed.

"Victor Scofield and Ruth Jeffers—how cozy!" the man said as he quickly stepped into the room and quietly closed the door.

"What? You got the wrong room! There's nobody here by that..."

"Please, do not speak," DeVarra said, as he pointed a rather nasty looking pistol at Victor's head. "And if you even think about getting up off the floor, I'm gonna put a bullet in this pretty lady's face! Sit down on the floor, indian style, and put your hands behind your head, now!" He swung the gun to point towards Ruth.

Victor did as he was told. Then DeVarra said, "You, go sit on the bed. Now! But not next to your boyfriend there." Ruth got up from the small table and sat down near the head of the bed.

"Get your hands up, too! If either one of you even twitches, the consequences will be most severe! Now, we have some business to discuss. I'm going to ask each of you some simple questions, and for each straight answer I don't get, the punishment will be extreme." He then drew out a large stiletto knife, opened it, and laid it on the table where they had been eating. He sat down in the chair, never taking his eyes off Victor and said, "First, I want to know why you're here!"

"Because I'm running from the police, and this was a good..."

"Mr. Scofield, please do not insult me. I am fully aware that the FBI is pursuing you. What I wish to know is why you chose this area."

"Hear me out," Victor said. "The FBI attempted to arrest me this afternoon, and I escaped. I couldn't very well stay in Knoxville, as I'm certain the FBI will check all the hotels. To answer your question, I chose this area because it's obscure and unlikely to be checked by the authorities."

SmokeFire!

"So what is it you are intending to do?" DeVarra asked. "Hide out here indefinitely, or do you have a greater purpose in mind?"

"To tell you the truth, I don't know what I'm going to do. I was going to hide here and think about how I could convince the FBI that they've made a mistake, I..."

"I can see that you have not taken me seriously, Mr. Scofield," DeVarra said, as he opened the briefcase with his left hand while keeping the gun trained between Victor and Ruth. He removed what appeared to be two handkerchiefs and a roll of duct tape. Setting them aside, he quietly closed the briefcase and said, "Now, here is how this is going to go. If you were simply hiding out, as you put it, why would Ms. Jeffers be here? If you do not answer my question, succinctly and to the point, I am going to tie both of you up and gag you. This will prevent any screams from being overheard. Then I am going to tie this pretty lady to the bed and cut away her clothes. I will leave the rest to your imagination," DeVarra said without emotion.

"I was going to plan who to contact next in my search for my lost friends. She," Victor said, nodding towards Ruth, "is here because her father was mysteriously killed in an accident almost fifty years ago, near the area where my friends disappeared. We are trying to find out what happened, not only to my friends, but to her father as well."

"That's better. Now, I wish to know, in detail, exactly whom you have contacted in relation to your search, and what information you have obtained."

"I will tell you, but first, who are you? Are my suspicions correct in assuming that you killed Steve Russell?"

"I can see that appealing to you on a rational level, without resorting to violence, is futile," DeVarra said as he leaned forward in the chair. Turning towards Ruth, he said, "Remove your clothes—all of them—and lay back on the bed. Spread your arms and legs apart." He then stood and picked up the knife and duct tape.

"Wait! Leave her alone! I'll cooperate," Victor said, pleadingly.

"I am afraid that that time has passed, Mr. Scofield. I am certain you will cooperate, and very soon."

As he was about to take a step towards Ruth, there was a pounding on the front door.

Chapter Thirteen

"Fire! Fire! This is the manager! The hotel's on fire! Everybody's gotta get out now!"

DeVarra switched his gaze towards the door and, like any professional, swung the pistol to follow his line of sight.

Victor, sitting on the floor with his legs crossed, turned towards Ruth and quickly nodded towards the shotgun. *God, I hope she knows what I mean! Pick it up and shoot the bastard!*

There was more pounding on the front door, and DeVarra quickly looked back at Scofield, then back at the door. Ruth reached down, grabbed the shotgun, and threw it to Victor.

He had jerked his hands away from behind his head just in time to catch it when DeVarra spun around to his left, the pistol slightly behind his line of sight. Victor caught the gun with both hands, his left on the pump and his right on the receiver. The barrel was pointed up towards the ceiling, and he quickly lowered it.

I'm not going to make it! Even if I do, the damn safety's probably on! I should've checked it! DeVarra stopped his swing and took aim just as Victor pulled the trigger.

The tremendous blast from the shotgun was overshadowed by the muzzle flash, which was, in turn, eclipsed by the recoil. The shotgun jerked up two feet and caused Victor to roll over on his back while still clutching it. He thought he'd been shot, and wondered if he'd hit DeVarra.

Franklin 'The Nailer' caught the high velocity magnum load mostly in the right shoulder area just below his throat. Ruth looked on, horrified, as everything above the tops of his arms virtually disappeared in a giant red cloud. DeVarra's headless corpse stood for perhaps one second, then collapsed onto the floor with the pistol still clutched in his hand. A shot from his pistol had hit the wall behind and slightly to the right of Victor's head.

Victor jumped to his feet while he jacked another round into the chamber and pointed it at DeVarra. Realizing it was not needed, he lowered the barrel just as the front door opened.

"Don't move! Drop the shotgun!" Dan Red Feather said as he pushed the door open. DeVarra's body, or what was left of it, had been blown backwards and prevented the door from being fully opened. Red Feather pushed the door harder, shoving DeVarra's body aside, and

SmokeFire!

stepped into the room as Victor laid the shotgun on the bed. He was carrying an old Navy Colt that was in mint condition.

"Just sit back down, Mr. Halloran! You, too, miss!" he said, keeping the pistol pointed towards the ground as he walked into the room.

Victor looked at Ruth. She had her hands covering her face, and although she wasn't crying, she was shaking uncontrollably.

"What a mess," Red Feather said, looking around the room. DeVarra's missing head and shoulders, which had almost been vaporized, covered the front wall and ceiling.

"Mr. Red Feather..."

"Don't worry," he said, smiling as he shook his head back and forth. "The motel's not on fire. Saw this dude," pointing to DeVarra, "drive by right after your Missus turned in, then turn around and park out back with his lights off. Decided to spy on him while he was spyin' on you folks. You came out to get some sodas, and after you went back in, this dude comes amblin' across the parking lot with a pistol in his hand. Now, I figured if he was a policeman, then he wouldn't come alone, so I figured he was up to no good, especially with the silencer. So I went back and got my trusty Dragoon here," patting the old pistol, "and listened at the door for a minute." He set the pistol on the table with the sandwiches and sat down. Casually kicking one of DeVarra's legs out of the way, he rested his elbows on his knees and said, "Now, will somebody please tell me what the hell is goin' on here, and who is this piece of crap? Pardon me, ma'am."

Victor asked if he could get up and then went to sit beside Ruth. He put his arms around her, and she buried her head against his shoulder. They sat like that for a few minutes, until Ruth's trembling diminished.

"Mr. Red Feather, you saved our lives, and for that I thank you. For this, I will tell you the entire story, but—and I realize I'm in no position to ask for anything—but I would like you to hear me out before calling the police. Could we please move to another room? This is going to take me about an hour, and after that you can do what you choose, and I promise you, sir, I will do whatever you say."

They moved to an empty room on the other side of the motel, and as they walked, Victor held Ruth tightly and whispered to her, "We're

Chapter Thirteen

safe now! It's going to be okay. Deep breaths. Let the adrenaline rush off. I'm with you. It's all right."

It took, in fact, about an hour to bring Red Feather completely up-to-date. They sat together at the table in an identical room, and Victor, as promised, left absolutely nothing out.

"And so, as far as that guy goes," Victor concluded, "I haven't the faintest idea who he is—was, but he damn sure wasn't a cop."

"Sounds like you're gettin' too close to somethin', Mr. Scofield. Somethin' big. I need to make a couple of phone calls. This is an Indian Reservation, and we have our own Tribal Police. From what you told me about that gentleman who broke into your room, it sounds to me like he's a professional, and somebody sicked him on you. Now, we don't take to that much around here—rape, murder, and such, and we got our own way of dealin' with it. It's not my decision, though, and I got to call the Tribal Police Chief in on this."

Victor's heart sank. *Just what I need, more police! Now the Indians and the FBI will be waiting in line for my head.*

Perhaps sensing Victor's despair, Red Feather said, "But the Chief—he's my grandnephew—hates assholes, pardon me, ma'am, worse than I do."

He stepped over to the phone, dialed a number, and spoke in his native tongue for a few minutes, which made Victor feel a little uncomfortable.

He had been holding tightly to Ruth's hand and she to his, during the entire conversation. She had regained her composure amazingly well, Victor thought, probably from her experiences as a nurse.

As Red Feather talked on the phone, Victor looked into Ruth's eyes. She wasn't crying, but her eyes had the blank look he had seen while in Vietnam. It was the look of extreme fear. He winked at her and nodded his head a couple of times, hoping to reassure her that everything was all right. She exhaled a deep breath and squeezed his hand tightly.

Red Feather sat back down at the table and said, "He's on his way here now. You'll like him, Mr. Scofield. He's a good man. He'll do the right thing. Now, I don't know about you folks, but I could use a drink. What about it?" he asked as he rose from the table.

"It's Victor, Mr. Red Feather, and yes, I think I would."

183

SmokeFire!

"Call me Dan then, Victor, and I know *I* would. Be back in a few minutes." He smiled down at Victor and Ruth, nodded his head of long gray hair and walked around the table to the door. When he passed behind Ruth, he paused, and then placed one hand on Victor's shoulder and the other one on Ruth's. Standing proudly, he said, "Listen, folks, I'm seventy-eight years old and I'm a good judge of character. You folks are good people—I know that—and we're gonna try to help you. But it ain't up to us. The Chief'll have to make some phone calls to the Tribal Judicial Branch. So just sit tight and I'll be right back." He squeezed Victor's shoulder, and then left the room.

"Oh, God, Victor," Ruth said, letting go of Victor's hand, "this is getting worse by the minute!"

"That was quick thinking, throwing the shotgun, I mean. You were fast, and it saved our lives." Victor said, leaning back in the chair.

"I didn't even know it was there. Then when you nodded, I just happened to see it. I didn't even think."

"What I want to know is who he was and who sent him. Dan's right. I'm getting close—way too close—and I'm going to see it through."

"Damn it Victor, you—we—were almost killed!" she shouted. "So far you've been framed—that's the right term, isn't it?—for murder, then somebody tries to kill us! We need to go to the FBI, tell them everything we know! It's the only way!"

"No! The FBI won't help us. They had their chance and blew it. No FBI! We're going to see what Red Feather's people can do. That's our next step. I've got three days to figure out what's going on here, and, dammit, I am going to get to the bottom of it!" he said, slamming his hand onto the table. Ruth flinched and he said, "I'm sorry, Ruth. I didn't mean to drag you into this!"

"You didn't drag me into it, Victor. I made you, remember? I'll wait and see what the Tribal Police have to say, then make my decisions, okay?"

"Fair enough, but you know something? I'm really glad you're here! I mean it," he said with a feeble smile.

* * *

Chapter Thirteen

Victor went over the entire story again, only this time to an audience. Red Feather stood leaning in the corner with his arms crossed while Victor, the Tribal Police Chief, John White Horse, and his assistant sat at the table. White Horse had brought his wife along, and she was sitting on the bed holding Ruth's hand.

To say that White Horse struck an imposing figure was like calling the Grand Canyon a ditch. He stood at least six feet six, weighted about two-thirty and was all muscle. Victor guessed his age at about thirty-five. His physique, combined with his dark skin, shoulder length straight black hair, and very serious blue eyes gave one the feeling that this was indeed a man to be reckoned with.

He was obviously intelligent and educated, listening quietly and only occasionally asking a question. His assistant sat silently, looking Victor straight in the eye. Neither took a single note during the discussion, nor was there any tape recorder that Victor could see.

"I see, Mr. Scofield," White Horse said when Victor had finished recounting the story. He looked in turn at his assistant, over his shoulder to Red Feather, and then to his wife. Victor didn't know what passed between them—there was never a nod, a blink, nor a word.

"I must make a phone call," White Horse said. "I'll be back in five or ten minutes."

After White Horse had left the room, Victor went to sit with Ruth while Dan poured himself another drink.

Resuming his leaning position against the wall, Dan repeated, "Like I said, he's gotta make a couple of calls. You're on an Indian Reservation, Victor, and we got our own way of doing things. He'll do all he can."

"Right now," Victor said as he put his arm around Ruth's waist, "we need all the help we can get."

After a few minutes, White Horse came back into the room and sat down.

"Here's what we're going to do, Mr. Scofield," White Horse explained. "We're going to get the other room cleaned up, if you know what I mean. Then we're going to try to find out all that we can about the individual who attempted to murder you both." He continued by saying, "That's a serious weapon he was carrying, and I found some

SmokeFire!

other items in his car, including a file on you," he said, pointing towards Victor.

"A file on me?" Victor asked, alarmed.

"Yes, complete with personal background and photographs. We're not certain at this time, but it looks like a professional hit to me."

Victor felt the blood drain from his head as if his blood pressure had just dropped by half. Ruth simply trembled and looked as if she were going to be sick.

"Listen, folks," White Horse said, leaning forward in his chair, "I've explained the situation to my superiors, and they are behind us on this, at least for the time being. From what you've told us, it sounds like you've gotten in the way of somebody—somebody who is very determined, and, very dangerous."

Victor had several questions he wanted to ask, but knew White Horse wouldn't know the answers. Instead, he simply said, "Chief, I've told you virtually everything I know about why we're here and what's going on with the FBI."

"The FBI is a fine organization," White Horse said. "But like any large organization, it is not without its faults. We're going to keep them out of it, for the present time, until we can look into this further."

Victor felt some sense of relief in that he had finally found someone who didn't want to throw him in jail, or worse yet, to kill him.

"In the meantime I got a little cabin not far from here," White Horse said. "Mary and Dan are going to take you and Ms. Jeffers up to it, and you'll be safe there. Just to make sure, I'm going to place a few of my men in the area, outside in the trees, so don't shoot them with that cannon of yours. Tomorrow morning I'll come around and let you know what I've found out. In the meantime, you and Ms. Jeffers go up, get situated, take a hot bath, and get some rest. When I come around in the morning, we'll talk some more."

White Horse stood up, and Victor joined him and shook his hand.

"Chief, I don't know what to say, except thank you. I'm sorry I brought this trouble to you."

"Mr. Scofield, you didn't bring this trouble. Whatever it is, it was already here and you just found it. This Reservation's ours, those mountains used to be. Now they belong to us all, and that's as it should

Chapter Thirteen

be. If these people want trouble, then it's trouble they're going to get," he said gravely.

"Now, go get some rest. You folks deserve it. Mary and Dan will take good care of you." And without another word he turned and left the room with his assistant in tow.

Red Feather pushed himself off the wall, walked to the table, and poured each of them another drink from the bottle. Then he handed them the glasses.

"Told you he was a good man," Red Feather said, smiling, as he chinked his glass against Victor's.

Chapter Fourteen

**11:45 p.m. Monday night, April 26, 1999,
Cherokee Indian Reservation**

After the meeting had broken up, Dan went back to Victor's room and got their belongings; then they all followed Dan up to the cabin—Victor and Ruth in Victor's Jeep and White Horse's wife, Mary, in Ruth's car.

The cabin—as White Horse had called it—was really a new log home, complete with three bedrooms, two baths, one of which had a Jacuzzi, and a huge mountain stone fireplace. Although it was well after eleven o'clock when they arrived, all of them were still too keyed up to go to sleep or to leave—all except Dan, who seemed unflappable Victor and Ruth chose the two upstairs bedrooms, and while Ruth unpacked, Victor sat on the bed, and Dan built a large fire in the fireplace. When they came downstairs, the fire was roaring, and Dan and Mary were sipping Jack Daniels. Ruth and Victor joined them, and they all sat around the warm fire.

"Dan, let me ask you something," Victor said. "You made a remark about discretion when I left the lobby. Then you saved the day with the fake fire drill. Where did that remark come from, when you said you were discreet, I mean?"

"Well, you said you had come in from Raleigh on business, but you had no credit cards. You said your wife had 'em. Now, I don't know much about business, but seemed to me that a businessman would have him some credit cards. I also noticed the new car registration tag on your Jeep, which isn't that unusual, but something to note. Then you paid for the room with three brand new, hot off the press, hundred dollar bills. It all just seemed a little strange to me. Wouldn't of said anything, though. Then later I saw Miss Jeffers there turn in the parking lot and that other piece of crap—pardon me—go up and turn around. At first I thought you might be the bad guy. Then I saw him walking across the parking lot carrying an automatic pistol with a silencer. That's when I figured he was a bad guy, and maybe you all were bank robbers or somethin'. When I listened at the door, I heard him threatening her," he said, pointing to Ruth, "and those, uh, remarks he made. I was going to shoot him when he opened the door, but you beat me to it."

"Well, you saved our lives with that move, and it's greatly appreciated."

"That was a slick move," he said, nodding towards Ruth, "tossing Vick that shotgun."

"We were lucky," Victor said, smiling and taking another sip of the whiskey. "It was a nice toss."

"What about White Horse's men? When do you think they're going to arrive?" Ruth asked.

"Already there, outside, I mean. They'll be watchin' the place all night and tomorrow, so don't worry. Won't nothin' get within a mile of here they don't know about," Dan said.

"Dan, you ever hear of a guy named Smoky Tobias?" Victor asked.

"Tobias! That piece of crap—pardon me ma'am. Man's mad as a hatter. Been livin' up in that old house since the early fifties. Knows a lot about the Smokies, though, kinda a walking encyclopedia, if you know what I mean, or used to be. Why, did you talk to him?" Dan asked.

Chapter Fourteen

"Yeah, I went up to see him Sunday. I wanted to talk to him about lost hikers and see if he could give me any perspective. Steve Russell suggested I talk to him."

"Poor Russell," Dan said. "Heard about that right after it happened. News travels fast up here. I liked that kid—only met him a time or two. What about Tobias?" Dan asked. "You get anything out of him, or did he just drink himself silly with that blackberry wine of his?"

"Mostly drank the wine, then passed out. Let me ask you something, though, when I mentioned Panther Creek, he got all excited, called it a bad place. Said there was evil spirits up there, then told me about an old Cherokee legend. He didn't go into detail about it, said it was called Ole Red Eye or something. Then he remembered the translation before he passed out," Victor said.

"Yeah, SmokeFire," Dan said. "Supposed to have one big red eye, lurks up in the high country at night, a soul stealer. It's an old legend known mostly among the Cherokees and hasn't been well documented."

"You don't really believe that, do you, Dan? I mean evil spirits and all. You seem too rational for that," Ruth said.

"Ruth, there's many an Indian legend. Let me tell you one, then you tell me what you think. Indians said when man came into the world—of course animals were already here—that the Great Spirit decided to open a huge chasm to separate man from the animals. So the great chasm was splitting open the earth—with man on one side and the animals on the other, and at the last moment, the dog jumps across the chasm to stand on the side of man. Now, let me ask you, do you believe that, Ruth?"

"Well, I don't..."

"Course you don't believe that, but do you believe that the dog stands on the side of man, is man's best friend, I mean?"

"Why, yes, I love dogs," she said cheerfully.

"Have you ever wondered why dog is man's best friend? What makes him different from the other animals?"

"He jumped across the chasm?" Ruth asked.

"I don't know about jumping across chasms, but it's as good an explanation as any, and, besides, it makes a good story," Dan said. "It's the same with SmokeFire. Panther Creek is the only really undeveloped area in the Park. There's no trails back there, and the terrain's pretty tough. It's a dangerous place. Makes a good story, don't it?" Dan said, smiling.

"Yes, I guess it does," Ruth said.

"Dan, you ever been back up Panther Creek?" Victor asked.

"Sure, many a time, but not for quite a while. Last time I went up there was maybe twenty years ago. Great fishin'!"

"So you never noticed anything unusual up there?" Victor asked.

"Nary a time! Used to go up there and spend a week or so fishin' and huntin', back when you could hunt and not get caught, but then I saved up and bought the Tomahawk. Now I got no time for it."

They talked until after one and then Dan and Mary left. Victor had really enjoyed their company, and it seemed they had talked about everything—the Cherokees, lost hikers, and, of course, the Smokies.

After they left, Victor fixed another drink, picked up the poker and stoked the fire. Then he sat down on the stone hearth, facing Ruth, who was sitting on the couch.

Suddenly, left to herself, the enormity of what had just happened seemed to hit Ruth again. She put her head down into her hands and said, "That was the most horrible situation I've ever faced. I was terrified—I still am. Look at my hands Vick, I'm shaking!"

"It was awful, but we're safe now—it'll pass. You just have to keep telling yourself that we're OK. I find it extraordinary that Red Feather and his friends are willing to help us, especially in light of the fact that they don't know us. What about that White Horse guy?" Victor said, taking a sip from his glass.

"He is a striking figure. He missed his calling by not going to Hollywood. He'd have made a great Indian Chief!" Ruth said.

"Or warrior. And that assistant of his, what was his name?" Victor asked, and then added, "He sat there and never said a word, just watched."

"Nobody mentioned his name," Ruth replied, "and what about before White Horse went to make his call, the way they just looked at each other? It was like something just passed between them without it being said."

Chapter Fourteen

"They are a little mysterious, I'll grant you that. You know, maybe when this is all over—if I'm not in jail, then we could get to know them better."

"You won't go to jail, Victor, we'll get it straightened out. White Horse will tell the FBI what happened here, or I will. Then they'll have to listen. I wonder if that piece of crap, as Dan refers to him, killed Russell?"

"I figure it's likely, as he was going to kill us, but what really worries me is this—who sent him? Who is he working for?" Victor asked.

Finishing off her drink, Ruth said, "I'm too tired to think anymore, but I do have a favor to ask, and I don't want this to sound wrong, but I don't want to be alone tonight. Would you stay in my room with me?" she asked pensively.

"Sure, it doesn't sound wrong and honestly I feel the same way. I don't think all of this has caught up to me yet. I've lost my best friends, I'm running from the FBI, I've killed a man, and now I'm hiding out on an Indian reservation with a beautiful woman and God knows who out there watching over us. Don't worry, I'm too tired to try anything," he said with a laugh as he stood up. "Let's get some sleep."

They walked up the stairs together and went into Ruth's bedroom. She kicked off her Reeboks, fell back on the bed, and said, "I feel like I've been in the O.R. for sixteen hours."

"And I feel like I'm the patient! I'll go get some pillows and sleep here next to the bed," he said, turning for the door.

"Vick! Please come back here," she said, sitting up. "You can't sleep on the floor. It'll break your back. We'll sleep together here, okay?" she said, patting the bed.

"Okay, but I'm going to get the shotgun and check the door locks. Be right back." He turned and left the room.

Life used to be so simple, she thought, and then fell back down on the bed.

Ruth changed into an old Atlanta Falcons football jersey while Victor was downstairs. When he returned, Victor undressed down to his slacks and lay down on the bed.

As they were lying next to each other, Victor said, "Ruth, I really like these people—the Cherokees. They are a kind, caring, fair-minded people. They take care of each other, they're intelligent, and not taken with themselves."

"You're right. I feel the same way. We live only fifty miles away, and there's a whole different culture in our backyard that I never really knew about. I knew about the Cherokees of course, but I've never actually met one."

Victor reached up, turned out the light, and lying back down he said, "I meant what I said, Ruth, I'm really glad you're here."

"I'm glad I'm here too, Vick," she said, and reaching over she placed her left hand gently against his cheek. "It's all going to be okay. We'll work it out together," and she was asleep in two minutes.

Victor lay awake for a while longer, staring up into the darkness, and thought about what he'd learned today. Before drifting off to sleep, he reached up and held Ruth's hand, which was still against his cheek.

Chapter Fifteen

Tuesday morning, April 27, 1999
Cherokee Indian Reservation

When Ruth awakened, she discovered that Victor had already gotten up. She showered and changed into a pair of blue jeans and a casual long-sleeved red blouse. It was nine-thirty when she walked down the stairs, and Victor was saying goodbye to Chief White Horse.

"Good morning, all," she said coming down the stairs.

"Good morning, Ms. Jeffers. You doing all right this morning?" White Horse asked with concern.

"Fine, thank you. This is a beautiful place you have here. Thank you for letting us use it."

"Glad to be of help. I was just leaving, but Mr. Scofield can bring you up-to-date. Sorry to rush off, but I have some things to attend to. You make yourselves at home."

Victor and White Horse shook hands and then he left, closing the door behind him. Victor waited until he had stepped off the front porch and then locked the door.

SmokeFire!

"So, did you sleep well?" Victor asked.

"I think I went into a coma. Why didn't you wake me when you got up?"

"You were sleeping so well, and after last night, I thought you could use the rest. So, want a cup of coffee?" he asked "It's pretty good if I do say so myself."

"Sounds great!"

She followed him into the small kitchen where he poured them both a cup. "How do you like it?"

"Cream only, please," she said, and Victor handed her the cup.

"Watch it, it's hot," he said and then fixed his with the usual cream and sugar.

"So, what did the Chief have to say?"

"A couple of things," Victor said as he took a sip of coffee and leaned against the kitchen counter.

"He talked with a Tribal Court Judge this morning and discussed the situation. The Judge gave White Horse the authority to give us some protection."

"You mean hide us out?" Ruth asked. "Why would they do that, especially with you being wanted by the FBI?"

"According to the Chief, after Russell's murder and what happened last night, the Office of Tribal Justice is concerned with our safety, since we're on the reservation," Victor explained. "As far as the FBI goes, the Chief said they feel that for the time being, you and I would be safer here than with the FBI. I think they agree with me that the FBI jumped the gun in issuing a warrant for my arrest, and that there's probably more to this whole thing."

"It still seems like they're taking a pretty big risk, hiding you out," Ruth said.

"Yeah, I think so too, but maybe they could just say that they were holding me for questioning about shooting that guy last night, and that they didn't know I was wanted by the FBI."

"I suppose so," Ruth agreed. "What else did he have to say?"

"The Chief ran the fingerprints of the guy I shot last night through the NCIC—National Crime Information Center—and they came back

Chapter Fifteen

with a positive match. His name was Franklin DeVarra, and he was from Chicago."

"Chicago! He came all the way down here from Chicago?" she asked, surprised.

"Well, they don't know that for sure yet, but listen to this. According to the Chief, it seems our friend Mr. DeVarra was a hood with the Cavennetti organization out of Chicago, one of the international crime mobs who specialize in more sophisticated activities like industrial espionage, insider trading, things like that. Evidently Mr. DeVarra had been arrested for manslaughter about fifteen years ago, and the Cavennetti's got him off. He's been in their employ since that time, and is suspected in at least ten murders—'hits' was how the Chief referred to them."

"A mafia hit man! Victor, you can't be serious!" she said loudly as she backed away towards the kitchen counter.

"I'm afraid I am, and what the Chief and I were discussing was why he was here. White Horse is convinced that DeVarra's the one who murdered Russell, and I agree."

"But why did he try to kill us?" she asked, shaking her head.

"I'll tell you what the Chief thinks," Victor said, sipping on his coffee. "It's like he said last night; he believes I'm getting too close to something—something big. He thinks that I'm getting in somebody's way, not because of what I know but what I might find out, and I agree with him."

"That's it, Victor! We're going to pack up and go to the FBI. We'll be safer with them—oh, man, the mafia!" she said, incredulous.

"Not so fast! Ask yourself a question—who sent DeVarra? Who has that kind of contact around here? It has to have been somebody I've already talked to, and the Chief agrees with me."

"If he was a professional hit man," Victor continued, "then that would seem to involve an organization or group of conspirators with a lot of resources."

"Or one very powerful and connected individual," Ruth pointed out.

"True," he agreed. "Powerful and connected, but why? What threat—and it has to be a threat—could we possibly pose?"

"I don't know. Victor, this is way out of hand, and we can't go on. The FBI will help us get this straightened out, especially with White

SmokeFire!

Horse's help and since the mob seems to be involved," she said, her voice taking on an intensity that Victor had never seen in her.

"Ruth, I started out on this alone, and I'll finish it alone if I have to. I'm sorry, but that's final. The FBI will throw me in jail the second they lay eyes on me, and at this point I don't trust them. Maybe they have an agent in the Knoxville office with contacts to the Cavennettis. Have you thought of that?" he asked.

"No, I haven't, but it seems unlikely," she answered.

"I agree, but the Bureau has had some rare incidences of corrupt agents, and I believe that thought has crossed White Horse's mind too. Anyway, I'm going to see this thing through, but I want you to go back home. It's getting too dangerous. I'll call you when I'm done, which will be Thursday night. If I can't find out what's going on by then, I'll go to the FBI on Friday, okay?"

"I'm going to stay with you, Vick. I meant what I said when I came along. If this has anything to do with my father's death, then I'm going to be a part of it." Without waiting for him to respond, she asked, "So, what's next?"

"The Chief asked me the same thing, and I told him I had some more records to check out, then I would get back to him in the next day or so. I don't think he believed me, but he didn't say anything."

"Why wouldn't he believe you, Victor?" she asked.

"Because I lied. I've checked out everything I know except one."

"What do you mean? What are you going to do, Victor?" she asked, with a degree of concern.

"I'm going into Panther Creek—alone. That's where the answer is."

"No! Absolutely not! You could be killed! You don't know what's up there!" she said stubbornly, laying her coffee cup down so hard that coffee splashed over the side.

"Ruth, I have to. I'll be all right, and I'll be careful."

"No, Victor! Your friends disappeared up there, and maybe there have been others. Dan kind of scared me last night with that old Indian legend story. I..."

"Ruth, I'm going. First, I don't believe in red-eyed, soul-stealing monsters. I'm not going in like Buddy and Donna, on a hike, I mean. I'm going in like we did in Vietnam, and I'm going to treat this as a reconnaissance operation in hostile territory—I used to be pretty good

Chapter Fifteen

at it. I've had a lot of training in situations like this and more experience than I care for, and it's not something you forget. If there's something up there, I'm going to find out what it is. Then when I come back, we'll go to the FBI together."

"All right," she said, "but I don't like it. When are we going?"

"*We're* not—*I* am! I can't take care of myself if I'm having to watch out for you, and one man alone can travel faster and under greater concealment than two people. I'm going in tomorrow morning, and I'm going to need some equipment, so we're going on a little shopping trip today."

Ruth just looked at him, her face wearing a look of deep concern and resignation.

* * *

They left at ten-thirty in Victor's Jeep. Victor had located the stores he wanted to visit from the yellow pages at White Horse's cabin and made a list.

They took highway 441 over the Newfound Gap into Gatlinburg, even though Victor had avoided it on his trip in because the authorities might be monitoring it. Since they were taking his new Jeep instead of Ruth's car, and with her driving, he felt that any chance of being intercepted was negligible.

Their first stop was at a large store named Smoky Outfitters, which in the large half-page yellow pages ad professed to be the largest camping equipment store in East Tennessee.

They went in and loaded up on the supplies that he would require for an overnight trip, including a compass, Bowie knife, waterproof matches container (with stick matches), snakebite kit, sleeping bag, rope, a small but powerful set of binoculars, a detailed contour map of the Smokies, and a small black aluminum frame canvas backpack.

Next they drove into Pigeon Forge to a large army surplus store, where they purchased his 'operational equipment,' as he referred to it. This included a set of jungle fatigues, bush hat, jungle boots, two pairs of green socks, rain poncho, field jacket, and two sticks of night cream for face coloring.

SmokeFire!

Then they proceeded to a gun store where he bought an infrared scope, eye-swivels and shoulder strap for the shotgun, a shell bandoleer, a dozen boxes of shotgun shells, a Swiss army knife, and a three-cell K-Lite flashlight (with batteries).

Their last stop was to a hardware store where he purchased fifty yards of black wire, a box of number six nails, a sleeve of brass rads, epoxy glue, a one-by-one six-foot board, carpenter's saw, eight four-inch threaded galvanized pipes (with end caps), a box of large number six rubber bands, a Black and Decker drill (with a carbide drill bit) and a box of wooden clothespins.

"Okay, Vick, where next?" Ruth asked.

"Next is the ultimate weapon all armies operate on—food! How about a late lunch back in G'Burg? Something nice, like smoked rainbow trout with a glass or two of Chablis," he suggested.

"How can you be so cavalier about this, Vick? I feel like I'm part of a terrorist team after going all over the place getting this stuff! How are you going to use all of this?"

"I'll show you when we get back to the cabin tonight, but first I need to relax with some good food, good wine, and some good company. I need to stop off at that little store and get some carbohydrate stuff on the way back, but right now I need to loosen up. You up for it?" he asked.

"Okay, what do you have in mind?" she said, somewhat annoyed.

"Oh, I don't know, a late lunch, dancing with disco music—I do a mean 'Hustle.'"

"I think you're out of your mind, but I'm starving so I'll settle for the late lunch," she said, turning her head to look out the passenger window.

They drove into Gatlinburg where Victor parked in a municipal parking lot. They then walked five blocks to a restaurant called the Trout House. They requested a table near the back, which afforded them some degree of privacy and was also in the smoking section.

Over lunch, they discussed many things but stayed away from the subject of Victor's trip the next day. She asked him some questions about his past. He told her about his marriage to Cathy, her illness, and his moving to Knoxville at Buddy and Donna's suggestion, and she

Chapter Fifteen

expressed her deep sympathy. He talked more of Buddy and Donna and told her some of his experiences in Vietnam.

She, in turn, discussed her past, the hospital, and related that she had never been married but had had a brief relationship with a surgeon, which had ended two years previously, citing his extreme self-centeredness as the primary reason. They each ordered desert and coffee, and left the restaurant about four o'clock.

Driving back to White Horse's cabin, they were both more relaxed, and Ruth remarked about various shops that she would like to visit at some future time. On the way home, they stopped off at a little supermarket near the Reservation, where Victor picked up some candy bars and toiletries while Ruth got some groceries for supper and breakfast the next morning.

They arrived back at the cabin around five, and Victor told her he had some work to do in preparation for his trip. Ruth went into the little kitchen while Victor unpacked his purchases in the living room.

"Victor, come in here please," she said, sounding a little surprised.

He walked into the kitchen and said, "What? Do you need..."

Looking down on the kitchen table he saw the object of her interest. It was a Colt AR-15 rifle, the civilian counterpart of the famous M-16 used by the military. Attached to it was a night vision 'Starlight' scope. There were also six twenty round ammunition clips and several boxes of shells. Lying beside all of it was a note—*"Thought you might need some additional protection while checking out the records. Good luck!"* It was signed *White Horse*.

"That White Horse, he doesn't miss a trick, does he?" Victor said.

"That is an evil looking weapon, Victor, what is that big thing on top, some kind of scope?"

"It's an assault rifle, and that thing, as you refer to it, is a starlite night vision scope. It's like a rifle scope, but if you look through it at night, then everything looks like it would in daylight, except it's kind of green colored."

He took the rifle and ammunition into the living area, then went out on the porch with the items purchased from the hardware store and went to work.

SmokeFire!

Ruth built a fire in the large fireplace, and about an hour later she came out with two glasses and a bottle of Chablis she had gotten at the store.

"What on earth are you making, Victor?"

"I call 'em 'poor man's claymores,'" he said.

"What's a claymore?"

"It's a type of antipersonnel explosive used by the military for defensive operations. It's like a mine, but it can also be detonated on command. They set them up around their encampments for defense and along trails as booby traps."

"Why are you making bombs, Victor?"

"Not bombs exactly, and like I said before, until I know what I'm up against, I'm not taking any chances. I'm going to be back in there overnight and I'll use these devices to set up a defensive perimeter."

"How do they work?" she asked, while looking down at all the parts.

"Well, first I empty out the powder and shot from eight shotgun shells, then I place one live shell into the pipe, and pour the shot and powder around the live round," he explained, showing her the last one, which he had just started to build. "I drill a hole in this screw-on pipe cap, then screw both caps on each end of the pipe. I bend a nail, on the back here, then I drill a small hole in this wooden block, which I cut off of that board there," pointing to the pine board. "I use the epoxy and glue the little block onto the cap, lining up the holes of the block and pipe cap. Then, when I'm out in the field, I'll string this black wire, say, between two trees. One end of the wire is tied to a tree, and the other has this clothespin on it. I take this rubber band, loop one end around the bent nail, and put the other in between the clasps of the clothespin. Now, if somebody trips the wire, the clothespin will separate from the rubber band, which will cause it to spring forward releasing the nail. The nail will hit the primer on the shotgun shell inside the pipe, and when it goes off, it will ignite the gunpowder placed around it, and whammo! The pipe explodes. Should kill or seriously maim anyone within about a ten-foot radius, I'm hoping. Pretty clever, huh?"

"Where did you learn to do this, Victor, in Vietnam?"

Chapter Fifteen

"Not exactly how to construct this device, I just made that up, but they did teach us to improvise. Buddy was really good at improvising. One time we took these M-40 grenades, and..."

"Vick, I'm really not in the mood for any war stories, with you going up there tomorrow and all. I really wish you'd reconsider. All this, this 'stuff'," she said, pointing to his handiwork, "scares me to death!"

"Ruth, we've been over this," he said while taking a sip of the wine. "I know you're scared, and I'm scared too, but I have to do this. I've come this far and I'm not going to turn back now. At least I know now that I'm getting close to something, and that something is up there and I'm going to find it. I owe it to Buddy and Donna."

"Vick, that something, as you call it, could get you killed. Please, I really care about you, and I don't want to lose you," she said, pleadingly. "Please don't go. Let's call Richter and go back tomorrow. It'll be okay. It's the sensible thing to do, and you know it."

Refilling their wine glasses, he said, "Ruth, I really care about you too, and you're right, it is the sensible thing to do. These people, whoever they are, probably killed my best friends, killed Russell, and tried to kill us. I'm not going to stand for that. There's not going to be any legal 'due process' here. My due process is going to come out the end of the barrel of the rifle that White Horse left. I know you don't like it, but that's the kind of man I am. Whatever *it* is, is up there, and I'm going to find it, and when I do, there's going to be hell to pay. I didn't start this, but I'm damn sure going to finish it, one way or the other!"

She raised herself off the porch railing that she had been leaning against and came and sat next to him. Setting her wine glass down on the little table among his 'claymores,' she put her arm around him and before he knew what was happening, kissed him fully on the lips.

"I've wanted to do that since last night, Vick," she said, sitting back and taking his hand. "I think I know what kind of man you are, and I know we haven't known each other but a few days. God, I can't believe I'm saying this," she said, releasing his hand and picking up her wine. "When I said I really care about you, I wasn't being totally truthful. I think I'm falling in love with you—I know it's stupid! But that's how I feel. There, I said it!" she said, sitting back on the bench.

"I'm glad you did." He leaned over and took her in his arms. Placing his mouth near her ear, he said, "I think I'm falling in love with you too!"

They held each other in a long embrace. With the setting sun and the accompaniment of spring crickets behind them, Victor felt something he had thought he would never feel again.

Later Ruth fixed dinner while Victor packed his gear. They ate on the floor in front of the fireplace and finished off the bottle of wine.

After dinner, they sat and talked, briefly about their feelings for each other, and of the past and the future, with each skirting the issue of any future that they might share.

"What time are we going to leave tomorrow?" Ruth asked.

"I want to enter the trail just before daybreak," Victor replied. "I want to go in while it's still dark, so set your alarm for about four-thirty, okay?"

Tentatively Ruth asked, "Will you sleep in my room tonight Victor? With me?"

"I'll sleep in your room with you, like last night, but, well..."

"I understand, Victor," Ruth interjected, "I shouldn't have asked, I'm sorry," she said, reaching across the table to his hand.

"Don't apologize. I haven't been with a woman since Cathy died."

"You don't have to explain anything, Victor."

"I want to. I want you to know how I feel," he said. "For a few years after she died, I was still grieving and I missed her so much I couldn't even think about another woman. Then, after that, grieving just kind of got to be a habit, I guess. It isn't about any false sense of loyalty I have towards Cathy, it's just," he hesitated and then said, "that, well—"

Hearing the sadness in his voice, she said, "Oh, Victor," and reached across the table and took his hand into both of hers. "I'm so sorry, I know it must be very difficult."

Regaining his composure, he smiled and said, "It was difficult, but it's different now. I meant what I said earlier, about falling in love with you. I just kind of need to work up to it, being intimate, I mean. Again, it doesn't have anything to do with Cathy, really."

"I would understand if it did, and I want you to know that."

"It doesn't, but if it did, then I'd tell you."

Chapter Fifteen

"I haven't been with anyone in a long time either," Ruth said. "It's a big step for both of us."

Putting his hand over hers, he said, "Yes, it is. And I want our first time to be special. When all of this is over, we'll put it behind us and spend a weekend together, an intimate one. I look forward to it. All right?" he asked.

"I look forward to it too, Victor," she said, then continued with, "I'm worried sick about you going in there tomorrow."

"Ruth, I'll be okay," he reassured her. "It's like I said earlier. I've had a lot of training in the military for situations just like this one, and I'm going in prepared."

"But that was a long time ago, Victor, and you're a lot older now."

"That's true," he said, "and a lot more cautious. I was really good at it, and learned a lot from Buddy because he'd done a tour in Vietnam before I got there. He used to call it the 'jungle creep'".

"Jungle creep?" Ruth asked.

"Yeah. We used to sneak up on enemy encampments and gather intelligence, then slip back out. We got so good at it they nicknamed our group the 'Sneaky Pete's.'"

"Well," Ruth said, "I still don't like it."

"Don't worry. I'll be fine. Now, let's go up and get some sleep," Victor said, standing.

They slept as they had the night before, with Victor in his slacks and Ruth wearing her jersey. However, this time they fell asleep in each other's arms.

Chapter Sixteen

5:30 a.m. Wednesday morning, April 28, 1999
Great Smoky Mountains National Park
Western Boundary Line, near Panther Creek

"Don't stop at the bridge. Drive on past about five hundred yards or so," Victor said, pointing down the road.

They passed the place where Panther Creek flowed into the Chilhowee River, through a large tunnel underneath the road. Ruth, who was driving the Jeep, pulled off into a gravel pullover and stopped the engine.

"Oh, Victor, the weather's horrible," she said, "It's raining cats and dogs."

"The weather's perfect! In the words of Charlemagne, 'let the birds, the rocks, and mountains be my army,' or something like that. This will provide good cover, and bad weather generally makes for poor performance of most untrained soldiers."

"You think there's soldiers up there?" she asked.

"A figure of speech," Victor replied.

"Why didn't we stop at Panther Creek?"

SmokeFire!

"Again, I don't know what we're dealing with, and I don't know who's watching. So I thought it would be a good idea to enter here, then I can cut back northeast and intercept the area near the creek," Victor explained.

"There's nobody within miles. The only thing we passed was that rock quarry operation across the river from Panther Creek," Ruth said.

"Yeah, Appalachia Stone, or at least I think that's what McAllister said it was called. A limestone quarry that evidently doesn't hire local labor. Anyway, I don't want to take any chances, so I'll jump off here."

He looked at the waterproof map one more time, before folding and placing it in the backpack, which was in the back compartment behind the seat. Then he leaned over and took Ruth's hand.

"Remember our plan. I have three cell phone battery packs fully charged. My phone will be set on silent ring. Even so, don't call me unless it's an absolute emergency. I'll check in with you periodically when I can. Don't worry, even though I know you will. I'll be all right."

Reaching over, he kissed her, and she hugged his neck with both arms. "Come back to me, Vick."

"I will, you be careful, too, baby." He stepped out of the Jeep, reached behind the rear seat and removed his backpack—which contained his claymores, shotgun, and other equipment. He then removed the AR-15 and slung it over his shoulder. Ruth started the engine, and Victor shut the door. As she drove away, she looked into the rearview mirror, but he had already disappeared into the deep undergrowth.

* * *

Victor scrambled up a niche in the rock face and dropped down among a copse of mountain laurel. Laying the backpack aside, he put on the rain poncho, and applied the night cream in green and black streaks across his face, using a small makeup mirror that Ruth had given him. He then put the black and green bush hat on and fixed the brim so the rain wouldn't run down his neck. He left the poncho's hood down so that it wouldn't interfere with his hearing and then put the backpack back on. Then he got out the map and compass and double-checked his position.

Chapter Sixteen

Okay, Vick, time to do the jungle creep, he said to himself.

He moved due east and came to Abrams Creek, where he snaked up behind some rocks and peeked around the side, scanning both banks of the creek. The area was clear, the water was moving swiftly, and he gauged its depth at one or two feet. The creek was about thirty feet wide here, and he crossed it quickly in a low crouch. Reaching the other side, he scrambled through a gap in the boulders and surveyed the woods. There was no trail, and the undergrowth was dense. The rain was coming down steadily, and when he squatted down to listen, all he could hear were the raindrops hitting leaves. Moving quickly he came to a small ridgeline and scrambled up the slope. As the first light of dawn was appearing in the east, he lay down among the leaves and scanned the ridge top with his binoculars.

Seeing nothing suspicious after ten minutes, he crossed over the ridge and dropped down the slope about three hundred yards, stopping periodically to listen and observe. He moved another couple of hundred yards and heard the sound of rushing water. Checking the map, he determined that he was near the north bank of Panther Creek.

His plan was to follow the creek upstream, avoiding the bank so as not to expose himself. The ridgeline paralleled Panther Creek, and he followed it upstream, staying undercover about fifty yards from the edge of the bank.

After about a mile upstream, he found a rock outcropping that was covered with rhododendron. He climbed up the back of the rocks, dropped the backpack, and slowly crept to the edge, staying low beneath the branches.

He set the rifle next to him and lay down, looking left and right. The outcropping provided an excellent vantage point from which to watch the area without being seen. He could see about a hundred yards both up and down stream, and he could also see into the bushes on the opposite bank. He decided he would stop here and keep watch for an hour or so. Getting out a Snickers candy bar, he unwrapped it and ate it. Buddy had taught them to eat candy while in Vietnam for the carbohydrates, to keep their energy level up.

He pulled some branches down nearer to the ground, which gave him extra cover, and settled in to keep watch. As he lay there with the rain rattling the leaves, he thought of Ruth. He had forgotten how good it felt to hold a woman close and to be held. She was like no other woman he had known—warm and caring and, at the same time, strong and resolute.

Get a grip, Vick! Don't let your mind wander! Focus!

He put everything out of his mind and maintained his vigilance over the area, lying completely still for the next hour. *Remember, patience is a weapon*, he recalled from his training.

Unlike a reconnaissance in Vietnam, he didn't know exactly what he was looking for, so he had to move more cautiously and be observant for anything out of the ordinary. Sometimes, the best way to be observant, he remembered, was to hide and watch.

Seeing nothing, he picked up the rifle and crawled backwards to where he had left the backpack, then moved back down the rock outcropping.

He checked the map again and moved upstream about a mile to where the creek bent back to the left. The rain had slacked off somewhat, but it was heavily overcast, and a light mist hung in the air.

The ridgeline was lower here, and he decided to move farther back from the creek. The going was tough as he picked his way through the deep undergrowth. About sixty yards back from the creek, he came upon a small game trail. Bending down, he examined the ground's surface for ten feet in both directions. He saw deer droppings, an occasional deer hoof print, but nothing else.

Being careful where he stepped so as not to leave any footprints, he followed the game trail that paralleled the creek and kept an eye out for other signs of human passage but saw nothing. After about another half-mile, the creek bent back to the right. The undergrowth was extremely dense between the game trail and the creek itself, so he left the trail and moved in closer to the creek.

When he was about twenty yards from the creek, he dropped the backpack and lay down in a prone position. Keeping his rifle in front of him, he crawled on his stomach until he reached a dense copse of undergrowth. He carefully separated the branches and looked out over the creek, which was about forty yards wide.

On the opposite bank was a small glade surrounded by large old trees of various types. He looked through the binoculars and checked the area.

Chapter Sixteen

What a beautiful place, he thought. The water in the bend was calm and deep. As he was looking along the far bank, he heard a noise, which seemed to come from the right on the opposite shore. He laid down the binoculars, reached behind him and carefully drew the rifle up, sighting it in the direction where he had heard the sound.

There it is again, something moving about ten yards outside the glade, he thought. His pulse quickened, and his breath was rapid and shallow. Memories of Vietnam flashed in his mind, and he remembered how afraid he had been as his team had stealthily moved through jungle.

Control your fear, Vick, he thought as he slowed his breathing and willed himself to calm down.

He lay perfectly still with the rifle butt against his right shoulder and his finger on the trigger. The only sound was the rain falling on the leaves and splattering on his bush hat.

He measured his breathing and waited as he kept the rifle sighted on the opposite bank.

Come on out, show yourself.

There was a crash as the branches of the thick undergrowth on the opposite bank parted. Instinctively, Victor took a deep breath and held it, preparing to fire.

At that moment, a large buck deer jumped through the mountain laurel and cautiously approached the creek at the edge of the deep pool.

A deer, and a big one at that! Must be about an eight point! As he lay the rifle down in front of him, he noticed that his hands were shaking.

He watched as the deer drank from the creek, occasionally looking up. After about five minutes, the deer moved off into the forest, and Victor back-crawled to where his backpack lay.

He opened the backpack, took out the cell phone, and dialed Ruth's cell number. After one ring he pressed the end key and replaced the phone in his backpack. This was the signal they had worked out to let her know that everything was okay.

Oh sure—everything's okay, baby, although a deer almost gave me a heart attack!

He put the backpack on and moved back into the bush away from the creek, then proceeded upstream.

SmokeFire!

* * *

Cooper came bursting into Bill Richter's office, "I just got a hit on Ruth Jeffers's cell phone, sir. It lasted only about two seconds, but it was enough for the cell company to get a general fix."

"What area?" Richter said, looking up from the desk.

"The signal hit two towers, one on Chilhowee Mountain near Look Rock, and the other in Gatlinburg. The weaker signal hit Chilhowee Mountain."

"If that's Scofield calling her, and I bet it is, then that means he's in the Gatlinburg area. Damn, what is he up to? Get Pike on the phone and warn him Scofield might be in the area. Also contact the Gatlinburg police department, and tell the cell company to keep monitoring her number. I want to know immediately if there's any more activity," Richter ordered.

* * *

Victor stopped among a cluster of mountain laurel and checked his position on the map. It was now about two o'clock, and he calculated he'd covered about a mile and a half as the crow flies. He wished he had had the photographs that he took from the helicopter, as he could have looked them over last night and maybe searched out the best trail.

It was slow going with the harsh terrain and dense undergrowth. That, coupled with having to move stealthily through the forest, caused him to cover only about a quarter of a mile each hour. After verifying his position, he sat down among the bushes, took out another candy bar, and thought about his operational plan.

He felt at an extreme disadvantage because of not knowing what he was looking for. Whatever it was, he concluded it would probably not be obvious, so he had to pay close attention to details.

What are the details, he thought. *What could they be? Terrain, trails, signs of passage?*

He was feeling discouraged, as he had only the rest of the afternoon, tonight, and tomorrow to come up with something. Then he had to turn

Chapter Sixteen

back and surrender to the FBI. *And let the chips fall where they may*, he thought.

He put the candy wrapper back into his backpack so as not to leave any sign of his passage. He checked his camouflage face cream in the little mirror, touched it up, and strapped the backpack on. He picked up the rifle and dried it off with a small rag, and then headed north upstream.

The temperature had dropped from the mid-sixties to the mid-fifties and there was a chill in the air. He had purchased a light field jacket at the army surplus store, but had elected not to put it on, so that he might have freedom of movement. It had started raining again, hard this time, and with the sound of thunder overhead, he trudged on. The mist rolled down the mountainside and visibility was becoming limited.

After about five hundred yards, the terrain became extremely harsh. There was a cliff face off to his left about a hundred yards away, and he was only about thirty yards from the creek. *If I get caught here, I'm in a world of hurt*, he thought, as the only places he could retreat to were either up or down stream. *Perfect ambush site. Be careful!* He was moving slowly in a low crouch as he advanced towards the cliff face for better concealment. It was pouring rain, and flashes of lightning amidst the thunder were coming about every ten seconds. He crawled up to within about ten yards of the cliff face, and the undergrowth was so thick he had to pick his way among the small branches. The sky had grown dark, and the heavy mist was getting thicker. He stopped and crouched down to listen, but could hear nothing above the din of the heavy rain and thunder.

This place is like something from a horror movie, he thought. He was getting cold, and the rain, the mist, and the thunder and lightning only heightened his anxiety. A large drop of cold rainwater fell onto his neck and trickled down his back, and he began to shiver.

Ignore the weather! Control the fear! Stay focused! If I can't hear them, they can't hear me, he thought. Gathering his courage, he got up and went further north.

After another few hundred yards the creek changed course to a more easterly direction. He stopped among a cluster of boulders near the cliff face. There was one large overhanging rock, and he crawled underneath it and unstrapped the backpack. Taking out the map and compass, he determined that he was a half-mile due west of Tarklln Ridge. Despite the rain poncho, his clothes were soaked, and he was beginning to get cold. He ate another candy bar, wiped off the rifle again, and headed east around the bend of the creek, fighting discouragement.

The terrain began to flatten out, and just ahead there appeared to be a small clearing. He dropped the backpack, and with his rifle in the ready position, slowly low crawled towards the edge of the undergrowth.

There was something man-made in the clearing, but with the rain and mist, he couldn't make out what it was. Reaching the fringe of the undergrowth, he slowly parted the bushes with the barrel of the rifle.

It's the old abandoned mine site I saw from the helicopter, he thought.

Taking the binoculars out of his pocket, he scanned the area. He counted three ore cars, two of them still sitting on rusting track and the third overturned about twenty yards back. There were many small saplings in the area, but he could still make out the old junk scattered among them.

He watched the area for about thirty minutes, and then decided it warranted further examination. To break cover and go walking in would be foolish, so he low-crawled back to where he'd dropped the backpack and piled some leaves over it. He then moved about a hundred yards north and circled around to the opposite corner of the site. Finding good cover among some bushes, he observed the site for another half hour. Seeing nothing, he decided to approach it. *Combat approach, Vick*, he thought, *be careful!*

Keeping the rifle pointed in his line of sight, he quickly crossed the open area, staying as low as possible, and dropped behind the overturned ore car. He scanned left and right, and then peeked around the bottom edge of the car. He could hear his pulse pounding in his ear, not from the exertion but from the tension.

Get a grip, Vick, be cool and calm down.

Prior to their first insertion in Vietnam, Buddy had leaned over in the helicopter and looked Victor directly in the eye, saying, "Sir, the first rule of combat is to just relax and take a deep breath—don't panic!"

Chapter Sixteen

He took a couple of deep breaths and tried to calm down. He scooted to the other side of the ore car, peeked around its edge, and again saw nothing.

He took stock of the site, noticing a number of rusted old tools, chains, and implements. Judging by their rust, they must have been here over a hundred years.

Lightning flashed, and a second later a thunderclap followed. He low-crawled to where the other two ore cars sat on the small mine gauge tracks, squatted down on one knee, and looked around. He was so fully alert now it seemed that everything was in slow motion, and he could see every detail where his eyesight fell.

Looking up at the ore cars, which were covered with rust, he noticed something. On one ore car the rust was worn off along the top edge. It was only a small area, but...

There's another one, he thought, *no rust there either*. They were about three feet apart, and he quickly scanned the bush line at the edge of the site. Seeing nothing, he approached the car.

The top of the ore car was about six feet high, and looking at the worn areas, he decided that someone must have pulled himself up to look inside, and rubbed off the rust. He looked down and noticed that along a flange at the bottom of the car were two worn places as well. Bending down, he examined them carefully. There was some black residue on the right one.

This is where they put their feet, he thought, *to boost themselves up*.

Rubbing his finger along the spot, he removed some of the black residue and held it underneath his nose.

Rubber—rubber soled boots!

He took a quick look around and boosted himself up to look inside the car in the same manner as the previous person had done, while being careful not to place his hands or feet on the same places.

He saw only a few old rocks inside. Stepping back down, he examined the marks his hands and feet had made, and they were identical. There was also some black residue where he had placed his feet.

Combat boots! The other guy had worn combat boots?

Most hikers, Victor knew, preferred standard hiking boots, which, he recalled from seeing them in the stores, had brown or tan soles.

SmokeFire!

Looking back up at the top of the ore car, he thought, *Buddy? Was this Buddy? Had he been here?*

Buddy had always worn combat boots on their previous trips, just like the ones Victor was wearing now, preferring their fit to that of hiking boots.

He'd been here! Buddy had been here! Knowing Buddy, Victor thought, his curiosity would have made him look inside the car. He scanned the area, thinking that Buddy and Donna may have set up camp at this site, as it was close to the stream, and the open area provided a good campsite location. He carefully grid-searched the entire site, looking for signs of a campsite but found nothing. Over to his right, away from the ore cars, he noticed several dying saplings. He approached the area and examined the small trees, which, like the others, were only about two feet tall. They seemed to be dehydrated, but nothing else was unusual. On a hunch, he went to the edge of the tree line and looked at the branches.

Yes, there! And there too! Someone had removed small branches from the dead trees.

They had been here! This is where they made camp! Buddy had taught Victor, among many other things, about how to build a fire in the rain by using small branches still attached to the trees.

His adrenaline was rushing now, and he crouched down among the trees and took stock of the area.

If they had been here, why don't I see any other signs? He silently asked himself.

It was now nearing five o'clock, and it was too late to move on farther upstream. Besides, this was his first real lead, so he decided to follow it up.

He carefully made his way back to where he'd left his backpack and brought it down to the rail cars. The rain had slacked off again, and he made a campsite by clearing away some of the saplings while always keeping his rifle nearby and maintaining a vigilant watch for signs of danger.

He thoroughly surveyed the area before getting out his claymores. He set them up at various points near the campsite, stringing the trip wires no more than ten feet as he wasn't sure of the blast radius.

Chapter Sixteen

Should've tested one to make sure they worked and to assess their damage effectiveness, he thought.

Although sunset occurred around eight o'clock this time of year, it was starting to get dark around seven due to the overcast sky. He had previously removed some small branches from the dead trees and placed them within a circle of stones. He had also gathered up some larger stuff that was sitting nearby.

Throughout this process, he stopped periodically and faded back into the tree line to watch, making sure that no one caught him by surprise.

He took out the sleeping bag, filled it with leaves, and placed it about ten feet from where the fire would be. Then he strung the backpack up a small tree, suspending it about seven feet off the ground where it would be visible.

He stood back and surveyed the site. Satisfied that everything looked good, he lit the fire, picked up his rifle and headed back into the trees, being careful to avoid the trip wires.

"High ground, sir. Always choose the high ground to provide a clear field of fire," Buddy had said. Victor chose a spot that was about twenty feet above the campsite but only thirty yards away, off to the right.

He made his way up the embankment and cut several bushes away so as to provide a good field of fire without the rifle being obstructed by the branches. He had brought along the starlite scope and the infrared scope from the backpack. The first he attached to his rifle and the second he laid down in the grass close by.

All his preparations completed, he lay down at the edge of the embankment and spread the field jacket over his back; then he covered himself and the rifle with the cuttings and settled down to wait. It was now eight o'clock, and the miserable drizzle had begun again.

He called Ruth's cell phone, let it ring once, and then disconnected. He wanted to hear her voice, but didn't want to risk making any noise. He had never been so cold, so lonely, and so afraid. Unlike Vietnam, he didn't have his team concealed around him. He had been afraid then, but had found some solace in knowing that his friends were close by. He was alone here, facing an unknown enemy, and the fear was almost unbearable. As he lay shivering, with the rain falling and the darkness

SmokeFire!

closing in, he thought seriously of calling Ruth and telling her to get White Horse and his men to come in and get him. He could hide deep in the bushes and wait for them to arrive, and then walk out and turn himself in to the FBI.

No, I've come this far, he thought, *there's no turning back now.* He picked up the rifle and placed it against his shoulder. Under his breath, he quietly said, *Okay! Party time! The door's open. Come on in!*

* * *

It was eleven o'clock, and the rain had stopped about an hour earlier. He had had to make a trip down to the campsite after it stopped raining to put more wood on the fire. He had crept up to the edge of the firelight and quickly thrown several large logs onto the hot coals before retreating back to his post.

His arms were cramping from holding the rifle for so long while in the prone position. He occasionally picked up the infrared scope, which could detect heat, and scanned the area, but saw nothing. He had not turned on the battery for the starlite night vision scope, as he wanted to conserve power.

He pulled another candy bar out of his pocket and was getting ready to unwrap it when he thought he heard a noise off to the left of the campsite.

He dropped the candy bar, picked up the rifle, and activated the starlite scope. He quickly scanned the area through the scope and saw movement: a light green blob amidst darker green.

Oh, God! Here we go! Potential target on the left, forty yards, he thought. He swung the rifle to the right and searched the area.

Second target, range thirty yards! Opposite approach patterns! Crossfire setup!

His pulse pounded in his ear as he swung the rifle back to the first target.

He lowered the starlite in time to see a red eye materialize from the proximity of the first target.

Laser sight! he thought, just as there was a phut, phut, silent noise.

The sleeping bag jumped with the impact of the rounds. *Silencers! Bastards are using silencers!*

Chapter Sixteen

He swung the rifle back towards target number two. A large red eye, the hallmark of the laser sight, was approaching through the bushes.

Using the starlite, he sighted in on target number two.

A small individual stood up among the bushes, and Victor could discern the classic shooter's stance even through the starlite. He brought the crosshair down to just below his throat and squeezed the trigger, firing a single shot. The four point flash suppresser guided the muzzle flash away from the starlite. Although the light temporarily blinded Victor, he could still see target number two drop his weapon and fall to the ground.

Swinging the rifle back to target number one, he quickly tried to draw a sight picture, but the target had heard the gunshot—as Victor's weapon wasn't silenced—and was retreating over to the right.

He rapidly fired four rounds in a spread pattern, shooting right to left. Just then there was an explosion, followed by a loud scream.

Found one of my claymores, didn't you, pal?

His fear temporarily forgotten, Victor rolled quickly to his left, and then slithered down the backside of the embankment.

Moving swiftly in a crouched over position, he circled back to behind where the explosion had taken place. He crouched among the bushes and waited, but all he could hear was moaning, about thirty yards ahead.

He sighted the starlite and saw a man writhing among the bushes, rolling back and forth. Victor was closer now, and he raised the Starlite, swung it left, and saw that the other target was down and still.

Kill shot!

He crept up to within about ten feet of the wounded man, and even through the darkness, he could see that he was seriously wounded.

He performed a fast scan of the area through the night vision scope but saw nothing. Standing up, he approached the wounded man.

The man wore a long-sleeved dark blue jumpsuit and lay on his back. Both of his legs had been completely blown off just below the knees, and Victor could see he was going into shock. His small Heckler and Koch HK-94 assault weapon lay in the grass a few feet away.

SmokeFire!

Victor approached him and kicked the weapon away. Looking down at him, Victor could see that he was oriental. Not Japanese, definitely not Vietnamese—*maybe Korean?*

"Why are you here?" Victor asked, while pointing the rifle at the man's face.

He was obviously in a tremendous amount of pain; his face was contorted and he was groaning loudly. Raising himself up about six inches with his left hand, he moaned.

"Don't move!" Victor commanded while keeping the rifle trained on his head. "I asked you why you are here."

The man grimaced, then spat at Victor and reached inside his jumpsuit.

Without hesitating, Victor fired a single shot that hit his target between the eyes. Opening the jumpsuit, Victor removed a small black pistol and threw it into the bushes.

He searched both bodies but found no identification of any kind. They were both oriental, wore identical jumpsuits, and carried the same type of weapons. They also wore identical wristwatches, cheap Japanese chronographs.

He took both bodies and, hefting them over the edge, dumped them into one of the ore cars. Then he took one of the weapons, and after removing the thirty round clip, threw it into the creek. The other he took with him. He then disarmed his booby trap claymores and stashed them along with the HK-94 and extra clip in the backpack.

Returning to the embankment he retrieved the infrared scope. As he placed the scope inside the pack and hefted it up, his hands were shaking from the adrenaline of the last few minutes. He felt absolutely no remorse about killing the two men. In all likelihood, he thought, these were the guys who killed Buddy and Donna. *But why?*

They're protecting something, he thought, *same uniforms, same professional weapons, and same wristwatches—organized!*

He needed to abandon his previous position in case someone had seen or heard his gunshots. Looking up, he saw that he could climb higher on the embankment where there was a gap in the rocks. After scrambling up the slope about a hundred feet, Victor was just below Tarklln Ridge and had a full view of Panther Creek below him. He

Chapter Sixteen

dropped the backpack and, taking the rifle and infrared scope, climbed up onto a large rock.

He scanned the area with the starlite, but saw nothing. Setting the rifle down, he picked up the infrared scope and sighted down to the campsite. He could see a deep red area at one of the rail cars from the residual heat being given off by the two bodies. The heat from the campfire appeared almost white.

He lowered the infrared scope, and from his high vantage point, Victor could look down Panther Creek from the bend to perhaps a half-mile downstream.

He raised the infrared scope back up to his eye and looked downstream, trying to determine if anyone else was moving towards his position.

What the hell?

He swung the scope in the opposite direction, and saw the same anomaly. As he turned the scope downstream, then back up, he thought, *What the hell* is *that?*

He saw a series of large red patches through the scope, not paralleling the creek, but forming a straight line from downstream to the slope of Tarklln Ridge. They appeared to be about two hundred feet apart and looked like large red landing lights on an airport runway, although some were brighter than others.

Studying them through the scope, he decided that they were stationary and must be about five feet in diameter.

Heat spots! Symmetrical—man made!

Looking to his left upstream, he noticed that they deviated from the far edge of the creek and stopped about five hundred yards to the east.

He put the infrared scope in his backpack, strapped it on, picked up the rifle, and headed toward the closest heat source.

Chapter Seventeen

3:00 a.m. Thursday morning, April 29, 1999
Great Smoky Mountains National Park
Panther Creek, at the slope of Tarklln Ridge

It had taken Victor two hours to cover the distance to the heat spot, stopping along the way to get his bearings. He had been forced to cross Panther Creek just below Tarklln Ridge's southern slope, and was now on the eastern bank of the creek. Taking out the infrared scope, he fixed the position of the last heat spot, which was his destination.

It appeared much larger now through the scope, and he calculated that it was maybe two hundred yards away. Stealthily moving up the short slope, he reached it in about forty-five minutes.

Whatever the heat spot was, it appeared to be embedded just beneath a small rock face about twenty feet high. Circling around, he watched the entire area through the infrared scope for about ten minutes before approaching it.

Parting the undergrowth, he came upon a large, heavy metal grate that was tilted at about a thirty-degree angle and sat flush with the ground. It was hinged and secured with a massive lock. He leaned down and looked through the grate but could see only darkness, although he could hear a faint whirring sound and feel a slight breeze coming from inside.

Examining the heavy lock, he surmised that shooting it probably wouldn't even dent it. Dropping his backpack, he got out two of his claymores and some wire, and packed the claymores next to the lock. He attached the wire to the clothespins and set them underneath a rock; then he backed out as he laid down his black trip wires. After moving about fifty feet way, he laid down the small wire spools and went back to the grate. Then he attached the clothespins to the rubber bands, attached the firing pins to the claymores, and retreated back to where he had left the spools.

Picking up both wires he stretched them, feeling the tension in the rubber bands. After looking around, he crouched down behind a log and simultaneously jerked both wires.

The result seemed like a single explosion, and he felt the concussion wave from the blast. Dropping the wires, he grabbed his flashlight, rope, and rifle and scrambled back to the grate, where he found that the lock had been blown apart. Removing the lock fragments, he swung the grate over and shone the flashlight down inside.

The shaft was definitely man made and fairly recently too, as there were many scratches and small drill holes along the jagged sides, probably left from drilling tools.

This is stupid, Vick, he thought. *Go back and tell White Horse about it—let them handle it. But let them handle what?*

He felt the fear slipping back in. He needed to think, so he sat down and turned off the flashlight. It was so dark he could barely see the ground, which didn't help his state of mind.

Tell them what? That I killed two guys up in Panther Creek and dumped their bodies into an old ore car? he thought. *Oh, and yeah, I found some kind of shaft and blew it open—hey, that's what it's all about. You guys need to check it out!*

Since it was on Park property, White Horse would have no authority. They would have to get Pike involved, and Victor would end up in jail faster than the FBI could say 'serial murderer.'

Chapter Seventeen

There would be only his word about the two Koreans he'd killed. If this was some kind of conspiracy, it wouldn't take them long to cover their tracks. *No, I need more evidence*, he thought.

He remembered the tunnel rats in Vietnam, specially trained personnel who would descend into enemy tunnels filled with booby traps. One of them had once told him that it was the scariest thing he'd ever done. Looking over at the shaft opening, Victor now knew what he'd meant. The thought of descending into the dark unknown sent a shiver of fear down his back.

I don't have any choice, he said to himself, *this has to be what it's all about. I've got to get more evidence.*

He stood up and turned on the flashlight. When he shone the light into the shaft, he couldn't see the bottom. There was no ladder, and he could see no footholds. Taking the coil of rope, he tied one end to a tree and threw the coil into the darkness of the tunnel. He slung the rifle over his shoulder by the strap. Then, calling upon all his inner strength, he let out a deep breath and descended through the opening. He had never felt more alone or more afraid as he dropped down into the darkness.

He stopped about ten feet down on a protruding rock and shone the flashlight downward. The whirring was louder now, and he memorized the positions of extruding rocks as he couldn't hold the flashlight and descend at the same time.

Putting the flashlight in his front pocket, he slowly dropped down the shaft while holding the rope, covering about three feet with each drop. Periodically he would stop and shine the flashlight down, picking out his stopping points. The mechanical whirring became louder, and the turbulence increased as he descended into the shaft. There was a musty smell, and a slight mist was circulating making the sides of the shaft wet.

After about a hundred feet, he stopped, pointed the flashlight down, and saw what he thought to be the bottom of the shaft about twenty feet below. When he switched off the flashlight, he could see light below him.

He carefully made his way down, and just short of the shaft opening, he stopped and tied the rope around his waist. Laying his rifle and flashlight on a protruding rock ledge, he turned upside down and, lowering his head beneath the opening, he looked left and right.

There was an extremely large industrial fan bolted into the side of an immense cavern, directed upwards into the shaft. The wind from it blew at him furiously, as he was only about three feet from the cage that covered the fan.

He lifted himself back up, untied the rope, and threw the remaining coil down onto the base of the cavern while directing it around the edge of the fan. Slinging the rifle around his shoulder, he stood on top of the caged fan housing, intending to drop over the edge and slide down onto the rock floor about twenty feet below.

He grabbed the rope with both hands and stepped off of the fan housing onto a small rock that jutted from the side of the shaft. The rock gave way and he banged his shin hard on the jagged edge, causing him to lose his grip on the rope.

He fell to the bottom of the shaft, crying out in pain as he hit the rocky bottom.

Crawling to the tunnel wall, he unslung the rifle and examined his shin. It was bleeding from a large gash. He removed the rag from his pocket that he'd used to dry off the rifle, and tied it around his calf. The other cuts he'd suffered in the fall were painful, but not as serious.

Crouching down, he moved along the edge of the cavern wall and looked around, keeping the rifle in a ready position. To his left he saw two large mercury vapor lights attached to a portable industrial light rack, which were facing forward and away from his position.

Keeping in the shadows, what few there were of them, he moved forward to the light rack. Two massive pieces of equipment were positioned in front of the rack. One was a crawler—or at least that's what he thought it was called—used for mining. It had a number of lights attached to the front, and two large drill booms extended forward, facing the end of the cavern, which was a solid rock wall. The other piece of equipment sat behind the light rack and resembled a tractor-scraper commonly used for moving earth.

Looking around, he tried to estimate the size of the entire cavern. It appeared to be about twenty feet high by thirty feet wide, and was carved out of solid rock. There were massive jack supports seemingly set at random along the shaft. And spaced in a regular pattern and

Chapter Seventeen

bolted into the ceiling were large square plates that had water dripping from them.

A mine? He thought, *A gold mine or something? There's no precious metals in the mountains, not enough to be profitably mined anyway. Is this is what it's all about, an illegal mining operation?*

He turned right and looked back up into the shaft from which he had descended.

Air shaft! They're ventilating the mine.

As he moved westward, he was struck by the immense size of the operation.

This must have taken years, he thought, *this is solid rock!*

Further on, he reached another shaft opening identical to the one that he'd descended. It, too, had a large fan that was pointed upwards into the opening.

I don't know what they're after, but it must be pretty important to go to this kind of expense!

About a hundred feet further, he came upon three large dump trucks, sitting idly in a straight line and facing away from the end of the tunnel. Just about every horizontal surface, including the machinery, was covered by black soot. Rubbing his finger along the side of a truck he smelled the residue.

Diesel soot from the equipment.

It was cool and damp, and a large drop of water fell down his neck. Looking up to the ceiling of the cavern, he could see water dripping down through cracks in the rocks.

Suspended by chains, a large pipeline hung against one wall of the cavern about six feet off the ground. A steady thuck-thuck mechanical sound was repeated about every ten seconds from pumps attached at intervals along the pipeline.

Water pumps! Ground water from the creek. They're pumping it back toward Chilhowee River.

Checking his compass and looking at the shaft, he estimated that the mine extended in a direct line from the river to his present position.

Appalachia Stone! The quarry must be a front for whatever it is they are after up here, he reasoned, as the quarry was situated directly across the river from Panther Creek.

That's all the evidence I need. I've got to get out of here!

Turning back to his right, a blinding light flashed into his face. He raised his rifle, and...

"Don't! Drop it! Now!" a voice shouted.

He couldn't see in front of him, but several figures appeared silhouetted against the light from the powerful racks.

He held the rifle at arm's length out to his right, and dropped it on the cavern floor.

"Get on your knees, hands behind your head! Now!"

He dropped onto the hard floor, and placed his hands behind his head.

Oh, Ruth, I've really screwed this up, I'm sorry!

"Never say die, sir, no matter what happens to us, never give up!" Buddy's voice rang in Victor's head.

Oh God, I wish you were here, Buddy!

"Mr. Victor Scofield, what a surprise!" a large man said as he walked forward out of the light. Two men, dressed in the same blue jumpsuits as those he had encountered earlier, walked on either side of the man as he approached Victor.

"Harrison Pike! I should've known!" Victor said.

"Well, well, Mr. Scofield," Pike said as he walked up and stood before Victor. "We've been expecting you!"

The men in the blue jumpsuits were both Asian, Victor noticed. While one pointed a weapon at him, the other went behind him, and, lowering one of his hands at a time, handcuffed both behind his back.

"Get him up," Pike said to the one who handcuffed him.

The man roughly grabbed the handcuffs behind Victor's back and jerked him to his feet.

"So what's next, Pike, you going to kill me, like you did my friends?"

"In due time, Mr. Scofield, in due time." Turning to the man on his right, Pike said, "Let's take him back to the shaft house."

They walked down the massive shaft back towards the river, with Victor and one guard in front and Pike and the other behind.

As they walked along, Victor looked at the walls, ceiling, and floor, all which were carved from solid rock. Turning back to Pike he said, "This is quite a feat of engineering; it must have cost millions."

Chapter Seventeen

"More than you can imagine, Mr. Scofield, more than you can imagine."

Still walking, Victor asked, "Why? There's nothing up there. There's no gold in the Smokies unless you're an amateur after a few flakes in some quartz. No precious gems, no minerals, no nothing. Why go to this expense? Nothing could possibly be worth it."

"Oh, but it is, Mr. Scofield, and we have almost attained our goal. Another two hundred feet is all that we require, and yes, it did cost millions. It took us four years to develop this access tunnel," Pike said while waving his hand around the immense cavern.

"Why? What could be worth that, and worth the lives of my friends, of Russell?" Victor asked as they walked on.

"Something much more valuable than gold, Mr. Scofield—uranium. Weapons grade uranium unlike any ever discovered on the planet, with the exception of a single mine in Australia. A massive deposit extending from the surface to over three hundred feet below ground, we estimate, maybe more."

"Uranium? And on National Park property? That's why you tunneled in underneath the river. You're going to take it out underground through this shaft, and no one will know the difference," Victor said.

"Exactly. It was our little secret until you came along," Pike said.

"You mean until my friends came along. What? Did they stumble onto your little secret too?" Victor asked as he stopped and turned around.

"We suspected that Mr. Tippins would disregard my orders and move into the Panther Creek area. Three of my men followed them to where they made camp at the abandoned mine site. While Mr. Tippins was gathering firewood, he evidently heard the noise from our drilling operation, and found one of our air shafts."

"Why kill two people for hearing a noise and finding an old grate covering a hole?" Victor asked, "Why risk drawing that kind of attention to yourselves when you could've explained it as some kind of geologic survey or something?"

"Quite correct," Pike said. "And we would have let them pass through if it had been just that. According to my men, however, your friend quickly surmised that something wasn't right, and quickly

SmokeFire!

vanished into the undergrowth. Unfortunately, when one of my men attempted to follow him, Mr. Tippins ambushed and killed him—bare handed, I might point out."

"Knowing Buddy, when he found the air shaft, he would have become highly suspicious," Victor theorized, "Then, when he saw a man following who was carrying an assault rifle, he would have perceived it as a threat and immediately eliminated him."

"Whatever," Pike said. "In any event he placed us in a position where we had no alternative."

"Yeah, well I whacked those other two who did it—blew one of 'em's legs off!"

The Asian guard hit Victor in the kidney with the butt of his rifle, and he went down on his knees.

"Move along, Mr. Scofield, we have business to attend to," Pike said.

Getting to his feet after the pain in his back subsided, Victor asked, "How? Who discovered the deposit? You?"

"Actually, it was discovered quite by accident, many, many years ago. An associate of mine was searching for something else totally unrelated and came across a strange looking rock outcropping. Fortunately, he knew something of geology and had a sample assayed, but was unable to capitalize on the information. When I assumed the post as Chief Ranger, he brought me into his confidence," Pike answered. "Now, move along!"

They walked through the shaft for about another mile, and Victor speculated that they were now underneath the Chilhowee River, since water was steadily draining through cracks in the rock ceiling.

Near what looked like the end, the shaft was well-lit. And as they walked to the opening, he could see they had hollowed out a larger rectangular area where extra equipment was staged, including large industrial generators that were operating at full capacity.

They approached an elevator, and the guard nearest Victor reached over and punched a red button on the wall. In a few moments, the elevator door slid open, and the guard shoved Victor inside, into the corner. Pike and the other guard joined them, and the guard pushed the red button on the inside. A moment later the door silently slid shut and the elevator ascended.

Chapter Seventeen

"You'll never pull it off, Pike. You can't keep something like this a secret. You're insane," Victor said.

"Oh, I'm quite sane, and yes, we will pull it off. In one more week we'll reach the seam, then two weeks of drilling and we'll remove over a billion dollars worth of weapons grade uranium. Minus our expenses for this endeavor, we'll clear over nine hundred million dollars. Then we'll seal the shaft and all will be as it was," Pike said.

"A billion dollars! Who can you sell it to? Nobody...you bastard! You're going to sell it to third world countries!" Victor said.

"You never cease to amaze me, Mr. Scofield," Pike said, stepping off the elevator. "Now if you'll please follow that gentleman," pointing to the guard, "we have a couple of matters to discuss."

The guard led Victor into a small windowless room, which appeared to be some sort of engineering office. There were blueprints pinned to the wall and rock samples sat among papers and reports on a table. Stacked in one corner were cans of chemicals with various markings.

It was cool, and Pike went to a small open-flame propane construction heater, and lit it with some difficulty. Then he picked up a steel chair and placed it about eight feet in front of the heater.

"Sit down, Mr. Scofield," Pike said, indicating the chair. Victor sat down leaning back on his hands, which were still in the handcuffs.

Pointing to one of the guards, Pike said, "Go get Mr. Yong, and tell him to bring his equipment."

Then turning back to Victor, he said, "Now, Mr. Scofield, we must have this little chat I spoke of. I will admit you are a diligent person, and we've been quite impressed with your persistence. It's a pity you're not working for us. We could've used a man like you. Now, before we begin, I'm curious about something. Would you possibly know what became of Mr. DeVarra?"

"You mean after I blew his head off? I really wouldn't know, but I suspect he's fish food at the bottom of Fontana Lake," Victor said, then asked, "Is that Chicago mob he was associated with in on this with you, Pike?"

"They are, shall we say, our investors," Pike replied.

SmokeFire!

"Killing Mr. DeVarra was quite an accomplishment. As I understand it, Mr. DeVarra was a shrewd professional, and you alone killed him, Mr. Scofield?" Pike asked.

"Professional, my ass! Yes, I alone killed him, and you know what, Pike? I'm going to kill you too, and all of these other assholes you got before it's all over with."

Pike nodded to the remaining guard who walked up to Victor and hit him in the ribs with a rifle butt. He actually heard more than felt his ribs breaking. He almost fell out of the chair before the guard grabbed him by his hair and jerked him up.

"Mr. Scofield, I urge you to be as cooperative as possible and save yourself a lot of pain," Pike said.

At that moment the door on the opposite side of the room opened and the guard led in a small, old, Korean man carrying an aluminum briefcase.

"Ah, Mr. Yong," Pike said, "allow me to introduce you to Mr. Victor Scofield," nodding towards Victor. "Mr. Scofield, this is Mr. Soon Yong. Mr. Yong is—how should I phrase it?—an expert of sorts in the art of persuasion." Turning towards the old man, Pike said, "Mr. Yong, I wish to ask Mr. Scofield several questions. I do not wish him to lose consciousness, nor be incapacitated to the point that he cannot talk."

The old man simply bowed, and set his briefcase upon a small table.

The pain of Victor's broken ribs made each breath excruciating, and he looked over as the old man opened the briefcase. He could see what appeared to be surgical instruments, but little else. Yong removed a small towel and spread it out next to the briefcase, then withdrew several dental instruments, a syringe, and a vial of clear liquid, and set them down on the white cloth. He then took out what appeared to be a small drill and inserted a small-gauge drill bit. After neatly arranging the instruments, he turned to Pike and bowed.

"Now, Mr. Scofield. I can assure you that Mr. Yong is a very skillful man, and you can make this as easy as you wish or as difficult. When I say difficult, I mean painful—very, very, painful. I strongly urge you to cooperate, and if you do, I in turn, will guarantee you a very quick and painless death. Do you understand?" he asked, bending down to within three inches of Victor's face.

Chapter Seventeen

Victor was consumed by anger, not about his own death so much as about the deaths of his friends and the fact that Pike and his cronies were probably going to get away with it. Uranium to third world countries, more deaths—maybe not immediately, but in the future. And all because of money.

He stared defiantly into Pike's face and said, "You can kill me, torture me, or whatever, but you don't know what I left behind. They're going to find out. You're close but you're not going to make it. I already knew about your mine. Why do you think I was here? You're an idiot!" and Victor spat in his eyes.

Pike reared back, wiped the spittle from his eyes, and then hit Victor viciously on the side of his face with his fist, knocking him completely from the chair. Victor lay on the floor, spit out blood and the remnants of some teeth, and almost passed out. Both guards grabbed him and sat him back in the chair.

"That was a mistake, Mr. Scofield, and I'm tired of your arrogance!" Pike said, "Remove his pants," pointing to the two guards.

While one held his neck in a chokehold with his arms, the other guard removed Victor's boots, fatigue pants, and jockey shorts.

"Mr. Yong, let's skip the dental work for a few minutes. I would like you to show Mr. Scofield the price of insolence."

The old man bowed, turned back to his briefcase, and withdrew a small black box about four inches square. It had three wires attached; two had alligator clips on the ends, and the other he plugged into the nearest electrical outlet. He then turned on a switch that was located on the top of the device and looked at it for a moment. A small green light illuminated, and Yong turned and bowed to the guards. While one guard held Victor around the throat from behind, the other held his ankles. The old man then took one wire and attached it to Victor's scrotum, and the other he attached to his lower lip.

He walked back to the device, turned, and bowed to Pike.

"Now Mr. Scofield, I can assure you not many people have experienced the pain which you are about to, so with that in mind, I would like to ask you exactly what it was that you left behind," Pike said.

SmokeFire!

Victor's ribs felt like someone was stabbing him with a hot poker. His mouth was full of blood from his missing teeth, and he could hardly breath with the guard's arm around his throat.

"Go to hell, Pike!" was all he could manage through his pain.

Pike had been right; the pain was like nothing he could have ever envisioned. An electrical charge—which only lasted about two seconds, but seemed like an hour—shot from his groin to his jaw. He heard someone scream in pain, but it didn't feel like it came from him. He slumped over in the chair and passed out for a moment.

The old man passed something underneath his nose, and Victor regained consciousness. His nostrils stung from the chemical.

"I warned you, Mr. Scofield, and I take no pleasure in this. Please answer my question," Pike said.

Victor raised his head forward, afraid that—hoping that?——he would pass out again. His vision blurred with the pain.

"What...question? I...can't...remember," Victor said.

"Mr. Yong, please help Mr. Scofield remember the question."

Again, the excruciating pain, although for perhaps only one second. Victor screamed—a scream like no other he had ever heard.

The old man repeated the process of putting the chemical underneath his nostrils, and Victor regained consciousness. The guard released Victor's ankles and stepped aside. Pike moved closer then asked, "Now do you remember, Mr. Scofield?"

"Yes...yes...the...the...letter...I...I...left...it...in…the…" Victor stammered.

"Much better, now where or with whom did you leave this letter, Mr. Scofield?" Pike asked.

"I...I...left...it...I...left...it...in...in..." he said, his voice now only a whisper.

Pike leaned close to Victor's face, grabbed his chin and said, "Where, Mr. Scofield, in what?"

"In your ass!" Victor yelled, and lashed out with both feet, striking Pike on the inside of his right knee.

Victor heard Pike's leg snap, and Pike screamed and fell backwards. He tried to regain his footing, but his broken leg gave way, and he fell backwards onto the open-flame propane heater. Cursing, he rolled off the heater but not before his coat caught fire. He rolled off to the right

Chapter Seventeen

with his coat now in flames and fell against the cans of chemicals that had been stacked along the wall. One of the containers ruptured, spilling its contents onto Pike's coat and pooling onto the floor.

Pike yelled and there was a loud whooshing sound, as the chemicals were ignited by the flames from his burning coat. He rolled off to the right, his coat fully engulfed in flames, and howled like something from the other side of hell. The guards, who had been busy restraining Victor, only stared as the events quickly unfolded. Pike tried to raise himself to one knee in a vain attempt to escape the deathly flames. His upper torso was now fully enveloped in flames that rose three feet above his head. When his hair caught fire, he yelled a piercing scream, then fell backwards onto the burning floor and was silent.

The guards, their initial astonishment now passed, rushed to him, flailing at his coat with Victor's pants in an attempt to douse the flames, but it was futile. The smell of burning flesh permeated the room.

Victor looked at the old man who simply stared at what was left of Harrison Pike. The guards stood and turned to Victor. One elevated his rifle and pointed it at Victor's face.

Here it comes! Oh, God! Forgive me, Father, for I have sinned..., Victor prayed.

At that moment there was a crash, and the door by which Victor and the others had previously entered burst open. Both guards turned their heads at the sound. Victor could not focus his eyes, but he did see the back of the guard's head nearest him literally explode, covering Victor's face with a red mist. He saw the other guard fall to the ground and the old man turn to run, but before he had gone a single step, he was shot in the back.

Looking into the darkened doorway, he saw Chief White Horse's assistant kneeling with a weapon identical to that which Victor had been carrying. Standing behind him were White Horse and several others. They quickly crowded into the small room, one man covering the left side and one covering the right. They held their weapons against their shoulders as they searched for other targets, but there were none. A man with long, black, straight hair, tied in a ponytail, whom Victor had never seen, went to the bodies and kicked their weapons away.

White Horse approached Victor and said, "Mr. Scofield, I would ask if you're all right, but I think it's safe to say that you've seen better days."

"Chief, I thought it was the Calvary, not the Indians, who were supposed to save the day," Victor said, leaning back in the chair.

"You've been watching too many paleface Hollywood movies, Mr. Scofield. In ours, it's us redskins who always save the day," White Horse said, smiling as he knelt in front of Victor. "You about ready to leave?"

"Yes, sir."

White Horse's men gently raised Victor to his feet and removed the handcuffs. He managed to put his pants on with the men supporting him, and White Horse's assistant put on his boots. Looking down, Victor saw that Pike, too, had seen better days. His coat was still smoldering, and he lay on his back. His face had been completely burned off, and sometime during the fire he had died.

With White Horse and three of his men taking point—two following behind, and White Horse's assistant almost carrying Victor—they proceeded out a door at the other end of the office and up some stairs. Victor was barely conscious, but he heard gunshots from up ahead, and along the way he passed several bodies of Korean men dressed in the same blue jumpsuits, all with fatal head wounds.

They opened a door and walked into a massive open area. The twilight of morning was in the east, and as they approached a large chain link gate, two guards heard them and turned. White Horse raised his rifle and ordered them to drop their weapons. As Victor passed by, two of White Horse's men searched and handcuffed the guards who were now laying face down.

White Horse walked to the side of the fence, pressed a button, and two large gates retracted.

As they walked the hundred yards toward the road, several vehicles came screeching up and slid to a halt along the shoulder of the road.

Victor hobbled, with the help of White Horse's assistant, towards the convoy of cars. A white Ford Taurus came skidding to a halt in front of Victor, and the doors flew open. The first person he saw was Ruth, who came running towards him.

Chapter Seventeen

"Oh, Victor! Oh, God! Are you okay?" she cried as she rushed to him.

"Be gentle with him, ma'am," White Horse's assistant said. "He's hurt, but okay."

Ruth put her hands gently on his bloodied and bruised face and said, "Oh, Victor! I was so scared! I'm so sorry."

Reaching out with his free hand, as the other was draped over the shoulder of White Horse's assistant, he rubbed her cheek and said, "It's okay, baby. Nothing a couple of weeks and a good dentist can't cure."

Behind Ruth stood Bill Richter, Clevenger, and another agent whom Victor did not recognize. Richter walked up, and Victor said, "I guess you're here to arrest me."

"I haven't the vaguest idea of what you're referring to, Victor," Richter said. Then turning back to the other agent, he shouted, "Get that ambulance over here now, our man needs help!"

The paramedics came up with a stretcher, collapsed it to almost ground level, and White Horse's assistant helped lower him onto it. Lying down, Victor looked up into their faces. The men were smiling, and Ruth and Clevenger had tears running down their cheeks.

Looking up at White Horse, Victor asked, "By the way, Chief, how did you know where I was?"

"Ruth called us late last night when you didn't check in, and told us what you were up to. We went into Panther Creek and tracked you. We found the bodies at the old mine site, but had a difficult time following your trail from there. We would've never found the shaft opening had you not left your pack. By that time we were probably about an hour behind you. We descended the same way you did, and, well, you know the rest."

Turning to White Horse's assistant, Victor reached up and offered his hand.

"I don't think we've been properly introduced, I'm Victor Scofield."

He bent down, and gently taking Victor's hand, said in a serious and deep voice, "Pleased to meet you, Mr. Scofield, I am Thomas Walking Bear."

"Please call me Vick," he mumbled weakly. "All my friends do."

SmokeFire!

The shock and strain of the past twenty-four hours suddenly caught up with him. His head fell back on the stretcher and he closed his eyes.

Chapter Eighteen

Saturday morning, May 1, 1999
Knoxville, Tennessee
University of Tennessee Memorial Hospital

Victor lay in his hospital bed with his ribs taped. A number of doctors had been to see him since his admittance, including an oral surgeon who said that they could completely reconstruct the four teeth that had been knocked out. The electrical shocks, he had been assured by a neurologist, would leave no impairments of any kind, except for possibly some nightmares.

Ruth had maintained a constant vigil at his side since his arrival, and many of her nurse and doctor friends had stopped by. Ruth told Victor he was getting the 'royal treatment,' and he believed it.

Richter and Clevenger had just left, and although there was still much to learn about the entire affair, Richter assured him the FBI was making rapid progress in the investigation.

The mine had been literally stormed by the federal authorities, and no less than sixty arrests had been made. Geologists were being flown

SmokeFire!

in to assess the mining operation, and as Richter had said, "There are so many bureaucrats getting into this you can't stir 'em with a stick. Everybody wants a piece of it!" The investigation was fully under way, he had said, including determining where financing for the operation had originated. The FBI speculated that the Cavennetti organization had fronted a lot of the funding, but there were many loose ends that could take their organized crime division months—if not years—to trace all of it.

The good news was that none of the uranium had been extracted from the mine. The government really didn't know what to do about the deposit, Richter had said, but he thought that the shaft would be sealed and the deposit left undisturbed.

"I'm hungry, why don't you sneak out and get me a Big Mac with large fries?" Victor asked Ruth.

"I can't do that, Victor, and besides, Dr. Gorman told me he's going to come by this morning and release you. You're coming to my house to recuperate—and no arguments!"

"My own private nurse. That sounds interesting. You know, these broken ribs could take months to heal. I might need to lie on the couch, watch Star Trek movies, and be hand fed with chocolate ice cream. My injuries are pretty serious, I hear."

"We'll see about that, Mr. milk-it-to-the-max Scofield, but I'll take good care of you. I can't get anyone to sub for me next week, but I've got Friday off. Besides, Richter wants both of us in his office a week from Monday 'no ifs, ands, or buts,' was how he phrased it! He said he has to get some formal statements from us, but he promised to leave us alone until then."

"All right. But hey, what about my house? I mean, I ripped off the end of it with the car, and what about my 'Z'? It's going to cost a fortune to restore it to showroom quality."

"Richter's already got a construction crew lined up to repair your house starting Monday, and your 'Z' is at Classic Car Works being repaired—all at FBI expense."

"Hmm, government contractors and lowest bidders. My house will probably have cardboard for a wall, and my 'Z' will be a disaster," he said, taking a sip through a straw from a plastic cup of water. "I need my Star Trek movies if I'm going to be laid up, and my VCR if you don't

Chapter Eighteen

have one. Oh, and my remote—I like to play it back when Spock talks. He's really cool."

"I'll get your movies, and I have a VCR with a remote, Captain Kirk," she said.

"And lots of chocolate ice cream, and some Glorsch beers, with the snap caps. I like peanut butter, too, and grape jelly."

"Oh, God, I hope this recuperation period is short," Ruth moaned.

"Oh, I don't know. This could last quite a long time. I don't feel so good," he said, his voice taking on a pitiful tone.

"Poor baby. Well, you get some rest, I've got a couple of errands to run, like getting Star Trek movies and chocolate ice cream. I'll be back by noon and we'll go home—my house, I mean," she said as she leaned over and kissed him. Smoothing his hair back over his forehead, she said, "I do love you, Vick, and I'm very proud of you!"

"I love you too, hon. Don't forget to come get me!"

She mussed his hair, made a fake frowning face, and then left.

Within an hour, Mae came to see him. She was naturally upset, but spent some time with Victor talking of Buddy and Donna and thanked Victor for his efforts. Evidently Richter and Clevenger had gone by to see her yesterday and explained the events to date. Victor felt sorry for her, and they had a long and candid conversation, mainly about her and Jennifer, and the future.

She had the name of an attorney with whom a will had been left by Buddy and Donna—information courtesy of the FBI—but she knew no details. Before leaving, Mae bent down, kissed Victor on the cheek, and said, "Everything will be okay, Victor. I'll be praying for you."

About thirty minutes later, Dr. Gorman paid a visit and released Victor. When Victor asked about the payment for treatment, Dr. Gorman explained that it had been taken care of by the United States government.

Ruth came back about noon and wheeled his wheelchair through the corridor and down to her car, which was parked in the pick-up zone. When he left the room, Victor noticed two policemen standing at his door. They turned and left by the stairs as Ruth wheeled him away.

* * *

241

SmokeFire!

The next several days were uneventful. Victor rested all weekend at Ruth's, and on Monday she drove him to see the oral surgeon, who began the reconstruction of the four missing teeth. Then on Tuesday, they went by Lakes Grill and had lunch and talked with Francis and Mark.

Victor had called Buddy and Donna's attorney, and made an appointment for Friday afternoon. Since their bodies had not yet been recovered, the attorney explained that there couldn't be a reading of the will yet, but that they would discuss it.

Early Thursday morning Ruth was preparing to leave for her twelve-hour shift at the hospital.

"Now, get some rest, Vick! I'll be back about seven thirty tonight and cook dinner. Do you want anything special?" she asked.

"Not really, I guess I can't handle a steak yet, so maybe some more spaghetti with that homemade sauce of yours. It was great!"

"You're going to start speaking Italian if you eat anymore spaghetti, but I'll stop by the store and pick some up. There's some books in the spare bedroom, and there are some of Dad's old books up in the attic, but be careful going up that ladder," she said, referring to the drop down attic stairs. "I don't want you to fall and re-injure your ribs." She kissed him goodbye, and left for work.

Victor went into the kitchen and poured himself another cup of coffee. It was a beautiful morning, and his ribs were feeling much better, so he went to sit outside on her small deck. Sitting in the sun, he contemplated what he should do next. The first order of business was to take the remaining money from his hundred thousand dollar withdrawal and put it back in the bank. He thought about updating his résumé, but decided he would take some time off and think about what kind of job he wanted to pursue. Not much appealed to him, and he really didn't think he wanted to get back into computers—at least not at a bank. He thought he'd ask Ruth if she could get some time off, and maybe they could take a vacation somewhere, just for a week or so. With the fast pace of events, he hadn't felt like they'd really had time to connect and talk about all that had happened.

He went back inside and looked for something to read. Finding nothing of interest in Ruth's spare room, he decided he would go into

Chapter Eighteen

the attic and see what he could find there. He lowered the drop panel in the ceiling and unfolded the ladder, and then climbed up into the attic.

There were many old boxes stacked along the walls, and an old bookshelf sat to one side. He opened the attic window to let in some air and then began looking through the books that lined the small shelves. Most were related to geography and geology, presumably belonging to Ruth's father. He flipped open a geology book and read a small section concerning uranium mining, and then replaced it on the shelf. There were some old maps rolled up with rubber bands around them, and he unrolled a couple and looked them over but found nothing of interest.

He began going through the boxes, but they were mostly old papers and junk like that, which most people have in their basements or attics. Near the back corner of the attic, he saw an old wooden box. He removed the cardboard boxes that were stacked on top and carefully pulled it out to the center of the floor. Inside were some old photographs.

They were very old, all black and white, and showed a young man, whom Victor took to be Ruth's father, in an Army uniform in various localities. Others showed a young attractive woman, *probably Ruth's mother*, Victor guessed, and in some she was holding a baby.

I wonder if Ruth knows they're up here? She might want to get these framed or reproduced, he thought. He laid them aside and poked around some more. Near the bottom of the box were some old letters, most still in their envelopes, which had been carefully cut open. He began reading them, and found that most were from Ruth's father to her mother. After skimming through several, he began to feel guilty about invading their privacy and placed them next to the pictures. He dug down into the bottom, found some more snapshots and a few more letters. Taking them out of the box, he laid them with the others, and then put the box back into the corner.

Going downstairs, he took the photographs and letters and laid them on the end table, and was about to get another cup of coffee when he saw an unopened letter on top. He picked it up and took it into the kitchen. Pouring himself another cup of coffee, he looked at the letter more closely. It was addressed to Mary Jeffers—at this address, and the return address was Capt. Geo. Jeffers, rural route delivery, Great Smoky Mountains National Park.

SmokeFire!

Turning it over, he verified that it indeed had never been opened, as the flap was still sealed. It was postmarked May 15, 1951.

Wasn't that about the time that her father had had the accident?

Succumbing to his curiosity, he opened the kitchen drawer, withdrew a knife, and gently opened the letter. It talked of a fishing trip Ruth's father had been on earlier in the day, of their plans after his retirement, and of an army buddy who was coming to see him. He was about to refold the three pages, when he saw the next paragraph.

He set his cup down, leaned against the kitchen counter, and read the remainder of the letter.

This is unbelievable! was all he could think. He folded up the letter and replaced it in the stack with the others, then rushed back up into the attic and started pulling out the maps. He went through four of them until he came across what he was looking for. He rolled the map back up and took it downstairs. Checking his watch, he saw that it was now eight-thirty.

That's probably enough time, he thought. He took the old map and put it in his Jeep, which had been delivered earlier in the week. Then he went back into the detached garage and found some tools, which he also placed in the Jeep.

He locked the house, quickly backed out of the driveway, and headed towards town. He had one more stop to make. Mark wouldn't be at the Grill yet, as it was too early. He would drive to his house and borrow his scuba equipment. Then he would find out if his suspicion was really possible.

Could it be, after all this time?

Chapter Nineteen

**10:00 a.m. Monday morning, May 10, 1999
FBI Field Office
Knoxville, Tennessee**

They had arrived at the FBI office promptly at eight o'clock and had given their statements to Richter and Clevenger, while a stenographer took notes, even though the interview had been recorded on a small tape recorder. After the interview, other agents came into the conference room to introduce themselves. They all paid Victor many compliments, and expressed concern about his recovery. He assured them that he was fine.

"Well, I guess that about does it, Vick," Richter said, sitting down on the edge of the conference room table. "There isn't anything else we need you to do, but there are a couple of things...That was a lucky break—you finding that letter," he continued. "The entire shipment of gold bullion was being moved from Seoul by an army detachment in February, 1951. It belonged to the South Korean government, and apparently they were afraid that the North Korean army was going to overrun Seoul, so they decided to move it. Obviously, it never reached its destination and was thought to be taken by the North. Forty-two men were listed as missing in action," he explained.

"Evidently, this Colonel William Anderson stole it en-route and had it transshipped to the U.S. He needed someplace that would receive the shipment where it wouldn't be looked into. We don't know exactly what happened, but the Defense Intelligence Agency thinks the shipment arrived early, giving Captain Jeffers time to hide it until he could get it sorted out, only Anderson didn't know that Jeffers had already discovered its contents and hidden it. Then Anderson must have destroyed the camp, only to find the gold wasn't there."

"I'll bet he was surprised," Victor said. "Have you found any trace of him?"

"No, but DIA says that he just disappeared with the convoy in Korea. Maybe he thought the gold got lost in shipment. Who knows?"

"How much is it worth?" Ruth asked.

"At today's price its value is about one hundred million dollars," Richter said. "The government is going to turn it back over to the South Koreans, who are absolutely ecstatic."

Victor said, "Let's see, that puts the shipment weighing about fifteen thousand pounds. I wonder how long it took Ruth's father to transport and dump it into his fishing hole?"

"Quite a while, I should imagine. He must have made several trips in a Jeep or something," Richter said. Then, turning to Ruth, he said, "Your father was quite a clever man, Ruth, and I'm sure the government will posthumously award him a medal."

"I just can't believe it," she said. "All this time, and I finally find out what happened to him. I wish my mother were still alive to see this."

"Oh, and our financial guys have traced some of the capital of Appalachia Stone's accounts," Richter explained. "It seems that the Cavennetti organization is heavily connected, and there will be some federal indictments handed down in Chicago. Funny thing is, though, there was about ten million dollars traced to your old employer, SNB. They were loans through some shadow companies, and there was strong evidence that your friend Vodeski was in it up to his eyeballs. We got a warrant, but when we arrived at his house to arrest him, we found that he had committed suicide—put a garden hose in his exhaust

Chapter Nineteen

pipe. Evidently his wife had left him several months ago, and we're trying to locate her, but she's moved out of state. It appeared he'd been dead about three days, and we think he knew that we'd connect him after your little episode at the mine, and decided to off himself."

"I always knew there was something about him I didn't like," Victor chuckled.

Just then the conference room door opened and the receptionist said, "Mr. Richter, they're ready for that call now."

"All right, put it through in here please, but give us a moment before you do." Then turning to Victor, Richter said, "Vick, there's an important call for you coming through, just pick up that phone when it rings," pointing to the one sitting on the table. "Folks, I think Mr. Scofield will need some privacy for this, so why don't we go get a cup of coffee."

"What? Who...?" Victor asked.

As Richter stepped through the door, he turned and said, "it's someone who wants to thank you for all your sacrifices," and then silently closed the door behind him.

In a moment the phone rang, and Victor picked it up.

"Hello?"

"Yes, is this Mr. Victor Scofield?" a male voice asked.

"Yes, it is. Who is this, please?"

* * *

After the call, Victor went out into the lobby where Richter, Clevenger, and Ruth were talking.

"Well, how'd it go?" Richter asked.

"Just fine, other than almost giving me a heart attack," Victor said.

"Well, it's not everyday that you get a call from the President of the United States. Probably *would* give me a heart attack!" Richter laughed.

"The President!" Ruth cried out. "You talked to the President?"

"Yep, pretty regular guy too."

"What did he say, Vick? The President, wow!" Ruth said with a giggle.

SmokeFire!

"That's classified. I could tell you, but then I'd have to kill you." Victor said, then added, "Oops, guess I shouldn't be saying that here," to which everyone laughed.

"Vick, there are a couple of other things. First, it seems that there's one-point-five million dollars missing from the gold shipment. Curiously enough, two off-shore blind trust accounts were opened last Friday in the Cayman Islands, one for one million in the name of the Cherokee Indian Reservation Scholarship Fund, and the other for five-hundred thousand in the name of Mae Courtner—Donna Tippins's mother. You wouldn't know anything about that would you?" Richter asked, somewhat seriously.

"No, sir. I wouldn't," Victor said, shaking his head.

Richter smiled and said, "Didn't think so. Oh well, I guess the missing gold must have been intercepted during shipment back in fifty-one. No way to trace it now," Richter said, smiling and shrugging his shoulders.

"There is one more thing, then I'll let you folks get out of here. I'm aware that the president of SNB, Brad Heron, has offered you the job as president of the bank, pending board approval, since he's going to retire. You going to take it?" Richter asked.

"I haven't decided," Victor said. "I will say the salary is good, but it doesn't have much appeal to me."

"Listen, Vick, you're not a banker," Richter said. "Now, we can't possibly match the salary that the bank's offering, but we can offer you a rewarding career."

"You offering me a job, Bill? With the FBI? As what?" Victor asked.

"Yes, we would like you to come to work for us, based here in Knoxville, of course. The FBI's increasing its tactical division, and we'd like you to be a part of it, as a special agent."

"An FBI agent? You've got to be kidding!" Victor laughed.

"I'm completely serious. You interested?" Richter asked.

"I don't know. We're leaving on a week's vacation tomorrow. Can I let you know when we get back?" Victor asked. His eyes met Ruth's, and he couldn't tell whether what he saw in them was incredulity or mirth.

Chapter Nineteen

"Sure. It's a good job Vick. We need you. By the way, where you guys going on vacation? Not up in the Park, I hope," Richter said with a smirk.

"Absolutely not! We're going to the beach, over to Kiwah, South Carolina. I think I'm about 'mountained' out," Victor said, laughingly.

"Well, have a good time. You both deserve it!"

They made their good byes, receiving handshakes from the other agents and a hug from Clevenger. As Victor was walking to the door, Richter yelled after him, "I'll order you some office furniture while you're gone, and we'll make arrangements for Ruth to get some time off and stay with you at Quantico," referring to the FBI Training Academy at Quantico, Virginia. "Call me!"

Victor smiled and waved without looking back. Then he took Ruth's hand and they went home to pack.

Epilogue

Six month's later

Monday afternoon, October 18, 1999
Chilhowee, Near The Great Smoky Mountains National Park

Victor drove the 'Z' into Smoky Tobias's driveway, and the old Ford truck was where it had been on his previous visit last spring. He got out of his car, approached the cabin, and knocked on the door.

After a few moments, Tobias opened the door and said "Yeah, whaddya want? You ain't no salesman, are ya?"

"No, sir. Remember me? I'm Victor Scofield. Came up here back in the spring and had some of that blackberry wine of yours while we talked about the Smokies."

Tobias stared up at him from the wheelchair for a moment, then said, "Yeah, young feller. I remembers you. Come on in an' we'll talk." He opened the door and moved the wheelchair back and Victor walked in.

"Hope I haven't caught you at a bad time, Smoky, but I was near the area and got to thinking about that fine blackberry wine of yours, and, well, I thought I'd stop in and say hi."

SmokeFire!

"Why hell, yeah, come on in and we'll have us one! You ever find them two friends of yours, the one's was lost, I mean?" Tobias asked as he wheeled the chair across the small room.

"Unfortunately no, I did not," Victor replied, sitting down on the small settee.

"Well...Hey, you want Ole Smoky to fix us a glass? Got plenty, just fixed up a new batch!" Tobias said.

"I was hoping you would ask, Smoky. I'd love some."

"Be right back," he said, propelling the wheelchair back towards the kitchen.

In a moment Tobias came back into the living room and said, "You'll have to fetch 'em, young feller, can't do it and drive this here contraption."

"No problem," Victor said, standing up. "Be right back."

He went into the kitchen and after a minute or so returned with two large glasses of blackberry wine. He handed one to Tobias and sat back down on the settee. Taking a sip, he said, "That's mighty fine, Smoky, mighty fine!"

"Thank 'ye," Tobias said, draining nearly half his glass. "Now, what you been up to, young feller? Tell Ole Smoky what's goin' on in the world."

"I've been doing some more research, Smoky, research that I think you'll find interesting."

"Research? What kind of research?" Tobias asked, again taking another swallow.

"I've been researching records, and it's pretty intriguing actually. For example, I know you moved into this place in June of 1951. You got no pension, but you still pay your property taxes every year."

"So what? You got no business messin' in my records. Now you get the hell outta here!"

"Not so fast, I want to show you something. I think you'll find this interesting as well." Reaching into his pocket, Victor removed a small manila envelope and opened it.

"Now, this is what's called fingerprint lift tape. It's used for taking fingerprints at crime scenes. And these," he said, "are fingerprints from the National Military Personnel Records Center in St. Louis."

Epilogue

Holding both up to the light, Victor said, "Well what do you know? Now isn't that a coincidence! You know whose these fingerprints belong to, Smoky? They're yours. These," he said, holding up the lift tape, "I took off the wine jug in the kitchen a few minutes ago, and these," holding up the other records, "belong to one Colonel William 'Wild Bill' Anderson. And both sets are identical."

"What are you talkin' 'bout? You get out of here!"

"I don't think so, Colonel," Victor said. "You know something else, I found your gold. Jeffers hid it in his private fishing hole. How long did you look for it? Months, years? Somewhere along the line, you found the uranium, had it assayed, then brought Pike into the picture."

Dropping the backcountry dialect, Anderson said, "I was still looking when I fell and got paralyzed. How the hell did you find it?"

"A letter. When you blew up the camp, you neglected to look in the mailbox. Captain Jeffers had mailed a letter to his wife just hours before you killed them all, and in it he said that you were coming to visit him. You were already dead—listed as missing in action in Korea—but he didn't know that. He went on to say that he'd opened some of the crates and found the gold. Thinking there had been a terrible mistake in shipment, he hid it in his fishing hole," Victor explained, and then continued, "In the letter he told his wife what he'd found and what he'd done. You were so close, but you overlooked the most simple detail."

"Son of a bitch!" Anderson said, draining the rest of his glass, then shook his head and added, "Unbelievable! But how did you figure out it was me?"

"You see, when I talked to you in the spring, I noticed a couple of things. First, your firewood was split. Who split it for you? Second, when you made the toast with the wine, you said, 'here's to us, and them like us.' Now, that's an old Army toast, and since I was in the Army, I recognized it, but didn't pay any attention to it at the time."

"That can't be all of it," Anderson said, "It was Pike wasn't it? He told you."

"Not exactly. Before Pike died, he said an associate of his found the uranium while looking for something else. I think the term he used was 'something totally unrelated.' When I found the letter and the gold, it got me to thinking, and I took a wild guess," Victor said, "Then I did the background check on you, and there was nothing prior to 1951, no history whatsoever."

"I'll be damned," Anderson said.

"Of that I'm sure. How many, Anderson? How many men did you kill for the gold? The detachment in Korea, Camp Thirteen, how many?" Victor asked bitterly.

"As many as I had to! There's nothing you can do about it! You can't prove anything, and even if you did, what are they going to do to me, put me in prison? Hell, at my age and in this chair," Anderson scoffed.

"No, not prison," Victor agreed, "I made a phone call before I came up here to some friends of mine at the FBI, and explained my suspicions, but I was already pretty sure who you were. They're getting the warrants together now." Then, checking his wristwatch, he added, "And should be along in the next hour or so. They'll arrest you, of course, and I have their assurances that you'll be committed to a psychiatric hospital for the criminally insane for the rest of your life. Prison's a picnic compared to that."

Victor could see that he'd struck a nerve with Anderson, so he added quietly, "But there is another way."

"What other way?" Anderson asked hoarsely. "Some kind of plea agreement?"

"I don't think the Army and the FBI are very open to any plea agreement. No, you're going to spend what's left of your miserable life in a psychiatric hellhole, unless, that is..."

"Unless, what?" Anderson interjected, leaning forward in his wheelchair.

"Unless you take the easy way out," Victor said.

Anderson leaned back, and Victor could see that he knew what he meant.

After a minute of silence, Victor stood up and said, "Goodbye, Colonel," and walked out the door.

Driving away, Victor popped a tape into the cassette player and rolled the window down, letting the cool autumn air blow through the

Epilogue

'Z'. He was about two miles down the road, listening to a new jazz band, and never heard the single gunshot that ended Anderson's life.

* * *

Late Tuesday afternoon, November 30, 1999
The Great Smoky Mountains National Park
Western Boundary Line, near Panther Creek

The weather, on the day it all ended, was much the same as it had been on the day it had all begun almost fifty years ago. The winds were out of the west at fifteen knots and were picking up, and with the wind chill, it seemed much colder than the twenty-seven degrees that the thermometer read.

Victor's '77 'Z' was pulled over on the shoulder of the road that bordered the Chilhowee river on the west and the National Park boundary to the east, where Panther Creek flowed into the lake. Victor and Ruth, who was holding a bundled Jennifer in her arms, stood staring at the gray historic style marker with its raised black letters.

A lot had happened over the summer and autumn.

The bodies of Buddy and Donna had been found buried in graves near the mine site. These had been recovered, and the funeral was attended by Ruth, Mae, the Knoxville FBI detachment, Francis and Mark, and Victor's Indian friends.

In their will, Buddy and Donna had left Jennifer under the care of Victor, stating that, "Maybe he could find her a good mother, as he was a good man," and that they loved Vick and Jennifer very much. As always, Victor thought, Buddy had attempted to account for all possibilities.

Mae was off on an extended trip to the Holy Land with her church friends, with funding courtesy of her new trust account.

Ruth and Victor had gotten married in June—yes, it was a short engagement period, many had said, but everyone agreed they were perfect for each other. They had been married in a Cherokee Indian ceremony on the Reservation. Again, all his new friends were in full attendance, including all the staff from the Knoxville FBI office, as well as Wally McAllister, the helicopter pilot. After the ceremony, they had all then driven down to Lakes Grill in Knoxville in one long convoy, Richter

255

SmokeFire!

leading the way in his FBI car with his blue lights on and siren blaring. They had had a long party that lasted well into the night, and once, Victor stood alone back in the corner of the room and just watched.

White Horse was engaged in some deep political conversation with Francis, while Ruth was dragging Walking Bear across the dance floor. Red Feather was showing Mark and Richter's kids how to make paper things out of cocktail napkins. Richter and his wife were talking to Clevenger and her husband about, Victor surmised, airplanes, since Clevenger's husband was a pilot for Delta and as he spoke, his hand was gesturing like airplanes flying.

Leaning against the corner he was overcome by a feeling he thought he had lost forever. Yes, he had suffered tragic losses, but he'd made many new friends. He had found a wife whom he loved dearly, a daughter he adored, and a new life.

I'm a lucky man!

"Hey, anybody home? Earth to Victor," Ruth said, waving her hand in front of his face as they stood beside the road.

"Oh, sorry, just gathering some wool."

"Oh, Victor, it's so beautiful. Everyone would be so proud! I suppose I can stop guessing what it was you asked the President to do six months ago."

"I don't know about it being beautiful, but it seemed the right thing to do. As far as anyone being proud, I'm not sure of that either. I just didn't know of anything else to ask for that would be reasonable when he asked me what he could do for me."

"I know Dad would appreciate it, and although I didn't know Buddy and Donna, I'm sure from what you've told me of them that they would appreciate it too, and I'm sure Steve would just love it!"

Victor looked up at the marker, and Ruth moved closer to him. Shifting Jennifer's weight to her left arm, she put her right hand around his waist and gave him a slight hug. As she looked at him, she noticed a faint trace of a tear forming in the corner of his eye as he looked up at the historical marker.

He is such a good man, she thought—*so strong, and so kind. He has come so far, facing more in one life than any ten men would ever face in a hundred lives.* And the unique thing about Victor, she thought, was that it had all made him stronger, kinder, and wiser.

Epilogue

"It's cold, Vick. Let's go home to our new house, and I'll give Jennifer her bath and put her in bed while you build a roaring fire in the fireplace. Then I'll put something sexy on me, while you put something sexy on the stereo, and we'll talk about what a great future Jennifer, you, and I have waiting for us. What about it, sailor?"

In spite of the cold and wind, Victor felt a warmth rush over him that he had not felt in a long time—maybe had never felt before. Looking at Ruth, he smiled, and asked, "You pick up sailors here often?"

"Only when they're about to become the best tactical agent the FBI has ever had!"

As they turned back to the car, he shook his head and smiled.

"First, Mrs. Scofield, you know me too well, that's bad! Second, your rather indecent proposition sounds decidedly decent, and that's good! I accept, but will you still respect this federal policeman in the morning?"

"Ooh, do you get a uniform? That could present all kinds of possibilities! Oh, oh, and what about handcuffs?"

"You're incorrigible, and I love both of you so!" he said, smiling, and kissed her while they stood in the blowing snow, then smoothed back Jennifer's hair and kissed her, too.

Never had Victor felt such deep emotions, so much belonging. Even with Cathy, it had been different, but he would always remember their love and treasure her memory and the ones he held of Buddy and Donna. But this was now.

Walking towards the car with his arm around his wife, Victor tilted his head towards the sky and winked.

Thank you, Lord!

The bronze 'Z' drove off as the snow began to fall harder. The raised black letters on the historic marker were becoming obscured as the snow blew against them and began to stick onto the sign, and although twilight was near, someone who stood very close could have read the inscription:

Russell's Creek
Tippins Mountain
Jeffers Bend

The names of certain geographic locations in this area, which were originally named at the time the Park was dedicated, have been changed in honor of those who gave their lives in the name of freedom.

From the time between 1951 and 1999, a conspiracy of unparalleled magnitude occurred in this area. Within this time, eight U.S. Army soldiers, two U.S. citizens, and one U.S. Park Ranger made the ultimate sacrifice, which finally exposed this conspiracy and preserved the cause of freedom, sparing the lives of countless peoples of many nations.

It is in their honor that the name of Abrams Creek has been changed to Russell's Creek; the name of Hannah Mountain has been changed to Tippins Mountain; and the deep pool located on Russell's Creek at Black Rock is named Jeffers Bend.

By Constitutional Amendment the names of these locations may never be changed, thereby preserving the memory of their great courage and sacrifice, for which nations throughout the world will forever be indebted.

Special Agent Victor Scofield *will be back* in *CrossFire!*

Author's Notes

All areas referred to in this manuscript, including Panther Creek, Hannah Mountain, and Tarklln Ridge in fact do exist. It is one of the few places within the Great Smoky Mountains National Park where there are no backcountry campsites, and is generally not open to hiking. I went back there while researching this work, and the terrain is rugged, and although citizens are permitted into this area, there can be no open campfires, and hiking is discouraged.

The abandoned mine site from the Civil War actually exists as written, and is along Panther Creek. Although I have not seen it, the Park Rangers described it to me.

The passage referring to getting branches off of dead trees during rain is true—I learned it in the Boy Scouts.

I have spent much time in the backcountry of the Great Smoky Mountains. It is truly a beautiful, wonderful, and safe place.

Acknowledgments

I wish to offer my appreciation to the following people and organizations, without whose help this work would not have been possible.

The Park Rangers of The Great Smoky Mountains National Park, who wished to remain anonymous and spent countless early morning hours with me over maps and coffee, discussing terrain, trails, and search and rescue techniques of lost hikers—you know who you are.

The members of the Cherokee Indian Tribe who educated me on the folklore of the Smokies and their heritage and were so hospitable.

Francis Cantwell, who read each paragraph and gave me that special encouragement to go on—thanks so much!

Shirley Clark, my well-read grammar critic, thanks for your questions, and your suggestions.

My personal editor, Dr. Mary Papke, Director of Graduate Studies, The University of Tennessee Department of English, who reviewed the manuscript and made many valuable suggestions.

My test readers, who spent so much time reading the manuscript, made notes and suggestions, and urged me to write more.

Frank Wood, who stayed up until the wee hours educating me on drift mining operations.

Very importantly, Olen Letourneau, my Editor, who was so patient and contributed so much during the rewrites, and the staff at American Book Publishing Group—thank you!

Cassie, who is forever in my heart and was with me in the 'back bush' of the Reservation—I'll always remember the sneaking and barking!

My wife, Judy, who sat and read each unedited chapter, questioned me, gave me faith, and then asked for more.

And to the readers of *SmokeFire!* I hope you enjoyed reading this tale as much as I enjoyed writing it!

About the Author

The author is a Senior Applications Engineer with an engineering technology company, and travels extensively throughout the United Sates and Europe. He has held previous positions as that of computer programmer and teacher, and served with the Tennessee Air National Guard where he engaged in search and rescue of lost hikers in the Great Smoky Mountains National Park.

As an avid yachtsman, the author and his wife, Judy, spend most of the time aboard their boat "*Foolish Pleasure*" during the summer.

SmokeFire! is the author's first novel. Judson Kennedy lives in East Tennessee where he is currently working on his next novel.